Daniel,

Thank you for the support, and
for the life chats over walks
and coffee.

MICHAEL CRISTIANO

THE BLACK

ORACLE

CURIOSITY QUILLS PRESS

A Division of **Whampa, LLC**
P.O. Box 2160
Reston, VA 20195
Tel/Fax: 800-998-2509
http://curiosityquills.com

© 2015 **Michael Cristiano**
http://michaelcristiano.net

ISBN 978-1-62007-872-3 (ebook)
ISBN 978-1-62007-873-0 (paperback)
ISBN 978-1-62007-874-7 (hardcover)

To Francis and Jolyne.

TABLE OF CONTENTS

CHAPTER ONE

RETURN

The village.

After two months on a hunt, he'd forgotten what it smelled like: coconut oil on his skin after a long day harvesting grain in the sun; salt water mist coating his face at the Black Rocks. It was sweet like Darcie's scent, soft like Darcie's smile, and radiant like the glow of her blossoming pregnancy.

It had indeed been too long.

Joachim walked the path that wove through the dwellings of baked mud bricks and sewn-together grasses of the jungle. When he came to the fire pit, children swarmed at his feet, whining for stories. One day he'd tell them to his own child. One day soon.

"Dad told me you almost got bitten by a boar."

The boy who spoke was the tallest in the crowd and had his father's eyes. But Rae wasn't just a boy any longer. Soon he'd be a hunter like Joachim.

"Did he?" he asked. "And you believe him?"

"Of course not." Rae laughed.

"Good."

Ben came from behind him, holding firewood. "What are you telling my son?"

He tossed his hair back from his face and scowled. His eyes were blue, bright like a sunlit lagoon.

"Nothing," Joachim said. "I'm just stopping a rumor before it starts."

"A rumor?" Ben put a log on the fire and laid the rest down. "That crazed beast might have killed you if I hadn't shot it with my arrow."

"Oh, don't lie. You're just covering up for all the times I've had to save *you*." Joachim winked at Rae.

"Baruch says I may be old enough to join you on your next hunt," Rae said. "I'm fifteen now, Mr. Joachim. Father says he'll give me lessons on how to use a bow."

The boy fixed his arms at an awkward angle, pretending to shoot prey. He'd need more than lessons—especially if Ben were going to teach him.

"Well, you'll learn from the best."

"And now he mocks me," Ben said.

"It's the only thing I can do after hunting with you," Joachim taunted. "I'd get bored of looking at all the rocks and trees and mud out there if I couldn't annoy you."

"It sounds so exciting!" Rae mused.

"It is," Ben said. "But it's no game. The jungle is a dangerous place. Now, go and see if your mother needs any more help, Rae. Mr. Joachim and I must speak."

"Yes, Father."

Rae looked down, his face flushing, and went toward the cookhouse. Ben brought Joachim away from the fire pit, and they started up the path that led out of the village and into the jungle.

"What does Ophelia think about her son going on his first hunt?" Joachim asked.

"You know her," Ben said. "That woman still worries about me and I've been going on the hunts since I was thirteen. Still, I don't think he's mature enough. If something happened, I'd feel like I failed to protect him."

Trees blocked the sun from the path, and the hunter within Joachim awoke. A parakeet chattered not far away, recounting some tale of flight to the rest of the jungle. An animal grazed to their right unseen, mid-sized by the sound of its patter, gnawing slowly, timidly—listening too. The creek's hum sounded smoother. It must have swelled in last afternoon's rainstorm, consuming the stones that otherwise caught in the current.

"But the next hunt won't be for another six full moons, I think," Ben said. He stopped and looked around.

"What's the matter?"

He drew Joachim in. Ben's face was close to his. "Did you hear?" he asked.

"Hear what?"

The parakeet gabbled still. Ben cleared his throat.

"What is it?" Joachim implored.

"There was an incident at the village when we were gone on the hunt."

"An incident?" Joachim swallowed. "But I just spoke to Darcie. She didn't mention anything…"

"She wouldn't. Not everyone in the village knows. Only the elders."

Joachim tried not to notice, but he couldn't ignore the strain in Ben's voice. It was as if he were pulling a clothesline tight for freshly-washed tunics or splitting bamboo for kindling. It strained Joachim too—it unnerved him. The mid-sized grazer had silenced.

"It was one of Them," Ben said.

Joachim looked around as if one might hear him. When he was a child, stories about Them circulated through the children that played at the beach. Stories that kept you out of the jungle, that kept you awake at night. But at that age, drunk on childhood pleasures, Joachim had never seen any truth to the tales.

And then They invaded and took his father. The creatures.

"The agreement stops them from coming to our village," Joachim said.

"Didn't matter. It came right onto our lands."

"But the elders made a deal," Joachim pressed. "We were kids, remember? They couldn't come near our homes anymore."

"Just because you can't see Them, doesn't mean They're not there."

The third voice was Baruch, their leader and the oldest man in the village. He'd crept up so slyly, so silently behind them that Joachim hadn't heard him coming. And if Joachim was a good hunter, Baruch was better. A bit unconventional, but when old age threatened a hunter's strength, he had to adapt.

"It found one of the children," Baruch said. "Jolyne tended to the boy in the infirmary, but the wound was minor. The child will be all right and this creature seemed to be alone. Perhaps it was more of a mistake."

"But it was one of Them?" Joachim's mouth was dry. "You're sure?"

"Yes, but we killed it before it could cause any real harm. No other creature has been seen by anyone else—not in years. He was a little one too, still coming to sexual maturity. I'll bet he just ran free of his colony."

Joachim saw the creatures in his mind. He remembered them most from when he was a kid, from the night when the village's dwellings burned like torches. They'd rushed out from the trees like a flurry of tadpoles in the low tide. They found their way inside Joachim's home and ripped it apart.

They found their way to his father.

"Relax, brave hunter. That was at the beginning of your time in the jungle. Your village is safe. Darcie is safe."

The man placed a hand on Joachim's shoulder. Though he was two generations older than him, he gripped with remarkable strength.

"I know," Joachim replied.

Baruch's workshop blended in with the trees despite being as tall as their highest branches. It housed the old man's living quarters and the library where he kept the largest collection of books in the village. Around back was a cellar. Trent stood outside it among wooden crates. Each held prizes of their hunt.

"Congratulations, Joachim," Trent said. "Baruch just told me that you will have a child. Darcie must be ecstatic."

"She is," Joachim said. "And so am I."

He wasn't as delighted as he should have been though, even as Ben clapped him on the shoulder, and Joachim forged a grin. In his head, the dwellings looked like charred wood in the fire pit. His father's blank eyes burned into his mind.

"Shall we get started?" Baruch pointed to the crates.

"None of the meat has spoiled," Trent said. "Not like before."

Trent and Ben lifted the lid of each crate, differently marked for different animals: boar, fish, small game, and reptile. Soon the villagers would salt and treat the meat, but that was the easy part. Squeezing all fourteen crates into the small cellar would be more onerous than the hunt.

Cool, humid air waved over Joachim as he and Ben descended the steps. Besides the jarred vegetables on the shelves and the dried meats dangling from the ceiling, the room was bare. An empty cellar meant a plentiful garden in the summer months, but in winter it could mean death, and the autumn equinox was just a full moon away.

"Here comes the first," Baruch said.

Joachim could smell the sour combination of bluefish and preservation salts. He and Ben hauled the crate to the corner and lowered it onto the floor. They steadied another crate down the steps and placed it on top of the first. It was heavier: small game.

Soon they found themselves moving along a narrow stretch of ground. Joachim counted thirteen crates. He hoped the last one would be fish filets. His arms weren't too excited for another crate of dense boar meat.

"We're ready," Joachim said.

But there was silence. Dark clouds obstructed the sun outside the doorway. The wind ceased to play with the branches of the palm trees.

"Baruch?" Joachim called.

Out of the silence, Joachim heard movement. He held his breath and listened, the hunter inside alert and ready for attack.

There was a scream.

Joachim tore up the steps. Trent lay on the ground in front of the cellar. Blood seeped from a gash in his leg, and tears squeezed from his eyes.

Baruch was pale. Sweat and blood layered his brow. The sweat came from an afternoon of lugging crates into the cellar, but the blood was something that Joachim couldn't so easily explain. It wasn't human. The spots were green on the old man's face. He held a knife.

"What happened?" Ben's voice was like the clothesline again, tight and strained, threatening to snap and coil.

On the ground, Joachim saw the same green blood that coated Baruch's face. And then he saw something else, another being sprawled out on the leaves.

It was one of Them.

"It attacked Trent," Baruch said. "It came out from the trees over there."

The creature was still. Blood bathed its skin, and its eyes had rolled back into their sockets. Joachim approached it. If it stood, the creature would have only reached his torso, but it exposed sharp teeth through the drool-drenched flaps of skin outside its mouth. Its breath was shallow and its whimpering soft, but that wasn't everything the hunter heard. He heard snickering. Clicking. Gurgling.

There were more in the trees.

"Run!" he cried out.

Too late. One had seen him. Watched him, rather. It had been in the brush, and now it sprang out. It leapt onto him, climbed, and dug its claws into the flesh of Joachim's stomach. He tried to pry it from him, but it held tight. Slimy, leathery skin.

A second came, wrapped around his legs, and knocked him from his feet. His head swung back, and he smacked it on a rock. He didn't need to touch the spot to know there was blood; he could feel its warmth on his neck. Ben ran toward him, mouth moving, but his voice could not pierce the buzzing in Joachim's head or the sound of creatures sprinting out from the trees. His vision blurred.

He thought he could hear Darcie and their unborn child. He could almost feel it in his arms. His stories of hunt would never be told to the little one. Not by him, anyway.

Joachim wasn't afraid: he felt sorry. He knew how difficult it would be, how sorrowful it would be, how sorrowful he had felt. Out of all the villagers, Joachim knew what it was like to grow up without a father, and now he would die by the same monsters that had left him without one all those years ago.

They were invading again.

CHAPTER TWO

DEPARTURE

Joachim awoke inside a dwelling that was not his own. He was cold, and his head throbbed. As his eyes adjusted to the light, he realized he lay alone.

When he stood, pain pierced the muscles underneath the bandages on his stomach. He could hear the calls of villagers. Joachim crossed the room, passing a small table with medicine and herbs on it, and opened the door. He had to force himself to take a breath.

He'd seen this before so long ago. Entire dwellings had collapsed into heaps of broken mud bricks and burnt bamboo timber. On the pathways that crisscrossed the village, arrows lay in the dirt. The air smelled like the times he helped his father roast boar meat for their suppers as a child. It reminded him of the burnt animal fat and crispy skin. It reminded him of the first time he had hunted and killed a living animal.

He felt nauseous.

Joachim saw corpses: adults, children, demons of all sizes. Some were so mangled, he couldn't even tell what or who they were. His father wouldn't recognize this place if he were alive. Joachim almost didn't either.

"Trent!"

The man looked pale, and his eyes were large. Even after hunting with him for years, Joachim had never seen his friend look this way. He was distracted. He wouldn't look Joachim in the eye.

"Trent, what happened?"

"We were attacked," he said. "They raided the village."

"How many were killed?"

"I don't know." He looked down. "One bit Rae's arm."

"Is he going to be okay?" Joachim asked.

Someone called to Trent from across the fire pit. Baruch strode toward them, a bow strung across his torso and his quiver full.

"You are to stay here, Joachim. I want you to stay in the village."

"Stay here?" Joachim asked. "What do you mean?"

Trent shifted, and Baruch rubbed his forehead. Joachim wiped sweat off his upper lip, and his bare chest warmed even in the absence of the afternoon sun. Where were they going? Worse: why did they need to leave?

"Where's Darcie?"

The words escaped Joachim's lips before he could stop them. The men didn't respond. What if the creatures killed her like they killed his father? His throat tensed, and his chest tightened as if he were being strangled by a Boa constrictor. If Darcie was dead, he was better off dead too.

"Where is she?" He repeated. His voice was loud. "What did They do to her?"

Baruch touched his arm.

"I'm sorry, Joachim. Darcie was taken during the attack."

He felt like he was pinned under a boulder. He had just returned from a hunt and barely given a chance to hold her in his arms, and now she was gone. But not just her: the child. They had been taken away from him like palm leaves dragged out to sea by the tide, never to come back.

It felt impossible to take a full breath. His head spun. He was sure he was going to be sick.

"They took her?"

"Yes," Baruch said.

"We have to go to find her. We have to get her back."

"We are, Joachim," Baruch said, "but you are too injured. I would like you to stay here and oversee the recovery of our village."

"Stay here? Are you insane? That's my wife they've taken. And my child too. They've taken my child!"

"And that is why I want you to stay here," Baruch said.

There was calmness in his tone. He spoke slowly, deliberately, as if Joachim might have trouble following. But Joachim was following just fine. In fact, his mind was racing.

"Trent, Ben, and I will go and retrieve her," Baruch continued. "I'm afraid if I take you, the tension will be too high. You may let your guard down and lead Darcie farther away from us."

Joachim felt like a child being chided for inappropriate behavior.

"That's ridiculous!" Joachim couldn't control his voice. "Listen to me, Baruch. I can't let Them take any more of my family. I won't let Them do to Darcie what they did to my father."

Baruch looked at him. Even through the blank expression on his face, the leader-face he always wore, Joachim knew that he had reached the man. Baruch had been there when the creatures took his father all those years ago and was the one who told Joachim that they could never get him back. Baruch couldn't argue with him now.

"Please, Baruch," Joachim said. "I have to come with you. If I don't, I fail as a husband and as a father. Besides, I am a hunter. I know the land, and I can hold out against the creatures. Four hunters will give us a better chance when we face Them again."

The man's eyes were wide and heavy. His skin flushed like the red of the harvest moon. Leader-face was gone.

"I will let you come on one condition."

"And what is that?" Joachim calmed his breathing.

"Don't assume that you understand the ways of the creatures or of Zupay himself. Such brash actions will not get Darcie back. Your foolishness will get us killed."

Zupay. The name made his stomach jump and each heartbeat burn. He was the leader of the creatures. He ordered the invasion of the village. He was responsible for his father's kidnapping and now Darcie's.

But Joachim was a hunter after all, and he had been successful in the jungle before. Surely he could take on some demon tyrant and its band of slobbering reptiles. Besides, he'd have to if he wanted Darcie home.

"Is that fair?" Baruch demanded.

"Yes, but I–"

"Then prepare to go. We are leaving immediately."

The man walked away.

⋆ ⋆ ⋆ ⋆ ⋆ ⋆ ⋆ ⋆ ⋆ ⋆

When he returned to his dwelling, he had to prepare. Joachim found his rucksack under his bed in the same spot he'd left it after the hunt finished just two days before. As his hand brushed the woven bed sheet, he saw Darcie's face. He remembered the nights they slept in each other's arms. He remembered her touch. He remembered her soft breaths on his cheek.

Darcie had been sitting in the doorway when he returned to the village not yet two evenings ago. The day had been hot, and Joachim was sweaty and dirty and tired. He lowered his rucksack, and she closed the book she had been reading, one from Baruch's Old Earth library, like all the others.

"Welcome home."

He'd spent the last six weeks in the arms of the jungle, the cold, dark, unforgiving wilderness that never truly felt right even on the most beautiful of days. Joachim had hunted in those trees all his life, but nothing compared to Darcie. In her eyes, he was home.

"How did the great hunters fare?" she teased. "Did you take

down three alligators this time? How about an elephant? Will we have enough elephant meat to last us until next summer?"

"Not quite," Joachim replied.

She stood with her hands on her waist. From the back, someone would think that she was upset if not for the expression on her face. She watched him from under her brow, her chin turned slightly downward. She smiled.

"I missed you," he whispered as he snuck his hands onto her hips.

"No, you didn't." She smirked. "You and Ben and Trent are like children out there—like young boys. And the jungle is your little paradise."

"What if I told you that you are my paradise?" He kissed her neck.

She snorted. "Oh, please. Think you can just walk in here and woo me with some flattery?"

"I know I can."

Darcie's arms snaked around him. Her lips were as intoxicating as barley sweetened in the sun, and soon, he lifted her off of her feet and pressed her against the wall.

"Joachim!" she exclaimed. "The neighbours."

"There's no one watching."

She laughed and hit him lightly on the chest.

"How was everything while I was gone?" Joachim asked.

"Fine," Darcie said. "Boring."

They went inside the dwelling. There was simmering jackalope stew on the stove.

"Ophelia's ceiling had a leak last week," Darcie continued. "A big rainstorm pushed through here, and it ripped some of the roof off. Did you get a storm out there too?"

"Yes," Joachim said. "I'm not even sure my rucksack is dried all the way through yet."

He dipped his finger into the stew. It tasted salty.

"And how are you?" he asked.

Darcie played with a lock of her dark hair and bit her bottom lip. She reminded him of the day they married. There had been no parent left to walk Darcie down the aisle, so she walked herself. The whole time she eyed him: shy yet eager. Almost childlike.

"I'm pregnant," she said.

He almost dropped his hand back into the stew. *A little boy*, she had just called him, alluding to his exhilaration whenever he entered the jungle. And Darcie was right: he often became so energized that he did feel like a little boy—and he felt like one again now. He felt like laughing, like scooping Darcie up and twirling her around. He could feel life bursting through his chest: ravenous innocence and maddening excitement. They'd been yearning for a child for so long.

"You are?"

"I found out into the second week of the hunt." She touched his face. "I skipped my cycle, and I told Jolyne. She ran a test and told me I was expecting."

Joachim cried. The hunter was supposed to be brave, but being brave sometimes meant having courage to show his emotions. He wept for her, smiling and laughing through the tears, and she cried too.

She spent the night tight to his chest and coiled in his arms like a huntress in camouflaging paints, like a butterfly in a cocoon.

Like she was protected by a shield.

He wished she were there for him to protect now. She hadn't mentioned the creatures that evening, and he doubted she even knew that They had come while he was away. But now she was gone, and so he had to be too. If he waited too long, They would keep her away from him forever. If she wasn't already.

Joachim opened the pantry door, the bamboo joints moaning as they rubbed against one another. He gathered three loaves of bread wrapped in cloth, a jar of soaked vegetables, and some dried meats. Joachim loaded them into his rucksack on top of a blanket and a water skin. He'd have to remember his knife and his bow. There were freshly carved arrows in the yard.

"I thought you died out there."

His mother had crept in and stood in the doorway, the same one where Darcie had awaited him. The bun atop her head looked messy, and tears streamed down her face. She crossed the room and passed the couch with the grass-stuffed pillows. She held him.

"We couldn't find you after the attack," Alena said. "When the other villagers found your body, I thought They killed you. I couldn't bear to lose you to Them too."

"I'm here, Mom." He tried to stop tears from reaching his own cheeks.

She released him.

"And Darcie," she started, "and the child…"

More tears.

"I know," Joachim said.

"I'm sorry," she said. "The village will do whatever we need to in order to return her home."

"I'm going with them."

Alena looked down at the rucksack on the table. Joachim remembered that it was the same table Ben had made when he and Darcie first built the dwelling. It had all felt so different then, so safe. But it was a false safety. The creatures had remained hidden for all those years. They'd even convinced him that there was no danger in the jungle he couldn't face. They returned now as a reminder: a predator lived not far away, one that only wanted to see his insides scattered along the jungle floor.

"But you're hurt, Joachim," his mother said.

"Trent and Ben will be there, and Baruch will lead us."

She stood silent, her eyes on the ground. When they lifted again, tears didn't drown out the hazel any longer.

"You remind me so much of him, Joachim," she said. "You're determined like he was—and stubborn too. Oh, was he stubborn." She smiled to herself. "But what I miss most about him, I find also in you. You are just as brave as he was. You'd make your father proud."

The waves sounded like drums as they sloshed through the dips and coves of the rocks. Rae sat on the largest one with his feet in the ocean. Sand blanketed the ground at the exit of the path that came from the village, but if one ventured to the right, the beach transformed. The Black Rocks.

Rae had visited ever since he was little. His father introduced him when he was a child, and he'd spent entire days there listening to every story his father told. Some stories were from the village itself, some of the Old Earth and the days before the Great Death, but most seemed from the fantastical world of dreams.

"You can see boats travelling across the ocean," Ben often told him. "Just over there on the horizon."

He would look to where the man pointed, widen his eyes, and grin. He had never seen them, and as far as he knew, neither had anyone else. But he found the stories to hold hours of intrigue. He would watch the horizon all day long, even when the other children played on without him.

He waited for boats to sail across the ocean and land at their village. Boats that never came.

Rae was fifteen now, and he sought out the stones for a different reason. He no longer believed the stories his father told him. Instead, he came to the rocks as a refuge, an escape from village life that had grown boring. Whenever his father left on a hunt, he would stare out at the ocean, frustrated with his own youth. He wanted to be out there with them—his father, Mr. Joachim, and the other men. He longed to go into the jungle. To hunt. But today was a different hunt. The bandages on his arm from the bite of the creature confirmed it. They'd kidnapped Mrs. Darcie, and the hunters had to get her back.

"Any boats today?"

His father came beside him and looked out at the ocean. His face seemed thinner than before the attack, and he wore his dark tunic. *Better to blend*, his father would say. It was his hunting tunic.

"Those are just stories, remember?"

"Just stories?" Ben asked. "I've seen them."

There was movement behind them. Ophelia stood back on the beach, not attempting the rocks. Rae's mother had never found the easy path across them like he and his father had. She never bothered to.

"Come and say goodbye to your father and the other hunters," she said. "They're about to leave."

"Can't I go with you?" Rae asked.

Whined. He was old enough now to know he was whining, but young enough not to care.

"You're staying here, Rae," Ophelia said. "We've already spoken about this, and I won't have you bother your father about it again. He has other things on his mind."

She was using her annoyed voice. She used it whenever Rae pestered her about how old he was now and how mature he'd become. Ophelia would never believe him though. She didn't want to see him enjoy the glory of a hunter.

"I'm sorry, Rae," Ben said. "This is not about hunting. It's about getting Mrs. Darcie back to the village. This is much more dangerous."

But Rae already knew that. He understood danger, and he could handle it. He was already old enough and strong enough and good enough. He just wished his father would see it.

"You're needed here," Ben said. "They'll need help constructing new dwellings for the villagers. Do you remember those knots I taught you?"

Like the stories, Ben had also passed on to his son his love of knots. He taught him all his favorites, how to tie them and how to untie them. After a while, it became a little game. Ben would scatter knots around the village, and Rae would find them, sometimes spending hours untying.

"Yes," he said.

"So will you promise me that you'll use them while I'm gone?"

Ben rested a hand on his shoulder.

"I will, Dad," he said.

"And what do you say to your mother for giving her a hard time?"

Rae cleared his throat and looked at the ground. A little crayfish bathed in a gap between the rocks.

"I'm sorry," Rae said.

At the spot where the Black Rocks met the sand, Ophelia smiled, half-sincere. But Rae didn't feel sorry at all.

CHAPTER THREE

IN THE JUNGLE

As a hunter, Joachim knew where the boars raised their young in the jungle. He knew where they migrated when the summer rains threatened to drown out their brush. He knew where the great leopard prowled and was careful to avoid her prey's remains. He knew where the ibis nests were, where the baboons swung from the trees, and where the anacondas swallowed jackalopes whole.

What he didn't know was where Zupay and his creatures lived.

Though no path led through the jungle, the four men embarked on their journey through a gap in the trees just behind Baruch's workshop. Other villagers watched in silence: Rae, Ophelia, Alena. It was not the joyous send-off Joachim normally received when he went on a hunt. No one spoke.

The hunters each carried a rucksack. Ben wore his on his bare back, the sun glistening off the sweat in his chest hair. Trent straggled behind, looking almost disoriented, and he turned his head at every chirp and animal call.

Baruch led them, draped in the same long, dark cloak he wore around the village. Joachim hoped the old man wouldn't forget how hot the jungle could become. The steel of his dagger glimmered from beyond the leather of its scabbard.

Joachim tried to concentrate. If he became distracted, he would open himself up to danger. He needed to listen to the jungle: the silence of crickets before an approaching predator, the clatters of deliberate movement disguised under wind, the growls and buzzes foreign to the trees. He couldn't let himself slip—not when he was in the belly of the beast.

Baruch stopped. They weren't yet far from the village, but Joachim couldn't see the workshop through the trees anymore.

"This is unlike anything you have undertaken before," he said. "Visiting Zupay in his village will prove easy. Getting there is the most difficult and dangerous. The closer we get, the greater the risk of attack. It is clear that the treaty is over between our two villages. If we come across one of Zupay's creatures, do not hesitate to kill it. They will give us no such hesitation in return. On this journey, we do not hunt. Understand that we are the hunted."

Blood raced through Joachim's veins. No emotion leaked onto Baruch's face, but that made his words more unsettling. It was like a clear sky the night before a storm, or the exposed seabed when the ocean withdrew before a relentless high tide. Ben's face looked expressionless too, but Joachim knew better than to think he was unafraid. He was wringing his hands. Trent didn't attempt to hide his discomfort. He swayed back and forth on the balls of his feet.

"How long will it take?" Joachim asked.

"I hope only the rest of the day," Baruch said. "But I can't be sure. The jungle is a creature of its own."

The elder faced the trees. The breeze brushed his pale face and pushed back his aging hair.

"We should move as quickly as we can," he said. "Zupay will be expecting us. I don't intend to visit when the darkness can shield him."

The sounds of the jungle both soothed Joachim and made him apprehensive. The humming of fluttering insects and the wind calmed him, but every croaking bullfrog and snapping twig was one of Them bursting through the leaves.

After a while, the trees became denser. The vines and branches above blocked out the afternoon sun. Joachim struggled to keep up with Baruch. Though he tried to blame his slowness on his injuries, he could hear grunts of exertion from Ben and Trent behind him.

Minutes rolled into hours, and the light faded. Lemurs traversed the treetops, laughing at some joke that only they knew, and horned jackalopes scurried into their jungle floor dwellings. A gentle rain swept through the branches of the trees. Afterward, flowers of all colors sprang from their limbs.

"We'll take a small rest here," Baruch said.

They stood in a clearing beside a river. Joachim lowered his pack but kept his knife out. Ben sat down on the jungle floor. Trent knelt down to the water and splashed some on his face.

"How long have we been travelling?" Joachim asked.

"Almost three hours," Baruch replied. "I want to keep good pace, so this rest will only last a couple minutes."

"Trust me," Ben said. "You keep good pace."

Joachim laughed, though nervously. He disliked the idea of being still in the jungle almost as much as his muscles disliked Baruch's speed. Jungle predators didn't remain in one place: they hunted ruthlessly day and night, stalking their next meal. He now knew that these predators were not the usual animals he and the other hunters had learned to avoid.

These creatures stalked and hunted villagers like him.

"How much farther?" Ben asked. "I've never been in this direction on a hunt."

"I don't expect any of you have," Baruch replied. "Other animals in the jungle, the ones that you kill during expeditions, flee before the creatures' presence. They can sense the blood-thirst from miles away.

"Beyond these trees"—Baruch pointed—"we will enter Zupay's territory. I suspect you will find a few things you've never seen in this jungle before."

"What kinds of things?" Joachim asked.

"Until we reach Zupay, our biggest threat will be the plant life. Remember, foreign flora shouldn't be touched or eaten for any reason."

Joachim saw that Ben smiled at the instruction. They knew better than to eat random plants found in the jungle. They were hunters after all, not toddlers.

But as they pushed on toward Zupay's territory, Joachim saw a glow. He moved farther into it, and it intensified. Beside him, he saw that both Ben and Trent had stopped. He stopped too. The glow was like moonlight but closer, as if the rippled stare of the setting sun over the ocean was in the air all around them.

"I've never seen anything like it," Ben said.

"Neither have I."

Mushrooms as tall as Baruch's workshop stood in clusters ahead. Dark smudges patterned the trunks and the underside of the mushroom tops which were as wide as roofs on dwellings back at the village. Each mushroom glowed with orange light, illuminating itself and the surrounding jungle.

"In all the science books I've read about ecology from Old Earth, I've never read about such mushrooms," Baruch said. "I can only assume that these too are a result of the evolution that followed the Great Death. But don't touch them. Their skin exudes a poison that causes hallucinations and flesh decay."

Though Joachim would have appreciated more time to admire the strange luminescent mushrooms, Baruch started walking again. The mushrooms pulsed in unison and went on as far as he could see. Each shower of light was refreshing like cool evening air.

But what he saw as he turned around stole all wonder from him.

Blood sparkled in the light. An animal had been slaughtered. Its blood coated the leaves, vines, and even the trunk of a nearby tree. Innards hung from branches like ornaments, and furry hides lay on the ground like the remains of snakeskin. Joachim felt the acid of his empty stomach climbing up his throat.

"Zupay's creatures are fond of slaughter," Baruch said. "They take a liking to shredding their prey and casting the entrails around the jungle. Be careful not to touch them. Doing so is a sign of territorial breach. They will think we have come to attack."

"Haven't we?" Trent asked. His voice was high.

"No," Baruch said. "Not unless you wish for our entire village to be annihilated."

Trent turned red and took a long gulp from his water skin. The men snuck around the entrails, careful not to nudge them with their feet. They wormed their way through many similar scenes. Each time, Joachim became dizzier and dizzier, and his stomach became more and more upset. It wasn't just the images that made him anxious: the thought of Darcie's mutilated body spewed across the jungle floor made him want to crumble and sob.

"Don't move."

Baruch's voice pulled Joachim out of his head. The wind no longer blanketed them. The sounds of insects and crickets and pattering paws could no longer be heard. Silence filled the jungle, but the periodic glowing of the mushrooms was undisturbed.

"What is it?" Trent asked.

"There's something following us. Don't turn around."

Baruch stayed facing away from them. Joachim didn't hear anything. Not a snicker or a click like he heard before, like when the creatures invaded the village after they loaded the crates into the cellar. Maybe Baruch was mistaken. Maybe nothing had followed them at all.

But Baruch was right. A branch snapped, and he heard a snicker. It was Them.

The sound of movement grew loud. Baruch was moving too, scanning every direction. Joachim lifted his knife, and the other two men readied their bows, but they didn't know where to aim.

With a call from behind, the jungle became quiet again.

Something whizzed past his ear.

"Arrows!" Baruch cried.

Joachim crouched down, and as he did he heard a cry. He turned around. Ben's eyes were wide. He clutched an arrow lodged into the right side of his chest. Blood leaked from the wound and onto the fabric of his tunic. He fell to his knees.

"Ben." Trent cradled him.

Trent put his hand over the wound, but the blood leaked through. Joachim's vision became fuzzy. He dashed forward and gripped Ben's leg. His body slumped in their grasp. Trent shook him, but Ben had closed his eyes. Joachim reached to get a pulse from his neck.

He felt nothing beneath his fingertips.

"Stop!" Baruch's voice boomed over the trees. "Enough with this nonsense. Come face me."

The jungle fell quiet again.

"Baruch," said a voice. "I knew you would come to visit me."

He came from behind a tree, a creature shorter than Baruch by a full foot. His skin was green and flaky. Atop his head was a patch of dark hair. He wore a cloak like Baruch's, and bony fingers peeked out from his sleeves—long and reedy and fashioned with dagger-blade nails. His face was thin, and his eyes shimmered in the mushrooms' light.

"You know as well as I do that the jungle is a dangerous place." A smile flickered across Zupay's lips. "I must ensure the livelihood of my people and protect them from intruders."

Joachim stood, and Trent rose beside him, his knife outstretched. Creatures swung from the trees. In comparison to them, Joachim realized that Zupay was tall.

"Leave the dead man here and follow me," Zupay said.

He then disappeared into the trees. Baruch followed, but Joachim and Trent didn't move. The creatures watched, but they weren't interested in him. They were eyeing Ben's body.

"What about Ben?" Trent asked.

"I said, leave the body." Zupay's voice rang again. "It's ours. My creatures hunted it and successfully killed it."

"No!" Joachim yelled.

Baruch looked back at them, his face flushed, but he followed the cloaked demon. Joachim didn't move. How could he just leave Ben behind? Ben didn't deserve that, and neither did his family. Maybe they could save him. Maybe they could make it back to Jolyne in the infirmary and heal him.

"There's nothing we can do," Baruch croaked.

But Joachim knew it too. The man was right.

"If you stay," Zupay began, "my creatures will be forced to kill you."

Joachim couldn't argue. He couldn't take them all on his own, and if he died, how would he get Darcie home? He grabbed Trent by his tunic and pulled him after them. His feet barely moved as Joachim dragged him. The mushrooms flashed.

"Now, let us show you some hospitality," Zupay said. "Welcome to the village of my people."

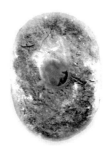

CHAPTER FOUR

DEAL WITH THE DEVIL

The trees thinned and opened to a path where mud stretched far into a clearing. Along both sides of the hunters, dwellings loomed high in the branches like tree houses of Old Earth. But they were vacant of playing children. Zupay's creatures swung down and hissed at the visitors, flashing sharp teeth. Joachim tried to scare them off with his knife, but Trent's weapons were at his side. He was whiter than the moon.

They passed a group of creatures guarding the mouth of a cave, and Zupay led them inside. There were markings on the walls, lit only by torchlight. The writing was different from theirs. It looked to be read vertically like an ancient script, one perhaps studied in a book from Old Earth, rudimentary but almost mystical. Animals accompanied other shapes and collections of lines: jackals, birds, and beetles. At the top and bottom of each line of script, there was an eye. They watched him.

Zupay sat cross-legged on a carpet of woven palms. He took drags from a pipe. In the back, smoke from sleeping embers drifted up through a thin shaft in the stone.

"You brought the whole village this time, Baruch," he said.

"Where's other fellow who used to come with you? I see you brought his son."

"You know very well where he is," Baruch barked.

"Indeed I do," the creature chuckled. "Come now, Baruch. Don't be so sour on a perfectly good gathering. Now, what brings you my village today?"

"You know why we're here."

"The girl?"

"Where's Darcie?" Joachim blurted out.

He felt his face redden. He was failing at staying calm. The hunter inside knew not to show his anxiety, to remain collected and wait for the proper moment to attack. That hunter was overshadowed. He was being smothered by someone frantic and wild—someone desperate, like a cornered boar mother protecting her young, snorting and growling and baring teeth.

"Hold your tongue or I'll have it served for lunch," Zupay snarled. "Honestly, Baruch, I don't see why you always insist on bringing men of such short tempers. It only complicates things."

"Give us Darcie back," Baruch hollered.

The old man's hunter was being smothered too.

"My, my, Baruch, you are a man of little patience today."

"You've broken the contract. A contract signed in blood cannot be broken," Baruch said.

"I believe the more powerful race decides when it is acceptable to break the contract, don't you?"

With that, Zupay stood and strolled around his cave. He took a final pull of smoke from his pipe and dumped the remaining herb into the fire. Within a moment, the dwelling reeked of the spicy odor.

"I asked you: where is she?"

"She is here," Zupay said. "But rightfully, my people found her, and we intend to keep her."

Joachim felt a fire ignite inside him. The fire crawled so hotly in his chest that it almost brought tears to his eyes. He thought of

Ben's body in the clearing, probably now half-devoured by Zupay's demons. The man was so young and so brave and so caring. What would Ophelia do? And what about Rae?

He could not bear to let Darcie await the same end.

"She didn't wander into your grounds!" Joachim cried.

"That doesn't mean anything."

"In the contract it does!" Baruch bellowed.

"To hell with the contract." Zupay eyes grew wider. "Besides, I can hardly call it a contract. You pleaded with me not to kill off your insignificant people, but *mine* didn't benefit at all."

"That's a lie, and you know it," Baruch said.

The creature tossed his empty pipe onto the ground and came closer to them so that the paleness of his skin offered a window to the veins underneath. The stench of faeces and rotting meat came too.

"In return for not slaughtering you all, I think we should be able to take as we please. We could call it population control, could we not? Your people struggled with overpopulation in the days of the Old Earth. I'd hate for you to suffer it again."

"But an innocent woman?"

"We needed to feed, and she was there. It could have been anyone, really."

"You haven't already killed her, have you?"

A tear brimmed and fell down Joachim's cheek. He wiped it quickly. Hunter's tears in Zupay's cave were not bravery; they were weakness.

"Of course not, you idiot." Zupay smiled. "I sometimes save the victims in case a more *juicy* deal should come along."

The mention of a deal made Joachim very warm. He could feel blood filling his face. A deal had killed his father all those years ago. Baruch and a group of men spent months away from the village. When they failed, Joachim's father remained as a penalty.

"What do you want?" Baruch asked.

"Well," Zupay began. "There is one small task I would need you to do."

Baruch relaxed, his shoulders lowering slightly. Joachim calmed too. Anything was better than wanting another human soul for ransom.

"I would need you to gather ingredients for a potion," Zupay said.

"What kind of potion?"

"You see, Baruch, I am getting older. I can't afford to die off and have my creatures fall into insanity. Besides, your village couldn't afford that either. If I die, there's no one setting boundaries on where they can feed."

"It's not like you respect the boundaries," Joachim mumbled.

Zupay glared. "That's not the point," he said. "Without the ingredients to this potion, I will inevitably perish."

"You've lived so many years, Zupay, much longer than any human lifetime," Baruch said. "How do you know you will die?"

"All things die, Baruch." Zupay looked at him. "Let us observe the trees. Some have been here since the Great Death. They surpass many lives, and some succeed to flourish for centuries. However, that does not mean that they live forever.

"Trust me, Baruch. A man knows when it is his time." He strolled around his cave. "When that happens, my tribe will lose the reason of my leadership and they will exhaust our food supply."

"Exhaust your food supply?" Joachim exclaimed. "Is that what you're keeping our village alive for?"

"It's not like you have any other purpose." Zupay examined the markings on the wall. The eyes in the script watched him too, almost fondly. "Between the four of us, I could raid your village and capture every human soul there if I wanted to. But that wouldn't be beneficial for the long term survival of my people, now would it?"

Trent knocked into a table, the scrape of the wood against the stone echoing behind them. Joachim had almost forgotten that he was there. He didn't look like he was listening though. He fingered the hem of his tunic.

"And you expect me to help you get immortality?" Baruch asked.

"You will if you want this man's lover and unborn child back."

Zupay observed their faces. Out of them all, he watched Baruch the most. Baruch stared at the ground.

"Take us to Darcie," he finally said.

Zupay led them back outside. He ventured left of the cave and followed another path into the jungle, one opposite from the way they had come. Nightfall darkened the sky, and the air was cooler. The jungle resonated with life, but it didn't sound like the nighttime Joachim recognized. Strange animals lurked through the trees, laughing and hissing as they passed.

Past guarding creatures, there was a clearing with a large wooden cage. Through the spokes, they saw that ropes tied Darcie's arms to two top corners. In the middle, sharp pieces of wood pointed into the interior, holding Darcie in a standing position. Yellowing bruises covered her face, and dried blood encrusted the ropes that bound her wrists.

Darcie's face was lifeless, and her head slumped to the side. Baruch called out her name. Joachim ran.

"What have you done to her?" he cried.

"Oh, don't panic," Zupay said. "She can't feel any pain. We've sedated her."

"Get her out of there." Baruch ordered.

"Well, this sweetens up the deal, doesn't it? Seeing her in this state *must* make you want to find a way to release her, and here's your chance. If you are successful, you'll get her back unharmed. If not, she's ours, and we will do what we please with her."

Baruch looked back at Darcie. Joachim could no longer hide his tears, and they fell onto the already filthy fabric of his tunic. Trent was biting the skin of his knuckles.

"Then tell me what you need," Baruch said. "I will get the ingredients for this potion of yours, and then you will set her free."

"You can't go it alone," Zupay said in mocking concern. "Frankly, we both know you're too old and weak to do it without an accomplice."

"I won't subject anyone else to it."

"Oh, but you must. You'll take one of them with you."

"I'll go."

Baruch's head shot around at the sound of Joachim's voice. Joachim didn't look at him, keeping his eyes on Zupay. Baruch shook his head.

"No, Joachim. You don't understand."

"Let the man go, Baruch," Zupay said. "Let him fight for the woman he loves. It'll be noble—poetic even. And should he fail, it'll be beautiful: a proper tragedy of epic potential."

Baruch's brow lowered on his eyes.

"I'll let your other escort return to your village," Zupay said. "He is as useless as a delirious boar after birthing."

Trent didn't hear him. He now stood by a small well in the corner of the clearing and stared off into the surrounding jungle. *Catatonic boar* would have been a better description.

"I won't hurt anyone until you get back or until the tenth dusk."

"I don't trust you," Baruch said.

"This I promise you." Zupay bowed. "I won't hurt the girl until the tenth night."

Baruch stared at him. The dark had almost completely fallen on the jungle, but the creatures didn't cease their snickering in the trees. A breeze swept across the clearing. It made Joachim shiver.

"You're not to hurt them. You're not to hurt Darcie or Trent or any of the other villagers when we're gone," Baruch ordered. "You must stay away from them all."

"Of course."

Immediately, Zupay walked back in the direction of the cave.

Baruch turned to Trent, grasped the man by the shoulder, and smacked him across the face. Redness grew on his cheek, and Trent's eyes widened. He looked like he was going to cry.

"Get a hold of yourself." Though Baruch whispered, his voice was hard. "I need you to return to the village immediately. Zupay won't attack because he knows that I'm getting something he wants. Tell everyone what has happened, and prepare them for potential assault."

Trent remained silent, his face twisting.

"Focus," Baruch said. "You are a hunter. Don't lose your composure. You must return to the village and relay the news. Do not fail your people. Can you do that?"

Trent eyed the jungle like someone might pop out and grab him, like a child straying too far from his mother. He nodded.

Baruch dragged him down the path, Joachim leading them. He followed where Zupay had gone and came to his cave. Baruch then turned Trent from the entrance and pushed him down the path that led out of the village.

"Make haste," Zupay called.

Trent looked once more at them, hesitating.

"Go," Baruch said.

With that, he ran. They watched him until he reached the trees on the other side of the clearing and disappeared into the darkness.

"What about Darcie?" Joachim asked. "Who is going make sure that they don't hurt her?"

"Don't worry about that."

Baruch entered the cave. The fire cast swaying light along the eyes on the wall. They were fond no longer.

"Think about the stupid decision you've just made."

CHAPTER FIVE

THE ONLY WAY

I t hit him. It smacked Joachim right in his stomach like the cold harsh waters of the ocean during a violent storm. He had just made a deal with Zupay, a deal similar to the one that took his father's life.

They re-entered the creature's cave. Zupay stood before the fire holding a small roll of parchment. Joachim wanted to run the other way. He wanted to hide as if we were a child, and Alena was forcing him to eat buckwheat. Though buckwheat tasted better than this, the feeling in his stomach was much the same: dread, disgust, nausea.

"Are you sure this is what you want, Baruch?" Zupay asked.

"Yes."

"And your companion?"

Joachim stared at the creature, a different expression painted on his face. He needed a new one. Buckwheat dread wouldn't do. He displayed one of determination, no longer fear or sorrow. It was the face of the hunter.

"This is what I want," Joachim said.

"Alright then," Zupay said.

The creature unrolled the parchment.

"So, the contract," Zupay started. "You and your comrade will gather the ingredients I need."

As he said this, words appeared on the page without him using a pen. The writing shone bright red and in English. Joachim would have been astonished if he wasn't so apprehensive.

"Firstly, you will go and contact a prophetess known as the Black Oracle. Her real name is Tilicea Shorciman, and she lives somewhere in the Realm of Zalm. Once you've found her, she will assist you, and the uncovering of the ingredients to immortality will follow. I am certain that all of those are in Zalm also.

"If you fail to find any of the ingredients, or you do not make the time limit, we will kill the woman that we have in captivity here and your friend Trent. If you succeed, they will be left alone."

The writing on the parchment stopped, and three lines appeared at the bottom.

"Trent?" Baruch asked.

"What kind of individual would I be if I subjected him to watch the slaughter of the woman?"

"That wasn't part of the deal."

"It is now. See, it's written in the contract. Any questions?"

Baruch's face grew as red as the ink.

"Why can't your creatures just get the ingredients?" Joachim asked.

"You'll get them because you want your wife back," Zupay said. "And because the ingredients are not of this world. They can only be found in Zalm, and the Empress will not welcome my creatures there."

"Where is this place?" Joachim persisted. "I have hunted nearly all of this jungle, and the only other civilization I know of is this village."

"Such a place is very good at hiding," Zupay said. "It only presents itself to those who seek to find it."

"It is just beyond Zupay's colony, Joachim."

He was surprised to hear Baruch's voice. The old man's eyes remained on the fire.

"Not far from here, there's a network of caves," Baruch said. "If we pass through them, we can cross the barrier that separates our world from the Realm of Zalm."

"Yes," Zupay said. "You remember it well, Baruch."

"How could I not?" Baruch said. "I have been there before doing your work. Besides, I passed near those caves on your last deal when we were not able to…"

Baruch's gaze trailed over to Joachim. He knew exactly what the man meant to say. When his father was still alive, there had been a similar journey. Joachim didn't know the details at the time, but he realized them now. The last time Baruch went past the caves to Zalm, he failed his task, and the village paid with his father's life.

"Well, I wish you better luck this time, for both our sakes," Zupay said. He pushed the piece of parchment at Joachim and Baruch. "Sign here."

"With what?" Joachim asked.

"Our blood," Baruch said.

He pulled his dagger out of his scabbard and poked the tip of his finger with it. A bubble of blood formed. Zupay held out the parchment eagerly. Baruch pressed his finger to the first line.

"Your turn."

Joachim took out his own knife. He held it shakily in his hand. He hadn't been this nervous since he asked Darcie to marry him. But that was a different kind of nervous, and this was a different kind of marriage. He was sacrificing everything.

He wiped the blade clean and pricked the top of his finger: a small sting. He pressed his finger onto the second line. The fire behind them crackled.

"Excellent," Zupay said, snatching the knife from Joachim.

Zupay cut into his finger as if he enjoyed the pain. The bubble of blood was dark green. He smeared it onto the parchment. All three smudges of blood glistened in the firelight.

Zupay's expression changed. The cheer fled from his face, and his brow lowered on his eyes. Joachim felt uneasy. The demon looked like he had just ingested rotted vegetables, except that probably wasn't too far from his actual diet.

"It is done, then," Zupay said. "Now, kindly leave my village, and do not return until you've brought me the ingredients I need."

ﾂ ﾟ ﾌ ﾟ ﾚ ﾟ ﾟ ﾟ ﾟ ﾟ

Joachim followed Baruch outside. The wind had calmed, and the air felt frozen on Joachim's face. Night had completely fallen on the jungle, and he could see glows from the fires illuminating the tree dwellings. Baruch led him around a stone wall and into the jungle to the right of the cave, taking them farther away from their own village and farther away from Darcie.

"Shouldn't we go back to the village for food?"

"We don't have time," Baruch said. "We can get more once we arrive in Zalm."

Baruch took a lantern from his pack and lit it, casting shards of light into the trees. Though he didn't see any of Them, Joachim knew they were there. He could hear their laughs and grumbles over the night's song. More than once, Joachim heard the rips and gnashes of flesh. A new kill.

"What happened the last time?" Joachim asked. "The time my father died?"

"We failed."

Baruch didn't slow.

"What were you meant to do?"

"The details aren't important, Joachim. The main thing is that we did not succeed, and we suffered for it, and I won't let that happen again."

Joachim gripped his arm. "Baruch, stop."

The absence of the sound of their footsteps made Joachim uncomfortable. In that void, the sounds of the jungle echoed louder. The creatures seemed to dwell closer, waiting for the perfect moment to attack.

"If we're going to do this, I need to know what happened," Joachim said.

Baruch shook his head.

"It will help us not to make the same mistakes."

Baruch paused and watched him a moment. He sighed. "Then walk with me, Joachim," he said. "Walk with me, and I will tell you it all."

It was a long time before he spoke again. His breathing would quicken and slow, and he'd open his mouth, but Joachim knew that he battled to find the right words to say. That is, if there were even any words to say at all. He tried to stay patient and listen to the jungle, but his mind itched to know. Alena had never mentioned what really happened. He doubted she even knew. The elders were full of secrets.

"Zupay had killed for many years," Baruch finally said. "Not frequently, of course. It was long enough between every murder to peel the scab off of the wound and make it fresh again. Each time, Zupay would come to the village after the kidnapping and send me into Zalm to do his work. Sometimes he wanted precious stones, other times he sent me to find information about the Empress and her people.

"Though we scoured the jungle during hunts, we could never locate Them. They used to be nomads, always stalking their food. There was no village to be a constant for them. They preferred it that way. Zupay said that it kept his enemies from descending on him."

"What enemies could he possibly have?"

"I don't know," Baruch said. "Either way, they decided to set up a village of their own after years of wandering. They claimed that they didn't need to chase their food; that the food would come to them."

"He meant us?" It was less of a question.

"Yes, and he was right. The attacks on our village became more frequent. One night, they launched the biggest attack we had ever experienced—"

"And they took my father."

"Yes."

Joachim took a breath. He had become more emotional than he wanted to. Baruch seemed to sense this and was silent.

"Then what happened?" Joachim asked.

"We set out into the jungle, but this time we knew where to find them," Baruch said. "When we arrived, we were not killed. They presented us to Zupay himself. He said the killing would stop if we helped him one final time."

The trees became so thick that they blocked out the stars and moon above them. Baruch's lantern was stifled by the darkness.

"What did he make you do?"

"There was another band of humans living on the other side of his village," he said. "Zupay needed our hunters."

Joachim didn't need to hear any more. He knew exactly what the man would say. It was one thing to hunt an animal, but to hunt another human being—to hunt a mother or a daughter or a son. To hunt a wife; one with Darcie's soft features. It made his stomach churn.

"He told us that if we wanted to save our people, we must obliterate theirs."

"Why?"

"I don't know. He said he could do it himself with his own creatures, but he wanted us to. He said that the other humans weren't aware of Zupay's existence and not even aware of our own village. They would be completely oblivious to the oncoming slaughter."

"But you said you failed," Joachim said. "You refused to kill them."

"No," the man said. He cleared his throat. "In the mess of our assault, we missed a few. But Zupay knew. Your father was forfeited."

Joachim swallowed. "How did he know?"

"Probably on a tally of the corpses. Zupay had been stalking them for a long time."

"But if you failed, why did he spare our village?"

"I told him that we did our best," Baruch said. "We killed most of their people. I insisted that Zupay benefited greatly."

"What about the survivors?" Joachim asked. "Have they ever been found?"

"Yes," Baruch said. "One family remained: parents and a daughter. In fact, we took them in after the assault. They didn't see the attack because they were out during our raid. They didn't know it was us who killed their friends."

Joachim tried to imagine it. The people who they had intended to kill now lived with them in the village. But who were they? One day they would realize the truth and turn on the village like the village had turned on them.

"Are they still with us?" He asked.

Baruch stopped walking and lowered the lantern.

"Isn't it obvious, Joachim?"

"No." He narrowed his eyes.

"Zupay has come back for the only living survivor of our attack," Baruch said. "That survivor is Darcie."

CHAPTER SIX

THE CAVE

For the remainder of their journey to the cave, Joachim and Baruch didn't speak. He completely abandoned his instinct to monitor the sounds of the jungle, and muttering filled the space in his head. As they travelled through the darkness, Joachim thought about everything he had just discovered.

The killings. He couldn't imagine such an act as a solution for Zupay. Could Zupay be so powerful that he could force his victims to kill for his mercy? Further still, how could Baruch and the other elders from that expedition all those years ago bear to look at Darcie knowing what they had done to her people?

Joachim felt disdain for the man who led him toward this mystical place called Zalm. Could he trust him after everything he had done to those people? The elders weren't just full of secrets anymore—they were full of lies. How did he know that Baruch wouldn't turn on him and his fellow villagers again?

Suddenly, light was in the air. As he looked up, Joachim saw that the trees and vines parted just wide enough to let moonlight fall on the jungle floor. He thought he could see a face in the moon. For a moment, that face looked like his father.

His father. If Joachim were in Baruch's position, would he not kill to keep his village alive? But then there was the slaughter of Darcie's village. If it were Darcie he had to kill, surely he would not, but what if he had to kill someone else? Could he completely deny he wouldn't sacrifice strangers to keep his village safe? Would he not have done everything to keep his father alive?

Would he not do everything for Darcie?

He watched the old man. Baruch walked unfalteringly onward, but Joachim could see weakness creeping into his step, and it wasn't something that had formed recently. The man had weakened over time, coming on fewer hunts and doing less manual labour for the village.

What sort of burden did being a leader entail? Though the village made most decisions democratically, Baruch remained the man in charge, the man with answers. The man ultimately at fault when things went wrong. Joachim tried to understand what it would mean to carry the whole existence of a village—what choices he would have to make, what sacrifices he would have to consider.

But the anger didn't go away. Murder was never a solution. It just couldn't be.

The ground underfoot became muddy, and the trees were thick once again, shutting out the moon. Even the dim light from Baruch's lantern couldn't shield the trees from the darkness. Baruch stopped, holding the glow at a length. In the obscurity, it took Joachim a moment to see why. A couple feet in front of them, he saw the opening of a cave.

"The journey will take roughly half a day," Baruch said. "I'm afraid we won't be able to sleep tonight, but we should arrive in Zalm in the early hours of morning. If everything goes as planned, we should reach the Black Oracle within two days."

The ground sloshed as the two men entered the cave, gurgles of mud echoing with each step. Vines hung from the ceiling covered with small, glowing shells, and water dripped on their heads.

Joachim could see the same animal markings from Zupay's cave on the walls of this one. More eyes.

They walked without speaking, and Baruch led rather incautiously. It didn't seem that he felt there was anything to fear. Joachim felt quite otherwise. He had to stop himself from drawing an arrow along the wood of his bow whenever a howl of wind passed through the opening behind them.

After half an hour, Baruch stopped. A smooth wall of rock blocked the tunnel. It was covered in markings and there were two large handprints of red paint on the stone.

"What is this?" Joachim asked.

Baruch didn't answer. He rested his lantern on the ground.

"How are we going to get past this, Baruch?"

"Just wait."

Baruch pushed back the sleeves of his cloak and cleared his throat. He placed his hands on the stone so that they were on top of the handprints. He closed his eyes and muttered words that Joachim couldn't understand. It was a language he didn't know, one he'd never heard. It was melodious and guttural and fluid, like all the vowels sang to him.

Baruch lowered his head then stepped away.

"What was—?"

As Joachim spoke, the cave shook. It didn't last long, just enough to alter his balance. When it ended nothing seemed damaged, but as Baruch lifted up the lantern, Joachim saw what had happened.

"Follow me."

The wall that had been a barrier just moments ago had changed. Ripples danced through the barrier like a pond disturbed by a rock. Baruch went forward. When he reached the stone—or the spot where the stone just was—he kept going. He disappeared into the rock as if there had been nothing blocking the path at all.

"Walk."

The old man's voice was muffled and blunted on the other side, but he was there nonetheless. Joachim stretched out his hands. Coolness consumed them, starting at his fingertips and moving up his arm as he moved farther. He closed his eyes. The wall felt refreshing on the flesh of his face and body like the freshwater springs of the jungle that he bathed in during his hunts. It was energizing like Darcie's kiss after months of being away. On the other side, the air was warmer. He opened his eyes.

The cave continued on.

Baruch led Joachim down the narrow tunnel. The walls were marked as before, but this script looked completely different, made up of lines and dots and lacking the jungle animals that were present in Zupay's, lacking the eyes. Lavish pictures accompanied the writing. Some of them showed people hunting, others worshipping a higher power, and even some of humans being eaten by horrible beasts.

He stopped and looked at them.

"The pictures tell the history of Zalm," Baruch said. "The first High Council needed a place to record past events. Books proved to be too easily tampered with and too easily burned. They searched for a place that would resist those who wanted to erase the history of their world."

"Can't people just come down here and tamper with them?" Joachim asked.

"They can get down here, yes, but they're not able to deface the pictures."

"Why not?"

"The last living sorcerers and sorceresses of Zalm put charms and curses on this cave to make sure no one could change the stories. Not even the High Council can erase Zalm's history."

"Charms?" Joachim asked. "Like magic?"

"Yes, indeed."

Joachim smiled. Magic? That was the defense against people

who wanted to alter historical accounts? He'd read about it in Baruch's library. Surviving books from Old Earth told about burning witches and ancient alchemy and childish folklore. But it was just that: it wasn't real. Joachim had never heard something so ridiculous.

But then again, he had just walked through a stone wall.

"Go on then," Baruch held his knife out to him. "Try to chip a piece off the drawings."

Joachim took the blade, uncertain. As soon as the metal touched the stone, Joachim felt a strange sensation in his fingers. He mounted the knife in position, ready to scrape off some of the stone, but the feeling in his fingers grew. In an instant, the knife in his grasp grew hot. He brought it right to the stone, and the handle became unbearable.

Withdrawing the blade, he looked at the flesh on his palm. The skin was red and puffy: the early signs of a burn. Baruch took his knife back and led him forward again.

"If you had insisted on damaging the images, the burning would travel up your arm and consume your body."

"Is this magic present everywhere in Zalm?" Joachim asked.

"Not any longer," Baruch said. "In fact, magic in Zalm is relatively rare. The 53rd High Council of Zalm outlawed all forms of it. When I last visited, many sorcerers and sorceresses were being executed to scare others into abandoning their practices. Others went into hiding."

Joachim looked at the pictures again. He noticed that they began to change. The violence was different in them now. The pictures showed battles and burning cities. Soldiers in emerald armour struck down other soldiers and women and children. Periods of peace were sparse.

"What about the Black Oracle?" Joachim asked. "Is she not considered a form of magic?"

"Yes, she is, but the Council knows of her powers. They make sure she is kept away from the citizens, but they continue to call on her when they need prophecies."

Joachim couldn't imagine what it would be like to abandon a force as powerful as magic. With its help, so much could be accomplished. In his own village, life would be easier. He could kill the creatures and Zupay. He could get Darcie back. He could bring his father back.

"They're a lot like us, you know," Baruch said. "They don't know how they came to be in their world, and they don't know when they are to leave."

"But our time on Earth already ended," Joachim said. "Sometimes I fear we're the only humans who survived the Great Death."

"Earth hasn't ended." Baruch looked up at the pictures. "It is still here, and it will continue to be here regardless of whether or not humans are alive to populate it. Our village is simply a new era."

No one ever really talked about the time before the Great Death. It never came up at dinners or at meetings held by the elders. There were seldom stories about it told around the fire pit or in the conversations of the children. It was simply a mystical time from the books of Baruch's library, complete with stifling pollution, war, and disease. But when the Great Death came all those generations ago, Joachim's people survived, and now they lived anew.

All the humans who remained could be crushed by a fleet of demons. The creatures were a species that emerged following the extinction of the human race. Zupay was the most evolved of them all. The villagers knew no reason for the hyper-intelligent mutation of the demon leader, but he was nonetheless capable of language and logic like they were—and calculated murder.

"But how were we like Zalm?" Joachim asked.

"The people of Zalm are ignorant and arrogant. Even those who aren't, the ones who try to save their world from implosion, hold no power against the control of the Council. But one day they'll see, hopefully quicker than we did."

"Did humankind ever see?" Joachim asked. "In all the books, it never seemed that humans before the Great Death ever worried too much about their end."

"The leaders talked a lot. For many years, it drove many political campaigns as leaders used the threats of annihilation to gain the following of their citizens. I don't know how that world ended, but it is evident that if anything was done, we did it far too late.

"But this is not the end," Baruch continued. "Earth will repopulate. I'm convinced there are more human survivors out there. We can't be the only ones. My only fear is that this time we are not alone. The creatures outside our village can't be the only things that evolved after the Great Death…"

Baruch looked over his shoulder.

"Something's following us."

Joachim tried to listen to the cave. Behind the dripping of water, he heard nothing. Despite this, he could feel his pulse pushing thick in his veins. He'd listened so intently to Baruch that he'd forgotten to monitor their surroundings. Now he felt as vulnerable as a baby boar alone in the jungle at twilight. He forced the hunter to return. He drew his bow.

Baruch lifted the lantern and shone the light around the cave. Joachim looked too, nervous at what might be there with them.

"I don't see anything."

"Be silent, Joachim."

A throaty growl resonated in the space behind them. Joachim looked, but he saw nothing. He heard it again, this time moving closer.

"What is it?" He whispered.

"There's no real name for them, but the people of Zalm call them 'cave dwellers'," Baruch whispered back. "They are nearly blind and almost impossible to see because they blend in with the rock. It'll kill us both if it finds us."

Baruch blew the flame in the lantern out, plunging the cave into darkness.

"Why did you do that?" The bow in Joachim's hands remained drawn. "I thought they couldn't see us."

"They may be blind, but they are still sensitive to light. This lantern could draw the creature closer."

Joachim held his breath and hoped that the cave dweller would leave them alone. The growling stopped, and he strained to hear anything at all. He could only hear Baruch's breaths behind him.

"Okay. I think it's gone now."

Baruch lit a match, and the cave filled with light again. It took Joachim a moment to adjust, but as his eyes accepted the light, what he saw in front of him made him jump backwards. The creature hadn't left at all. The cave dweller hung upside down just inches from his face.

Flaps of skin covered the creature's eye sockets, and its flesh was pale and slimy. Its body was so skinny that bones stuck through the flesh. The cave dweller sniffed wildly and let out a screech. As it opened its mouth, drool dripped from its teeth.

"Run, Joachim."

He dove just as the creature snapped its jaw, missing him by a couple of inches. It dropped from the ceiling and landed close to where he was. It sniffed the ground. Joachim had hunted vicious creatures before, but he had always remained far enough away to strike it with an arrow, hidden in the trees. He never went to prey until they were too injured to fight back.

But now Joachim was injured. His muscles ached from fatigue, and the wound on his stomach stung as he struggled to crawl away. Maybe Joachim couldn't fight back.

Just as it opened its mouth to bite him, Baruch's voice tore through the air. The cave dweller spun and sprinted the other way. Before Baruch could move, the creature jumped on him and sent the lantern smashing into pieces on the floor. The cave dweller dug its teeth into Baruch's shoulder. The man cried out, and the oil from the lantern ignited a fire. Joachim ran over, baring his knife.

Joachim grabbed the creature by the back of the neck and threw it onto the ground. It sprang to its feet and dashed toward him, letting out another screech. He swung. The blade missed the creature, and it jumped onto his chest. The dagger flew out of his hand, and Joachim fell to the ground. He grabbed the creature by the throat, holding it from his face as he felt around for his dagger with his other hand. Inching around the dirt, Joachim felt the hilt just out of his grasp.

The creature broke free from his grip and sunk its teeth into his forearm. Blood sprayed from the wound like a hot summer rain. Tears seeped from Joachim's eyes, burning his cheeks. He could feel the panic setting in, feel his limbs giving way to the franticness of death. He had to center himself. He had to summon the calm, calculated hunter. Darcie needed him.

Joachim felt the knife slip into his hand, and he pushed it through the back of the cave dweller's head.

The creature flopped dead on top of him and coated him in smelly blood. Joachim sat up. The gash on his arm stung, but that wasn't what concerned him. Almost all of the oil from the lantern had finished burning. The shadows closed in on them.

"Baruch?"

"I'm here, Joachim. Are you hurt?"

"Only a little," Joachim lied.

Joachim stood, but the ground started to shake. An earthquake? Tiny stones rained down. He dropped the knife and fell onto his stomach in another strong tremble. He was bleeding now there too from the wound that was still healing from Zupay's attack. In the distance, larger stones crashed onto the ground. The cave then became still.

"What just happened?" Joachim asked.

He squinted through the haze of dust.

"I'm not sure," Baruch said. "Did you bring a medic kit with you?"

Joachim reached around to his back. He was generally the medicine man when he went out on a hunt, though he never encountered cave dwellers. The contents of his rucksack were flattened and damaged from the brawl, but he found bandages.

He looked at Baruch's shoulder. Blood stained the entire left side of his cloak. He poured alcohol on the wound.

"Your arm."

"I'm fine," Joachim said.

"Go bandage yourself," Baruch said.

"I can wait. Your shoulder can't. Now stop moving so I can wrap it properly."

"No, you need to—"

He heard footsteps. Joachim stood, pointing his blade in the direction of the sounds. His stomach burned. The fabric of his tunic rubbed against the wound. The light was so dim he could barely see, but he could make out three dark figures coming toward them.

"Who are you?" A female voice called.

"We are victims of a cave dweller attack and an earthquake," Baruch said as he struggled to stand. "We are on our way to the city of Zostrava."

"Well, my dear Baruch, I can certainly help you get there."

A light erupted through the darkness, one much more effective than Baruch's now smashed lantern. The woman in the middle of the three figures walked toward them. She wore a long black cloak. Flowing locks of ginger hair brushed her shoulders. Like her, the two women on either side wore dark cloaks, but their hair was darker than their leader's. A strikingly odd beauty accompanied all three of them—olive skin, light blue-green eyes with golden highlights.

The women formed a circle and surrounded the travellers. They closed their eyes. A growing breeze fluttered through Joachim's cloak, and he clutched his rucksack, too bewildered to ask what was happening. Light surrounded them, obscuring the stone of the cave.

Joachim hoped that Baruch was right to trust these women.

CHAPTER SEVEN

PREPARE

Breaking through the last barrier of trees, Trent emerged into the clearing of Baruch's workshop. Though the memories of what happened in Zupay's village were blurry and jagged, the journey back had had a sobering effect on him. He spent much time in the confusion of the night, dodging shadows and predators on his way, but he didn't stop running. He tore down the path that led to the rest to the village. The coming dawn warmed the sweat on his face.

Though it was early, the villagers were very much awake. There had been little sleep on the previous night, Trent knew. The entire village would have felt anxious with four hunters gone to Zupay. With the news he would tell them, he knew their fears wouldn't subside.

He came to the fire pit. Three villagers roasted slices of boar meat on skewers above the flames. The smell of meat normally made his mouth water and his stomach call out, but not today. It made him want to scream. It made him want to collapse into the sand like the pile of firewood, like the dwellings that didn't survive Zupay's assault.

"You've returned."

Ophelia was at the fire pit. Her face lit up, and she hugged him. Alena turned to him also. Her eyes looked swollen and heavy. Even at her age, Trent had never before seen her look this old and frail. She smiled as she embraced him.

"Are the others at Baruch's workshop?" Alena asked, looking down the trail through the trees.

"Yes, let us go to them."

Ophelia started forward as the words left her lips. Trent caught her before she ran.

"Trent?" Alena's eyes narrowed. "What happened?"

He tried to calm himself, but he did quite the opposite. He could feel tears gnawing at his eyelids. He wiped the first that crept down his cheek.

"They made a deal with Zupay to get Darcie back," Trent said.

More villagers gathered. Alena's eyes widened, and she became paler than she was before.

"Bring them here, Trent," Alena said. "Baruch must address the village."

A crowd had assembled now.

"They aren't here," Trent squeaked. "Zupay has sent Baruch and Joachim away to find ingredients needed for immortality. They have ten days to bring them back to him, and if they don't, the creatures will attack."

The crowd became a clamber of voices. They were like a flock of gulls discovering food scraps, fluttering and squawking and poking around, but ultimately not going anywhere at all. Many tried to delegate roles in case Zupay attacked, but most were too distraught to cooperate. Only a woman's cry brought silence back to the villagers.

"What about Ben?"

Ophelia's long face peered at him, illuminated by the morning's struggling light. They all listened for his answer. Rae came toward him through the crowd. His face was furrowed with the remnants of sleep—or the lack of it.

He couldn't lie to them.

"They killed him."

ㄅ ㄥ Ⴟ ㄐ ㄷ ㄱ ㄷ ⅁ ⴤ

The Black Rocks felt different to him now. Rae had listened to Trent talk. He heard about the trek through the jungle. What Zupay had done to Darcie. What Zupay wanted them to do. What had happened to his father. He didn't feel anger toward his fellow villagers or a longing to join the adults on their hunts anymore. Now, he only felt sorrow.

Tears streamed down his face as the sun began to set on this desolate day, sending a glow across the ocean. Rae realized that this was the only place left where he could find his father.

"Rae?"

The voice called from behind him. On a normal day, he would have heard somebody coming. It was hard not to stumble over the minefield of stones and gaps if a villager hadn't found the safe way across. But today was not a normal day, he knew, and he didn't care how the person got to him. He just wanted to be alone.

"Go away."

"Rae, please come with me."

He turned around. In the salty breeze, the woman's features were blurred, but he could still recognize Mr. Joachim's mother standing there. Her long hair was pulled back in a bun, and she held a leather-bound notebook in her hand.

"Why?" Rae asked, wiping his cheeks.

"The village is deciding what steps we must take. Baruch told Trent to warn us to prepare for a possible attack."

"Then why do you need me?"

"You are part of this village."

"That doesn't matter," he spat. "My father was right. I'm too young. I can't hunt. I can't help. I can't do anything. And now he's gone."

The woman came closer to him, mastering the rocks as if she had walked them many times. She stood just behind where he sat. He wanted to will her away, but she put her hand on his arm.

"That's not what your father meant at all," Alena said. "He grew up with Joachim, and I know him as if he were my own son. Your father didn't mean that you're not capable of doing any of those things. He meant to protect you, Rae. He wanted to protect you from the things that want to harm you in that jungle."

"Like the things that killed him," he said.

Rae felt the tears again. Before he could stop himself, he was standing and holding the old woman. He buried his head in her shoulder, and he realized that she wept also. She eased him away from her.

"We need you at the village, Rae," she said. "With two of the main hunters and Baruch gone, we've lost some of our protection. Now, more than ever, we need everyone in this village to help us get through this."

"But, what if I—what if I *am* too young?"

"It doesn't matter, Rae." She put her hands on his shoulders. "You are not alone. We together are a village, and we will help you. We can all help each other."

"But—"

"Do it for the village. For your father."

Rae knew she was right. His father didn't stop him from hunting because he felt Rae was inadequate. If he were in his father's place, knowing how dangerous the jungle was, he would hesitate to let his own son hunt in it, especially now that he knew just exactly what that loss felt like.

"Okay, I will."

"Good." The woman wiped her eyes. "Let's go back."

The two climbed over the rocks back to the sand. Despite the terrain, the woman didn't slip once even though Rae did in places where the stone was wet. They crossed the beach until they came to a gap in the trees then followed the path toward the village.

"My father used to take me to those same rocks," Alena said. "We would walk down there every night just as the sun went down when I was a little girl. That seems like so long ago."

"Better days?" Rae asked.

"Yes and no," she replied. "Better because I was more naïve, I suppose. This village seemed like the safest place back then, even though the threat from the creatures was just as prominent. I could spend all day in the sun, catching frogs and listening to the voices of the jungle. However, nothing is more painfully sobering than finding out that the bliss of childhood was no more than an illusion."

Rae thought about what she said. Though he tried to believe that he always took the threat of the creatures seriously, he had to agree that often those threats seemed far away from the village, far away from his life. Perhaps this was the moment where he fell out of childish bliss like Alena had. Perhaps now he started adulthood.

As the path widened, the village came into view. Though it remained busy with people, the atmosphere had changed. Barely anyone chattered as they worked on tools or gathered items or wrote things down. Those who spoke did so in whispers.

Alena led him past the infirmary and into one of the other dwellings. It remained standing after the creatures' attack, though there were holes in the mud brick of the wall. This was the new headquarters for the village, Rae knew, a new command post for a village at war. Whatever happened from then on, he felt that most decisions would have to be made by a few in that very place.

Inside, there stood a long table of bamboo. The shades were pulled across the windows, but sunlight still pushed through, plunging the room into an obscure twilight. On the table, someone had lit candles and laid out a large map of the jungle. Trent and two other villagers sat in chairs in the back corner. They stood as he and Alena entered.

"I'm glad you've decided to help out," Trent said.

"Me too." Rae shook the men's hands.

"As you've heard, this village is in danger," Trent started. "We may have a deal with the creatures, but that has never stopped an attack before. Now that Baruch and two of our hunters are gone, this village is more vulnerable than ever.

"If Joachim and Baruch should fail, our village is officially Zupay's to pillage and destroy. That gives us only nine days after today before their attack."

"Okay," Rae said. "So what's the plan?"

"We prepare for a war," Trent said. "We have women and children who are old enough working on arrows and knives. If we have to face Them, everyone should able to fight and be armed for an attack."

The thought of women fighting worried him. How would his mother be able to protect herself from a swarm of demons? As he thought about it, he realized that he had not seen her in the village when he returned from the Black Rocks.

"Where's my mother?" he asked.

"She's in the infirmary," Alena said. "She has been given medication to help her sleep. She's spent a very sleepless night, and I fear she may have many more to come."

He wondered if he would be able to sleep himself. The emotion crept so close to the surface, swelled so near to the brim that Rae feared if he took a moment to rest, he would never escape the sorrow again.

"So everyone just waits for the attack?" Rae asked.

"Not exactly."

Trent rested his palms on the table. He then pointed at various locations on the map as he spoke.

"We will have the men working in shifts. They will patrol the jungle as far as a mile from the village. Any sign of Zupay's demons, and they will launch a flare into the air. On that signal, we prepare our village for the attack."

"Do we have a chance against them?" Rae stared at the map. A dot in the middle of the jungle indicated where Zupay's colony lived. "My father said that there are only one hundred and fifty villagers. Even with everyone fighting, is that enough?"

"Do we have any other choice?"

Rae looked at the man and then at Alena. From the look in their eyes, he could tell that this was not something they wanted to do. Having everyone fight meant that everyone could die if they failed. And failure didn't seem unlikely.

"Then where does that leave me?"

"You and I have a special job, Rae," Trent said. "This plan doesn't only outline the defensive actions we must take. This outlines our offensive moves too."

"*Offensive?*"

"Yes. The only way we have a chance in this war is by bringing it to Zupay when he doesn't expect it."

Trent traced a line between their village near the beach and the village in the jungle.

"You and I will visit the creatures."

"Why?" Rae felt his heart beat surge in his chest. It leapt at the idea; it coursed in dread.

"We must find a weakness: a way we can reduce their power," Trent said. "If we do, we'll be better prepared for their assault."

"And how can we do that?"

"We spy on Them."

CHAPTER EIGHT

THE HIGH EMPRESS OF ZALM

The light faded and Joachim found himself in a large room. He squinted as his eyes adjusted to a light that was considerably brighter than the caves. He marvelled at his new surroundings. The walls were an elegant off-white, and the carpet was a light shade of emerald. Bookshelves lined all the walls except the one where a wide desk sat in front of an enormous window with a view of a cloudy sky and cityscape.

Joachim had never been to a real city. He'd only read about them and seen pictures in books about Old Earth in Baruch's library. In those pictures, cities were all pollution and concrete, and Joachim couldn't understand why anyone would want to live there. But this was different.

Buildings sprawled out as far as he could see. Most of them were built of white stone and supported by giant pillars. Statues of pale marble posed at street corners and city squares. In the gardens directly below, Joachim saw an obelisk. The gold of its tip shone bright in the rising sun.

People, animals, and carts crowded the narrow streets, but Joachim noticed something about them. The citizens didn't look as elegant as the three women who had brought them from the caves. They wore rags.

"This is Zostrava," the woman said. "The capital of this mighty kingdom. And above you is a portrait of my mother."

She pointed to the ceiling of the office. Joachim looked up and saw that there was indeed a woman painted on it. The woman wore dark green robes and looked very much like the other three women.

"When she died, she left me in complete control of Zalm. Quite a legacy, isn't it?"

The woman walked to the desk and removed her cloak. Underneath it she wore the same dark green robes as her mother. The other two women remained immobile, arms crossed over their chests.

"Valeska, Panthea, I want the both of you to go into the apothecary and summon herb treatments from the laborers. And find these gentlemen new clothes. They stink."

The two women bowed and left the room.

"Take a seat," the woman said.

She motioned to the two chairs near them. Joachim and Baruch sat. On the desk, there were quills, ink, books written in strange letters, and a large map labelled 'The Kingdom of Zalm'.

"A thousand thanks, Nelda," Baruch said. "This is Joachim, my accomplice on my journeys in Zalm."

"The pleasure is yours, I'm sure," Nelda said, smiling thinly.

She took several objects from her pockets and placed them on the desk. Each was a smooth stone that could fit into his palm. Markings were painted the surfaces, each symbol different from the next. Nelda met his eye and smiled, holding out one of them for him to examine more closely.

"They are called runestones," she said. "Each holds a different power. There are ones for seeing in the dark or calming the weather or setting a fire. This one I used today." There were three lines running parallel to each other down the expanse of the stone's face. "It holds the power of transportation."

"Baruch told me that magic has been outlawed in Zalm," Joachim said.

"This isn't magic, you fool." Nelda snapped her palm closed on the runestone and put it in a drawer with the rest of them. "This is just one of the special privileges of the High Council. Rightfully so: Zalm would be nothing if not for the knowledge and leadership of my ancestors and myself on the Council."

Joachim looked at Baruch.

"Now, my dear Baruch," Nelda began again. "It has been many years since you have come to see me. Almost two decades. What brings you back to Zalm?"

"I'm here to see your sister," Baruch said. "The Black Oracle."

Nelda laughed. It seemed as if it would be short, but soon she became hysterical, her laughter shrill and sharp and condescending. She then was silent, and her eyes became distant. Her face flushed.

"What's the matter, Empress?" Baruch asked.

"What would you want with her?" Nelda asked. "That woman is nothing but absurdity. Surely Zalm has more to offer than that wayward witch woman."

The door of Nelda's office opened, and Valeska and Panthea returned holding green bandages and dark clothing. One of them took the old bandage off of Baruch's shoulder and placed the herb bandage onto his wound.

"Take this," said the second woman to Joachim.

Joachim pulled off the old bandage on his arm, revealing a deep gash and crusting, dried blood. He placed the herb bandage on the wound. It soothed the remaining sting and sent a cool sensation throughout his body.

"Could I get another?" Joachim asked. "I have one on my stomach."

"Of course."

The woman handed him a second one. Joachim lifted his tunic, removed his soaked bandages, and put the clean one on it. When they were done, the wounds had almost completely disappeared, merely marks on the skin. Joachim and Baruch put on the fresh clothes.

"Leave."

Nelda glared at the two women. Her associates looked at each other, then back at her.

"Now."

They hurried out of the room. Nelda shifted her stare to Baruch.

"The Black Oracle, or *Tilicea Shorciman* as my mother named her, has been placed in a high security prison."

"What?" Baruch asked. "Why?"

"My mother's High Council, the 53rd High Council of Zalm, outlawed all forms of occult and magic—"

"I know that, Empress, but she was allowed special privileges because she could be of use to the kingdom. She can see the damn future, Nelda."

"Do not interrupt me!" Nelda slammed her fists on the desk, the quills and ink bottle tumbling over. "Our mother failed to see the harm my sister posed to our world. She may be family, but I work for the good of Zalm, not for that wretched whore. I couldn't let her stay in public. I avoided widespread panic. Her prophecies were an annoyance and fed unneeded fear to my people."

"*Unneeded?* Have you lost all sanity?"

"She was prophesizing the end of the High Council's reign," Nelda said, calming. "It was scaring the nobility and bringing our society to the brink of chaos. I had to get rid of her for the sake of my kingdom and my people."

"Do you honestly think you are doing any good by locking her away?" Baruch asked.

"Yes. But you do not understand me fully, Baruch. Just because I cut her off from the rest of Zalm, it doesn't mean that I am not using her."

"What do you mean?"

"I confiscate her prophecies and consult them regularly," Nelda said. "The Council and I discuss her claims and decide together whether or not to take action on her predictions. Some of them do come true, after all. How do you think I found you and your associate in the caves, Baruch?"

"Tell me which prison she's in." Baruch stood.

"Don't you dare use such a hateful tone with the High Empress of Zalm. Baruch, I don't know what you're up to, but my people and I will have nothing to do with it."

"It's about Zupay," Baruch said. "Has the Oracle spoken of him?"

She paused. "He has been mentioned."

"And what does Tilicea say he will do?" Baruch asked.

"Nothing to me, if I keep my distance," Nelda said. "What does this demon ask of you?"

"The Black Oracle."

"Why?"

"He wants her to find immortality for him."

Nelda snorted. "And you'll do his bidding?"

"I have to," Baruch said. "Without it, he will annihilate my people back in the other world. Even still, if he dies, all his creatures will fall into disorder and slaughter us. They may even come through the caves and terrorize Zalm."

Nelda crossed the room, looking at the books on her shelves. Some of the titles were written in English while others were written in the strange writing that he saw back on the cave walls. Curves and dots.

"Well, Baruch," Nelda sighed. "It does seem we have a predicament."

"A predicament, indeed." He went to her. "Now, I need your help, Nelda. Where is your sister Tilicea?"

"She's in the prison at Guluki. It is a lengthy trip, perhaps a full day of walking."

"I don't have a full day," Baruch said. "I have only ten days before Zupay attacks my village. Perhaps I can borrow a couple horses for the trip."

"That will not be necessary."

"What do you mean?"

"I can get you there without you having to do anything."

Nelda clapped her hands. Both Panthea and Valeska came back into the room, awaiting instructions.

"Get me four guards."

The assistants bowed and left again.

"I thank you." Baruch bowed too.

Joachim looked into the Empress' face. He didn't want her help. The hunter inside didn't trust her at all.

The doors of the office swung open, and the assistants returned with four thick guards, each wearing leather dyed emerald green.

"Take these men, and lock them into a cell at Guluki," the Empress said.

"Lock us into a cell?" Baruch's eyes widened.

Joachim stood and drew his dagger, but before he could use it, they held both Baruch and him in their arms. Hunting prey and fighting armed guards were indeed very different, Joachim knew, and this time he felt like the prey.

"What do you mean by this?" Baruch asked, pulling against the men's holds.

"I can't have you cause panic in my kingdom, Baruch," Nelda said. "Rebel movement against the High Council has begun again in the south, and we've had to squash protests twice this week in this city alone."

"We want nothing to do with your civil war," Baruch said.

"I don't imagine you do," Nelda replied. "That said, I can't let you gallivant around my kingdom crying about demons and immortality. Besides, Tilicea's prophecies did say that if I helped you, I could be inviting those things into my realm. I can't have that either."

"Then deport us. Let us go back to our world."

"No," Nelda said. "I will keep you at Guluki until the rest of the Council and I decide what to do with you. I will organize a tribunal for you in two weeks' time. However, deportation would be something very merciful to wish for indeed, if I were in your place, Baruch."

Two weeks? In two weeks, Darcie would be long dead, and their village long obliterated. Joachim tried to wriggle free, but the guards' grasps were firm, and the movements made his muscles ache. Nelda then retrieved a stone from the drawer—the one with three parallel lines: the teleportation runestone. She handed it to one of her assistants. Both Valeska and Panthea joined hands with the guards.

"Goodbye Baruch and associate." Nelda walked back to her desk.

"To Guluki you go."

Chapter Nine

The Prison

The light faded, and they were in the prison. Torches cast shadows along the stone walls, and the guards ushered Joachim and Baruch through a foyer and into a corridor. Valeska and Panthea joined hands again and disappeared into a sparkle of light.

The guards took their rucksacks and emptied the contents. Mostly food and blankets remained in them, but the men took Joachim's knife, bow, and quiver full of arrows, freshly carved. They found the same weapons in Baruch's pack.

Though Joachim struggled against the guards, pulling and bolting around like a hog caught in a snare, Baruch didn't resist them any longer. He dangled limp in their arms, watching the men and women inside the cells they passed on the way to their own. Joachim watched them too.

Upwards of four prisoners crowded each cell, though he could tell that they were built for two. A few times they even appeared to be solitary confinement cells, but he could hear the groans and cries of multiple people inside. Some prisoners thrashed around, yelling at them as they passed and clawing through the bars. Most, however, didn't move at all. They lay on the ground or slumped against the wall, their bodies frail and the only sign of life their heavy eyes that followed as the guards dragged them past.

They climbed two sets of stairs. On the next floor they passed a room carved into the stone. There were chains and whips and hooks hanging on the wall. Two guards taunted an old woman. She lay in a ball on the ground, completely naked. Blood poured from a gash on her back and onto the stone. One of the guards lashed her again.

Even when the guards brought them to an empty cell in the middle of a long corridor, Baruch didn't react. He remained still, complacent even, when the guards closed and locked the gate.

"We don't get any cellmates?" Baruch asked.

"No," one of the men grunted. "Under orders from the High Empress herself, you are to be put in a private cell. She doesn't want your poisonous words causing uproar."

The guards disappeared down the corridor, and Joachim turned to the old man, his breathing heavy.

"What was that all about?"

"What was what all about?" Baruch asked.

"You struggled against the guards in the Empress' office, but completely stopped once we reached Guluki!" Joachim fought.

"It was all an illusion."

"What are you talking about?"

"We needed the Empress to think that we didn't want to come to this prison," Baruch said. "If I hadn't acted like that, she might think that we aren't threatened by her authority."

"Why would we want to be in this cell?"

"Remember, Joachim, we are here to seek out the Black Oracle."

Joachim stared at him, not understanding. All he could understand was the consequence of two weeks captive in some prison while the creatures destroyed their village.

"Listen," Baruch began. "Nelda said Tilicea is imprisoned here at Guluki. If she foresaw us coming into Zalm for immortality then she knows that Nelda has brought us to this prison. Now that we're here, she can find us."

"Even if she did, how do you know she would help us?" Joachim asked.

"I don't. However, we are in the same prison as her now. That is a lot closer than when we were in Zostrava."

Joachim could feel his face turning red. This must be one of those unconventional adjustments an old hunter had to make, but Joachim found it annoying rather than admirable. Passivity was not something he practiced on a hunt, and frankly, there was no time for it now. He gripped the bars.

"Well, I sure hope she has as much compassion as you think she does."

ﾂ ﾝ ﾗ ﾈ ﾊ ﾟ ﾓ ﾘ

Hours passed, and Joachim became anxious. When they first crossed the caves and came into Zalm, it had been the early hours of morning, but as they waited in the cell, Joachim watched the daylight fade. Two guards came in just before dusk and offered them food. He ate it all, barely chewing enough to swallow, attempting to fill the emptiness in his stomach but still leaving hunger in his mind. The tins were then cleared away. The night began.

Though he felt exhausted, his mind wouldn't rest. He dozed in and out of sleep and woke often. Each time, he thought he was in his bed at the village, back in Darcie's arms. Each time, he was disappointed. He just wanted to go home.

Just before dawn, he couldn't escape the thoughts of her any longer. He remembered the first day they met. Darcie had worn a light pink dress. Baruch announced that humans had been found in the jungle and called for a feast to welcome them. All day Joachim had helped his mother cook boar meat and fish, mix salads and soups, and they laid them out on the communal supper

70

table and waited for their new villagers.

Joachim hid behind Alena's leg when Darcie and her parents came down the path from Baruch's workshop. He was eight years old at the time, and his father had just died. He had barely grasped what that meant, and now strange jungle people were coming into their village, inhabiting the dwelling next door.

They didn't look like jungle people at all. The kids that played at the beach said they would have paint on their faces and feathers in their hair. They said they would wear grass and bark for clothing, and they would speak a strange tongue like the jackalopes, like the sparrows in the trees.

But Darcie's parents sounded very much like his mom. They introduced themselves and their small daughter. She looked as nervous as he was, as little and woeful and frightened. They took a seat at the table, but Darcie didn't eat. She stared at the food, picking at the roasted boar and the tomato and onion salad. Joachim barely ate either. He was too busy watching her.

When supper was finished, they sat around the village fire pit. Alena was speaking to Darcie's parents, and soon the children went off. Ben and Trent wanted to play Hunters in the twilight. Trent was going to be the boar.

"I don't want to," Darcie said. She still eyed her parents not far away. She toyed with the hem of her dress.

"Then what do you want to do?" Ben asked. Trent's nice supper tunic was already covered in dirt.

"I'm just going to stay here." She turned and went back toward the fire pit.

"Do you want to be a hunter, Joachim?" Ben asked. "Or will you be a boar?"

"I don't want to play either," he responded.

"Why not?"

He looked back at Darcie. She was sitting with her parents, but she didn't look like she was having any fun. She stared at the flames.

"I'm going to go sit with her."

ㄅ ㄴ ㄨ ㄣ ㄈ ㄖ ㄈ ㄡ ㄖ ㄅ

From the small window in their cell, Joachim saw the first rays of dawn. Baruch was sleeping well, stirring only to get more comfortable on the stone floor. He couldn't believe that Baruch could sleep. It was astonishing—astonishing and frustrating. Joachim knew that the first night had passed, and now only nine days remained. If they didn't find Tilicea, their entire journey would be for nothing.

Rusted wheels on uneven stone echoed through the corridor. Joachim pressed his face against the bars, but he couldn't see anything except the empty cell opposite their own. He heard voices, but the commotion moved too slowly for him to see.

Baruch seemed undisturbed. He took to grooming himself, cleaning grime from under his fingernails and spit shining a spot of dirt on his leg. Two men appeared, guiding a wooden cart. They were both tall and meaty, the muscles of their arms easily twice the size of Joachim's. In the village, they would have been mighty hunters.

"Your meals have arrived," one said.

"Excellent," Baruch said.

He stood. From the cart, the men unloaded two slices of bread and two bowls of brown sludge. They passed the food through the bars.

"Beans," Baruch said, tasting the contents of the bowl.

The guards pushed the cart away, and Joachim took a bite of his loaf. The bread was chewy in his mouth, clearly left too long on some counter. Baruch vocalized his satisfaction all throughout his meal, *hmm*ing and *oo*ing as if he enjoyed it. Maybe he did.

They spent the rest of the morning and the afternoon staring at the walls of the cell. Joachim couldn't help but feel he was wasting time. He thought of Darcie and the village, of what would happen if they couldn't find the ingredients in the eight and a half days that remained. He nearly succumbed to tears several times. He should be finding a way to break out of there.

Baruch napped much of the afternoon away. Joachim wanted to slap him.

The sky darkened in anticipation of another night at Guluki. The guards came and went a second time, and they ate their dinner. Once they had finished, Joachim felt a shudder in the rock below him. He looked over to Baruch. He felt it too.

With a crash from beyond their cell, the entire prison shook. The guards' cart spilled over, brown gunk flowing through the cracks in the stone all the way back to Joachim and Baruch.

From the other side of the corridor, guards called out, barking orders at prisoners and other guards alike. More crashes echoed around them. There was a glowing red light at the other end of the corridor.

"What's happening out there?" Baruch asked.

"Whatever it is, we need to get out of here. I see fire."

Guards rushed past holding buckets full of water. For a few moments, it seemed they had pacified whatever had happened, but then it erupted again. The stone rumbled beneath them, and the guards fell to the ground, the water in their pails adding to the food-slush on the floor.

Yelling rang through the corridor, and more people ran by the door of the cell. These people weren't thick and muscled like the guards. In fact, none of these people even wore leather. Prisoners from the other cells had somehow escaped and fled.

This was an uprising.

Baruch stood with Joachim, their faces pressed against the bars. They called out to the people, but no one stopped for them. The fire burned and guards became sparse in the crowd of swarming prisoners.

"How do we get out of here?" Joachim asked.

"If I knew, we'd be out of here by now."

"Maybe I can help."

As they were watching, Joachim hadn't noticed the woman who

spoke on the opposite side of the bars. She stepped into the firelight, and her features became clear. She was small, shorter than Darcie by almost a full head. Her dark hair flowed past her shoulders in cascading ringlets, and she had green eyes. She wore a long dress, stained with blood and dirt.

"It's an uprising for my people," she smiled.

"Your people?" Joachim asked.

"Yes. Those imprisoned here are rebels who oppose the High Council's oppression and violence. Most haven't even committed real crimes."

In her hand, she held a stone. It looked like one of the runestones Nelda had in her desk drawer. On its face, a cross glowed yellow.

"Step back."

Baruch pulled Joachim away from the bars, and the woman placed the stone against the lock of the door. With a dull thud, the lock burst, and she pulled the door open.

"Come with me," she said. "We must be careful to avoid this chaos."

Baruch followed her down the corridor in the opposite direction of the fire. Joachim trailed behind. Inmates ran in every direction, holding torches or runestones of their own. A few guards lay dead, and those remaining were swarmed by the rebellion. The voices of freedom echoed loud through the night.

"There's an exit at the top of the stairs," the woman called behind her. "There, we can discuss the conditions of our new friendship."

She smiled at both Baruch and Joachim. It was then that Joachim realized that the woman resembled the High Empress herself. Odd beauty.

"Excellent," Baruch said. "It's nice to finally meet you, Tilicea."

CHAPTER TEN

OINTMENT

A fter a few hours of rest, Rae rose with the sun. Even though it had disappeared the night before, slumbering in the darkness behind the horizon, the villagers didn't disappear, not like Rae. He couldn't say he actually slept though.

The villagers readied the village for an attack, working like puppets moved by strings. Some carried wood back and forth from the collection near the fire pit, and others carved the pieces into bows or arrows or hilts for blades. A woman carried baskets of berries and jugs of water from the well near Baruch's workshop. Though Rae knew that the last hunt had gathered enough animal meat to last a few months, protein would be saved until it was needed.

It would be saved in case they couldn't enter the jungle to hunt.

Rae crossed in front of the fire pit and entered the command post. Trent stood above the table, looking at the map.

"Are you ready?" Trent asked.

"Yes."

"Did you sleep well?"

"Not at all, really," Rae said.

"Then that's two of us. I studied this map all night. I'm confident that we can sneak around the creatures and then spy on them without being noticed."

"And you think that's enough?"

"No," Trent replied. "We're going to paint ourselves."

"Paint ourselves?"

"If we color ourselves in dark greens, we should be able to blend in more with the jungle. I remember reading about fighters using the same technique before the Great Death."

He thought about it. It seemed like a smart enough idea, but then he remembered something his father once told him. All of the creatures' senses were heightened in comparison to the humans', not just vision.

"What about our scent?" Rae asked. "Won't they be able to smell us as we approach?"

"Good thinking." Trent smiled. "Follow me, and we'll begin our disguise."

They left the dwelling and walked past the fire pit. A few of the women had lit it and roasted peppers from the village garden over the smoldering coals.

Trent led them into the trees. Before they reached their destination, Rae knew exactly where they were going. Not many villagers built their homes in the jungle. Most liked the safety of the village, the protection of a tightly packed herd. In fact, Rae only knew of one who didn't.

Her name was Tabitha, and she opted to grow her own food. Though she visited friends, the old woman stayed away from the other villagers. Children made up stories about her, about how she spoke to animals and gave people nightmares, but Rae knew better than to believe them. The woman was an elder like Baruch or Mr. Joachim's mother who just enjoyed spending a lot of time alone.

The path to Tabitha's home was not clear. The plants overgrew onto the dirt, and the trees narrowed so closely that Rae could barely squeeze through in some spots. After he tripped over roots twice, they came to a small dwelling nestled in the trees.

The wood of the walls had rotted, and ripped curtains showed slices of furniture through the windows. Trent knocked on the door, each one pushing slightly into the dwelling. After a while, it was apparent no one would answer.

"I hear from the trees that our village is under attack."

The voice that rang behind them sounded hollow yet strong. Though Rae expected to find a woman crippled by age, he found quite the opposite. The woman was short and muscular. She looked like she would have the strength of a twenty-five-year-old man, perhaps two.

She had tied her fuzzy hair into a thick braid. The skin on her face and arms bore the marks of her feat of being the only female hunter in the village. In her hand she held a jackalope by its hind legs, its lifeless eyes watching them.

"Good morning, Tabitha," Trent said. "Unfortunately, you are right."

"Then why have you come?" she asked. "I have said many times that I am ready to fight for the sake of our village."

"We aren't ready to fight yet. We must measure our enemy."

"Ah, you're wise," Tabitha said. "Come inside. I'll make you something to give you energy and strength, and we can discuss this plan you speak of."

They followed her into her home. On a wooden stove, a pot of water simmered. She plopped the dead horned rabbit onto the counter and washed her hands in the wash basin. She then took three stone mugs and some herbs that dried over the fireplace. After picking enough leaves for the three of them, she placed them on a strainer above each mug, running the water through the herb. She passed one out to each of them. The dark contents smelled bitter.

"Drink," the woman said.

Trent drank it all in one swallow. Rae was a little more conservative. He took a sip, the bitterness making his nose burn. Though he tried not to, he couldn't hide the disgust from his face. Tabitha smiled.

"Very good," she snickered. "Helps with the growth of chest hair, I'm told."

She took Trent's empty mug, some more herbs, and refilled it. He drank it just as quickly as he drank the first. Rae simply stared at his, the liquid making his stomach churn.

"What is the village's plan?" Tabitha asked.

"First, we will have guards about a mile out, ready to signal if an attack is coming," Trent said. "The next part is where we need your help. We will need camouflage. Everything from body paints to something that will obscure our scent. I'm sure you know the creatures will be able to smell us if we get close to them. We want something that will allow us to spy on their village without being noticed."

"Spying?" She tasted the word on her tongue. "And what do you expect to come of this?"

"A soft spot. A weakness or a place where we can hurt them before we engage in battle."

"No disguise will completely fool them, but as long as you keep some distance, I don't see why there isn't an effective one."

"Yes, I was thinking we would paint ourselves in dark greens and smell like the jungle."

"Smell like the jungle?" Tabitha snorted. "No, no. That won't work."

"Then what will?" Rae asked.

"You will need something better than that. You will need to blend completely."

"What could be better than the jungle's scent?" Trent asked.

Tabitha began rummaging through her cabinets. She read the labels of many containers and tossed them carelessly aside. When she found the one that she had been looking for, she removed the cork and took a long sniff. Content, she passed the bottle to Rae. As he inhaled, the bitter tea in his stomach clawed at his throat. The ointment smelled like rotting carcass and feces.

"What is it?" Rae asked.

Trent took a long inhale and coughed. "It's Them."

"Exactly," Tabitha said. "Why smell like the creatures' surroundings when you can smell like you are one of them?"

"But we don't look like Them," Trent said. "They'll realize when they see us."

"Who says they'll see you?"

With that, Tabitha disappeared into a room connected to the kitchen. The sound of more searching filled the house as she rustled through cabinets and drawers. Finally she returned holding a wooden container. She opened it and presented it to Rae. Inside was a bubbly orange cream with specks of glimmering dust.

"Take some," Tabitha said to him.

"No, please. If I smell anything else, I may be sick."

"No, you foolish boy." She scooped some of the cream out of the container and put it on the back of his hand. "Now, rub it in."

He rubbed, and a tingling grew. He could feel the cream settle into his pores, the coolness making him shiver. After a few moments, something odd happened. Rae watched as his hand became blurry and then glimmered. In a flash, his hand disappeared completely, and he stared right through it to the wood of the table underneath.

"It's an invisibility ointment." Tabitha beamed. "It will last for a few hours at a time."

Trent laughed aloud. Rae did too.

"Where did you get this?" Trent asked. "I've never seen anything like it."

"Being an elder has required me to go to some very strange places," Tabitha said. "In fact, some journeys have even taken me right out of this jungle. Another realm, you might say."

"Well, it's perfect," Trent said.

"And you can use both of these ointments if you can do something for me in return," Tabitha said, holding the demons' scent and the invisibility cream.

"Anything," Trent said.

The men looked at her. Another odd smile crept across her lips.

"You must allow me to accompany you."

CHAPTER ELEVEN

THE PROPHECY

Joachim could hear stones clinking in Tilicea's pocket as they followed her up the stairs leaving their cell at Guluki.

"You have runestones," he said, nervous. Empress Nelda said only members of the High Council had access to runestones. If Tilicea was seen as a criminal, a *wayward witch woman* as Nelda called her, how had she managed to get them? Worse: was she too dangerous to be using them now?

"I do," Tilicea replied. At the top of the staircase, she led them into the main hall.

"Where did you get them?"

"Joachim." Baruch nudged him. He clearly saw no problem with Tilicea's stolen goods. The elder didn't want him to question her, but Joachim wouldn't be a good hunter if he didn't.

"I have informants in Zostrava," Tilicea said. "Along with the information they provide, they take back the magic that has been stolen from us."

An escaped prisoner crossed the foyer and came toward them. In one hand, he held a runestone, and in the other was a rucksack. He handed the rucksack to Tilicea and bowed. She threw the pack over her shoulders and nodded.

"Follow me," she said.

They slipped through the front doors of the prison. Joachim was surprised no one stopped them, but whenever a guard got close, one of Tilicea's allies took them. They fought them off with knives and bows, weapons that probably took calculated smuggling, but they almost didn't need them. The guards were outnumbered. Joachim remembered the crowded cells. Four prisoners crammed in one.

Outside, stone showered down on them from an explosion. Joachim covered himself from the assault, stumbling over the uneven, cracked cobblestone. When he looked back at Guluki, fire burst from the windows—licks of hostility and anger and freedom.

Tilicea led them toward trees.

"Where are we going?" Joachim called to her.

"The ocean," she said. "It's not too far from here. I fear if we remain close, the High Council's army men will arrive and find us."

They travelled for what seemed like hours. Though Joachim knew not much time had passed, his muscles still ached from the journey through the caves and the stone floor of the cell. A crisp breeze pushed through the trees, chilling him. The cold didn't help either.

As they travelled deeper into the forest, he saw that a white substance blanketed the trees. A bit of it fell onto his face as they dashed through the branches. For a moment it burned, but soon it was only water on his cheek. Snow. He knew about it only from the books about Old Earth. He scowled. Snow seemed much more pleasant in the descriptions.

The trees thinned, and Joachim saw the dark waters of an ocean. The blackness extended right to the horizon.

Tilicea stopped them, took a runestone from her pocket, and laid it on the sand, saying words in a strange tongue. Tiny flames ignited and flickered in the breeze. Though the fire was small, Joachim could feel the heat from where he stood.

"My name is Baruch, and this is Joachim. His wife was kidnapped by Zupay."

The woman touched Baruch's hand. When she took Joachim's, he felt a tingling grow in him, one not from the cold. Though hard to tell before, Joachim realized that she was indeed something for Nelda to be apprehensive of. A strange radiance came off of her, something that faded the more he tried to focus, like the distant stars that existed only in his peripherals. He could tell she was probably a very influential woman. Influential and formidable.

"I have heard of your struggles, Joachim," she said. "And those of your village. I promise to do all that I can to help you."

"Who told you?" Joachim asked. He'd already hinted his distrust; why not make it clear?

"The gods, of course," she said.

"Gods?"

"Yes. As the Black Oracle, I am this world's connection to them."

First magic and now talking to gods? Did Zupay really believe all this nonsense?

"How so?" Joachim asked.

"They speak through me," Tilicea said. "And I interpret and spread their word. That is how I knew where to find you. That is how I knew about the trials of your people."

"Then you must know what Zupay needs for immortality."

"Not yet. I have feared to enter that trance. The gods warned me against accessing that information in front of those who would use it improperly." She sat down. "But now that you both are here, I believe that it's safe to find out."

Baruch sat beside the woman, slipping a little on the cold sand.

"Here?"

Joachim looked around. In the forest beside the beach, each shadow seemed to move like a travelling guard waiting to emerge and take all three of them back to Guluki. This hardly seemed like a good place to enter a trance.

"Shouldn't we use a transportation runestone and find somewhere safer?" he asked.

"A transportation runestone?" She snorted. "My associates were only able to bring me runestones crucial to the storming of Guluki. By order of my sister, the transportation runestone is exclusive to people only she approves of. She would not allow these runestones to be easily stolen. Aside from the runestones for locks and fire, I have little other magic with me. Only the prophetic magic invested by the gods, I'm afraid."

"Then how will you enter the trance?"

"Is he always this distrustful, Baruch?" Tilicea sighed. "It is a wonder you were able to get to Zalm at all."

Baruch laughed, but Joachim hardly found it funny. His wife and child had been taken from him. After this night, only eight days remained to retrieve all the ingredients and stop Zupay before he destroyed the whole village. Now some crazed sorceress babbled about trances without the slightest inclination to conceal herself or their mission.

"Sit down, Joachim." Baruch eyed him. "Let Tilicea access the prophecy."

He sat but faced away from them and watched the forest. He wouldn't let another lunatic come onto the beach. One was bad enough. But then he heard Tilicea making strange grunting sounds behind him, something like a mix of drowning pelican and a boar in heat. Though he tried to resist, he found himself watching.

In her throaty symphony, she took the rucksack from her back. She brought out a long wooden pipe and several small corked bottles labeled in writing he couldn't read. From the first bottle she smeared cream on her arms, legs, and face. Out of a second she placed a small lump of herbs into the pipe. It smelled even worse than the cream. Joachim had smoked many times before, often tobacco and other herbs grown in the village, but he had never smoked something with such a stench.

Tilicea found a stick and lit the tip of it with the fire.

"Whatever happens, don't try to stop me," she said. "I am the will of the gods in the trance. Pay attention only to what they say."

"Of course," Baruch said.

Gazing out at the sea, Tilicea lit the pipe with the stick and took a long inhale. She held it for many moments and took another once she exhaled. With each exhale, her beautiful face grew pale, and her eyes got narrower and narrower. After a few minutes, Tilicea began to sway where she sat, unsteadily sucking smoke from the pipe. Joachim thought to hold her up, but he wouldn't want to interfere with the gods' will. Or *whatever*'s will.

As she exhaled the last puff of smoke from the now-empty pipe, she stared at the sand, barely able to keep her head up.

"Is she okay?" Joachim asked.

"I don't know," Baruch said.

There was a rustling in the trees. Though it was barely a sound over the song of the ocean and breeze, many years as a hunter told him that something was happening. Baruch heard it too, and he turned to look. Maybe something waited to confront them.

"What do you suppose that was?" Joachim asked.

"I don't know," he replied. "It wasn't a guard. You would be able to hear their boots on the frozen ground."

A thud near them made Joachim jump. Tilicea lay on her back in the sand now, her eyes so narrow they looked like the shards of a crescent moon. Her mouth moved slowly as if she spoke without sound.

"Has she fallen asleep?"

"I hope not," Baruch said.

Joachim heard the noise again from the forest. This time it wasn't so subtle. Something rustled through the trees, but it didn't come from one place. The rustling could be heard from all over, as if beings approached from behind every tree. When he heard the sound of laughter, he realized that Tilicea was still alive in her stupor. How fortunate.

Another noise then overcame her giggling. A ringing built in Joachim's ears, starting softly and growing until it drowned out the laughter and the sound of the ocean. Baruch heard it too. The man clutched his ears and winced. The ringing became so loud that Joachim's head ached.

A glowing grew across the ocean. It started dimly from far away then pushed as a wall through the air, consuming everything it touched. It crawled in from the trees like the arrival of the tide worshipping the full moon. The ringing in Joachim's ears became unbearable.

The light was blinding. It felt hot around him, making him sweat in his cloak. Before he could try to escape it, the heat disappeared, and the ringing in his ears ceased. The forest and ocean were still.

"Joachim, look at her."

He realized why Baruch sounded so alarmed. The woman's skin glowed as if her body had absorbed the light. She hovered a couple inches from the ground, her eyes closed and mouth mumbling. Her body shuddered and her eyes tore open. Her pupils were white.

As she twitched, she spoke with a voice thick with a hundred men and women.

"In order to achieve immortality, one must obtain the window to the Great Druid's soul, a half a quart of blood from the enchanting water nymph, and the Harpy's child still unborn."

$$ \text{᚜ ᚛ ᚜ ᚛ ᚜ ᚛ ᚜ ᚛ ᚜ } $$

"The Great Druid of Zalm is buried under a willow tree near Ionia," Tilicea said, the color now returned to her face.

After the gods recited the prophecy through her, she fell asleep. Though Joachim wanted to leave her on the beach and start collecting the ingredients for Zupay, he knew that he and Baruch didn't know where to find them, let alone what they were. Instead, they waited and wished that her slumber wouldn't last long.

Now that the sun emerged beyond the ocean and commenced their third day, she had awoken. Finally.

"And water nymphs, the Undines, can be found at Deadman's Bluffs in the south, west of Minua." Tilicea took a sip of water from her canteen. "On the way there, you two can stop off at the Cliffs of the Gods for the harpy egg."

"*Us* two?" Joachim asked.

"Yes," Tilicea said. "I cannot accompany you to find the ingredients. I must aid the revolution of my people."

"My dearest Tilicea," Baruch began. "Joachim and I don't know where we are going, and you yourself know what will happen if we fail. Not only will our people perish, but Zupay will send his demons into this world."

"Even with my help you may fail still. If you do, my people will need guidance not only for our war against the High Council but for our impending war against Zupay in the other world."

"Can we at least find a transportation runestone to help us get the ingredients faster?" Joachim asked. "We could go back to Zostrava and steal it from the Empress."

"I cannot help you there either," Tilicea said. "Even if we could get one, it would be tracked. Now that the uprising has liberated Guluki, Nelda will investigate all uses of that runestone."

"So we're supposed to wander around this desolate world with no guidance and no effective transportation in the middle of some petty civil war?" Joachim asked, heat building in his ears.

"This war is not petty, Mr. Joachim," Tilicea said, her face becoming flushed also. "This is about the repression of my people."

"Then what about our people?" Joachim's voice was low. "If we take longer than ten days, they will all die. Without your help, my wife and unborn child will perish. I'm begging you, Madam Shorciman. We won't be able to do this alone."

She stared at him for a long moment. Joachim regretted his words immediately. He barely knew the woman, let alone the struggle she led. He didn't understand her situation just as she didn't understand his. He'd be lucky to get any of her help now.

"Fine," she said. "I will take you to Ionia only because it is on the way to my people's base at the Zalmish Sea. But we must hurry. The journey will take a full day. If we only stop to rest once for a couple hours at night, we can make it there by tomorrow at sunrise. Do you have enough food and supplies to last until then?"

"All of our supplies were taken from us at Guluki," Baruch said. "We have nothing."

"All right." Tilicea took a final sip of water and tightened the lid on the canteen. "I think I have enough to last us until we reach the Eye of the Druid. We will figure out how to get you more supplies once we get there. Now, let's get off this beach before those filthy army men from the High Council find us."

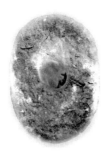

Chapter Twelve

A Soft Spot

After they stripped their clothing and covered themselves in the ointment, Rae, Trent, and Tabitha became invisible even to themselves. They stumbled around Tabitha's house until they found each other, deciding to put on at least one garment of clothing for their journey to Zupay's colony and taking it off again once they arrived.

"We'll have to reapply the ointment," Trent said. "The trek will take a couple hours."

"And how long will their stench last?" Rae asked.

"Until we wash it off," Tabitha said. "Just let me gather some dried meats and water, and we can leave."

Tabitha tore through the house, breaking more things than usual. Trent and Rae wore their underclothes, the garments hovering near the doorway. Finally, a floating rucksack appeared from the pantry, bulging with goods for the trip.

"Are we ready?" she asked.

"Should we bring weapons?" Rae asked.

"I have a couple daggers in the rucksack," Tabitha said. "But we shouldn't need them. The stench of Zupay's demons will be protection enough against the other predators of the jungle."

Two pairs of undergarments and a rucksack exited the house and pushed through the jungle, heading away from the village. Though they began their journey at the peak of the sun's intensity, the shade of the trees and the freedom of nakedness kept them cool.

It took Rae a few minutes to realize this constituted his first hunt.

The thought was bittersweet. With it, the jungle leapt alive. Each sound seemed clearer, and each color shone bright. When he closed his eyes, he could make out the distinct sound of crickets and those of much larger creatures. At that moment, he longed to hold a bow or a dagger and hunt like his father did.

His father. As soon as the image of him entered Rae's head, the jungle became a different place. Each buzz and ring frightened him. Each branch was a hand clawing out to grab him and consume him whole. The jungle had killed his father after all. It had mercilessly murdered him. How would he even feel knowing that Rae had entered it and approached the very demons that took his life away?

"Is something wrong?"

Tabitha's voice brought him back from the storm in his head.

"No."

"Then why have you stopped walking?" she asked.

He didn't speak. Trent's undergarments stood with them now too.

"What is it, Rae?" he asked. "Do you hear something?"

"No—" His voice caught in his throat. "I just… what if I can't do this?"

"What do you mean?" Trent asked.

He was glad to be invisible when he began to cry. He worried it might wash the ointment off, but when he touched the tears with his fingertips, they remained hidden. He tried to steady his voice but couldn't stop the shuddering that overcame him.

"Maybe my father was right," he said. "Maybe I'm too young. What if something happens to me? What if I die? How would my mother live without both him and me?"

"You will not die." Trent's voice was soft. "I promised your father long ago that I would protect you and Ophelia. I won't let anything happen to you."

"But how can you be sure?"

"Because I will fight until death to keep that promise."

A flight of air cooled Rae's sweaty skin. He longed to see his father, and he longed for things to return to normal. But what was normal? Was it living with a fear of Zupay's creatures?

If so, it wasn't a normal he wanted to live anymore.

"As will I." Tabitha's rucksack hovered beside him still. "But you must promise to fight alongside us to protect not only yourself but our village."

"How can I handle the responsibility of protecting the entire village?"

"Because your father did," Tabitha said. "And so does your mother. So does Trent, and so do I. In fact, every villager born to us has a responsibility to protect because without unity, we are destined to die alone."

The words seemingly rang in the jungle—on the breeze, in the messages of the birds, through the trees. In a place so desolate, one with such malice, it was hard to find any comfort. But now he felt differently. He didn't feel alone at all. Though he travelled with only two others, he knew that the entire village supported him and would protect him, just as he would them. And above all, he knew that his father would protect him. He had died to prove that to him.

"Okay," Rae said. "I can continue."

Tabitha's pack moved again and cut a path through the fallen leaves and rotting tree trunks. Trent stumbled around him, placing a hand uncertainly on Rae's arm for a moment before his undergarment followed the woman. With a final survey of the trees, Rae followed them farther away from the village.

The sun was no longer visible through the gaps in the trees. They had travelled all afternoon and had become lost, doubling the length of their trek. What should have been a three-hour journey had turned into a six-hour one in the heat, and they had to reapply their invisibility ointment. Though it was still long from dusk, the afternoon progressed quickly. Rae knew they would have another three hours of light, perhaps four. He just hoped there would be enough time to gather information about Zupay and his demons.

Besides the sound of their movement and the droning breeze, very little commotion echoed through the trees. Rae hadn't seen any animal scurry around or heard any birds in the branches. At first he thought his untrained ear was not yet used to the world of subtle sounds and slow changes. However, he began to think that there were no animals on this side of the jungle at all.

None besides the creatures.

"We're close." Tabitha stopped. "I can smell them."

"Are you sure that's not me?" Trent snorted.

"No. Look at those marks on the trees to the left. Blood."

Rae looked over. Red smears painted thick lines on a tree trunk. Then he saw more stains on the neighboring tree. And there were more behind a gathering of bushes.

"Blood?" Rae asked. "Why?"

"It's the entrails of their victims," Tabitha said. "A token of the kill, of sorts. They use it to mark their territory."

"Then we're close."

"Yes," Trent said.

"Don't they monitor their territory?" Rae asked.

"No," Tabitha replied. "The animals who know better won't come anywhere close to this place. I haven't seen another living thing since we started walking."

"Neither have I," Trent said.

Rae's heartbeat rang in his ears.

"Then why mark their territory?" he asked.

"It's a warning to potential prey."

Rae stopped. He had been warned.

"What's the plan?" he asked.

The rucksack glided to the ground. Tabitha had taken it off her shoulders. She rummaged through it and presented a dagger.

"Beyond the trees ahead, Zupay's village is not too far off," Trent said. "We'll approach the back and circle around the trees to Zupay's cave."

The rucksack rose again.

"Let's go."

They passed more trees marked with blood. For a short while, everything seemed drenched in it: the leaves below and above, the rocks, and every branch on the trees. They had to be careful not to get any on their feet. Then Rae saw something else beyond the red.

"I see something flashing behind those trees," he said. "Is the sun setting already?"

"No," Trent said. "Those are the giant mushrooms."

"*Giant* mushrooms?"

"Yes. They use the glowing to lure prey. They're highly poisonous."

They continued, and the flashing diminished. Rae felt relieved. Though he knew better than to touch them, the idea made his head spin. Just as he settled himself down, the jungle produced something equally unsettling.

Noise filled the trees ahead. Growls. Sneers. Screeches of laughter. Rae had heard nothing like it before, but he knew what was on the other side. His whole body trembled.

"It's Them."

"I know," Trent said. "Keep calm. Remember, we are protected in sight and in smell. It's time to take off the remainder of our clothing."

Two sets of undergarments and a rucksack went to the ground beside the trunk of a willow tree.

The villagers crept along the leaves. Rae jumped every time he heard a loud screech. The creatures resided just a hundred feet from them. The trees thinned and through the gaps, Rae could see jagged pieces of rock.

"We will enter the colony here," Tabitha said. "Zupay's home is just on the other side."

They moved slowly, careful not to make too much movement through the foliage. They stopped at a rock wall that extended toward the mouth of a cave. The sharp tips of stone reached up to Rae's chest, and he saw a clearing. There wasn't any blood on the surfaces of the rock or ground.

To his left, a path pushed through the trees to the remainder of the creatures' village. To his right, strange markings and pictures covered the walls inside Zupay's cave. Across from the villagers, another path extended into the jungle.

"Where does that path lead?" Rae asked.

"That's where they're keeping Darcie," Trent said.

Rae looked down the path, but something drew his eye to the cave. The sound started as a low growl, but grew into a screech. He heard metallic objects crashing onto the stone and yelling that sounded strangely human. At the peak of its fury, two creatures scurried out, their hands and feet kicking up dirt as they went.

"And tell that to the others." Another creature emerged. He stood on only two legs. "I will not have any further incompetence disrupt my plan."

Rae looked at the thing and could feel his breathing quicken. The creature wore a long cloak that concealed much of his body, but underneath he was frail and bony. His skin was green and there was only a small tuft of hair on his head. His large eyes narrowed as the slits of his nostrils sniffed the jungle.

"It's Zupay," Trent whispered.

The creature then turned from his cave and walked down the path toward Darcie.

Tabitha's fingers grabbed onto his wrist. "Rae, hold onto Trent. We're going to follow him."

"Follow him?"

"Yes," Trent said, grabbing his other arm. "Let's go."

Hands pulled him through a gap in the rock wall. They crossed the clearing in front of the cave and went down the path. Zupay had stopped in a clearing, peering up at the only structure there.

Though Darcie's head was down, they could hear her weeping.

"Did you enjoy your meal, my lady?" Zupay asked, feigning concern.

She didn't speak. Zupay waited, then took a sharpened log and poked her thigh. Darcie squealed.

"You will answer when I talk to you," Zupay spat. "I asked you a question."

"It was hardly a meal." She lifted her head, looking at the demon. Dark circles colored her eyes, and filth layered her face.

"Well, I offered you some of the meat we caught, but you declined."

"I can't eat it raw."

"Then I guess you won't want any this time either. I'll have one of my creatures bring you more moss."

Darcie lowered her head again, and more tears fell down her cheeks. Zupay left the cage and went to a well at the edge of the clearing. He lowered a bucket into it and pulled it back up. Water sloshed over the side.

"Water, my dear?"

"I thought you said it was too precious for prisoners?" Darcie asked, pulling at the ropes on her wrists.

"Never mind then, if you're going to be ungrateful."

Zupay took the water in the pail and hurled it at the cage, drenching Darcie. She wept more, slouching a bit, held up only by her bonds. Zupay lowered the pail again.

"Goodbye, wretch."

He took the pail in his long fingers and walked back up the path that led toward his cave. They didn't move as he walked past them.

"I know what we can do," Rae said once the creature had gone.

"What?" Trent said.

"We can poison the water."

"What about Darcie?" Trent asked. "What if she drinks the water?"

"We'll warn her not to," Tabitha said. "The next time we come, we'll tell her the plan. Once the creatures are weak, we'll return and break her out of this place."

"Is this the only water source?" Rae asked.

"I think so," Trent said. "I haven't seen any other wells."

He stopped. He heard something growing loud through the trees. The creatures sneered and laughed. Rae stood still, barely breathing. He tried to silence the beating of his heart. If it thumped any louder he was afraid they might hear him.

"They're about to feed," Trent said. "We should leave."

The villagers dashed through the trees, not wanting to chance an encounter on the path. Just as they reached the second clearing, they saw the creatures. Rae watched through the branches. Zupay and some of his demons had found dinner.

Blood bathed the entire clearing as the creatures tore through meat. Rae could hardly watch, his stomach churning like it had for Tabitha's tea. He tried to look away, but he noticed something. The meat that the creatures ate wasn't of an animal. Their meal was still clothed. The demons were eating a human being. The stench of death and rot filled the air. It was like when they roasted boar at the village, except he could smell splattered insides and hear them grinding the bones.

The human they ate was Rae's father.

Trent vomited behind him. Tabitha spoke softly to calm him down. The creatures didn't notice. They were too preoccupied with their food. Rae could do nothing but stand there, fire tearing through his veins. He heard every rip of flesh, tear of muscle, and slurp of blood. It took everything in him not to go out into the clearing and slaughter every demon in his path.

When the creatures finished, they left the clearing. Zupay returned to his cave, and his minions went down the path to their dwellings in the trees. Only blood remained, drenching the trunks of the trees and the stone.

His father was theirs. His blood was the token of their kill.

"Let's go," Tabitha said. "Before they return."

When they reached the willow tree, they took their undergarments and the rucksack and started again through the jungle. They travelled in silence, the failing light of dusk making their journey back to their village long—almost longer than their initial journey, it seemed. When they arrived, it was completely dark.

Rae thought only of avenging his father.

CHAPTER THIRTEEN

PHANTOMS IN THE WOODLAND

They travelled along the ocean for some time. Tilicea said that if they took the path they had used to reach the beach, they would have to pass Guluki again, risking an encounter with the High Council's army. Instead, they would take another path that connected the prison and the seaside town of Zerna and then head south toward the fortress at Ionia.

With the rising sun leading them, they left the glassy waters of the northern Zalmish Sea and entered the trees. In the sunlight, the once ominous woodland sprang to life. Joachim heard the shuffling of small creatures and the songs of the breeze, all blending over a drone of swallows in the morning's gentle mist.

It wasn't long before the thin layer of snow on the branches melted and the sun warmed the forest. The change in temperature was remarkable. He hardly believed that he now removed his cloak, letting open air trickle through the fabric of his tunic, when there had been snow on the ground hardly two hours ago.

As the morning wore on, he found his mind wandering to thoughts of Darcie and his village. Though he had started his journey in Zalm with his hunter instincts elevated, he faltered now. Even when he tried to focus on the trees, his mind was hazy and blunt from the days of sleeplessness. He became so unaware of the forest that he didn't realize Tilicea and Baruch stopped.

"Joachim." Baruch tugged at his shoulder.

"What is it?"

"Look up."

He did, peering to the tips of the trees. Just above them, he could see a vulture circling, weaving in and out of sight through the ceiling of leaves.

"You think it's going to try and kill us?" Joachim asked.

He laughed at his own joke. No one else did.

"It only feeds on dead things," Joachim remarked.

"That is likely the case," Tilicea said.

"Then there is probably some dead animal around here."

He rubbed his eyes, trying to push the fatigue from him. He tried to remember when he had slept last. Unlike Baruch, he had no sleep at Guluki, and they had travelled through the cave systems the night before. It seemed likely that he had not slept in nearly three days.

"The Great Druid's Road lies ahead," Tilicea said. "Despite the will of the late Great Druid himself, the route is marred by murders and violence. It is the quickest route between the precious metal mines at Zerna and the Empress' Palace in Zostrava. It's heavily patrolled by the council's army. It would appear that vulture marks a night of bloodshed on the road."

"Can we get around it?" Baruch asked.

"Not without wasting days."

"Then we have to cross it," Joachim said. "We need the ingredients."

His tone was drier than he would have wanted, but he was too tired and too irritated to change it. Tilicea eyed him, set down her pack, and sat on a tree stump. She took out her canteen and some dried meat wrapped in cloth.

"First, you will sleep. It is early in the morning still." She ripped a piece of meat and chewed. "We will recommence around the dinner hour, when the Great Druid's Road will be least guarded."

She passed the pack to Baruch and he, too, looked through it.

"But we don't have enough time." Joachim glared at them.

"An exhausted and clumsy hunter is as useless as a crying toddler on this journey," Tilicea said. "Sleep."

"Here." Baruch took something from the rucksack and held it out to him. "This will help you sleep. I slept plenty at Guluki. Now it's your turn. We'll keep guard."

Joachim knew he couldn't argue. They weren't moving, whether he decided to sleep or not, and he could definitely use it. He knew he was being unreasonable. He could feel an anger lingering inside him, one whose reasons he couldn't quite decipher. It wouldn't be long before he made a choice, some sleep deprived decision that could lead them all to danger.

He took the herb from Baruch and placed it in his mouth. It exploded, sickly-sweet, and he swallowed hard.

He spread his cloak on the ground, and the forest blurred.

ꝗ ꝭ Ꝯ ꝧ ꝫ ꝝ ꝟ ꝯ 8 ꝡ

Joachim felt his feet moving beneath him, jumping over fallen logs, and running across leaves. The jungle rang with the sound of creatures and collapsing trees. Though he didn't know where he headed, he didn't stop.

Billows of smoke rose like hands reaching toward the sky. He could smell burning on the breeze and feel heat on his body. Screams joined the other sounds, consuming the jungle into a symphony of chaos. Wretched cries that begged for mercy. Screams that called his name.

Flashes filled the sky, each blast shaking the ground and sending animals out of their burrows. As he ran farther, each crash became louder, each hiss of fire crisper. Another smell reached him, one that wasn't charred wood. He could smell the sea blast of the ocean. He was nearing the Black Rocks.

"Joachim."

His feet stopped. Someone waited for him.

"Ben?"

The man embraced him. Joachim looked at him. Ben was the cleanest that he had ever seen him, far too clean to still be an active hunter. His hair was nicely combed. His white tunic and pants appeared to be without any dirt or mud on them. It was so strange, it made Joachim uncomfortable. That, and he became aware of his own nakedness.

"What are you doing here?"

"You must hurry," Ben said. "They await, but cannot much longer. And neither will he."

"Who?" Joachim's eyes widened. "Zupay? Has he already hurt them? I have seven days!"

"Seven days."

Something boomed overhead, something a little more powerful than a tree crashing to the ground.

"Beware the road of the Great Druid, Joachim."

"What?"

"You are immersed in a conflict far greater than you understand."

Another crash, more forceful still. He could feel it shudder through the trees. He could feel it rocking him.

"Hurry, Joachim. The village needs you."

"Ben, stop," Joachim said. "You're not making any sense."

"Go now," Ben said, almost singing. "Tell the others, and take care of my son."

The man shoved him, pushing Joachim in the direction that he ran just moments earlier. Joachim stared. The man was fading away, his body disintegrating into the air and his smile blending in with the swirls of bark on the trees.

"The fathers say hello." Ben said. "You must go."

His voice echoed through the jungle just as another crash shook him. Joachim looked back, but the man had disappeared. Before he could stop and think, he ran again, his feet taking him toward the smoke. Palm trees stood like lit candles in front of him.

Pushing through another wall of greenery, he stood in a clearing. He didn't have to look around long to realize where he was. Books littered the ground, and a pile of scorched wood and broken stone lay where Baruch's library once stood. He raced past the old Tabitha's home. She and a few other villagers tried to extinguish the inferno. Rounding the curve in the path, Joachim came to his village.

Fire consumed the beach. His dwelling. His mother's dwelling. The infirmary. The other homes of his friends. Each smoldered in glowing embers. Some villagers tossed sand and water on the wrecks, but it was no help. They were just rubbish now, the remains of a village he no longer knew. Others gathered, tending to the wounded and calming the children.

How did these fires start?

Through the faces of the crowds, Joachim spotted Trent and Rae and Ben. Their weapons were drawn, and they eyed the skies and the other villagers. Joachim saw his mother holding a bow in her arms. She had arrows slung around her shoulder. When he saw the woman beside her, he felt his chest ache. The woman's dark hair lay on her shoulders, and her eyes glimmered in the glow of the embers. She rocked a babe in her arms.

"Darcie."

As the sound left his lips, a crash echoed through the village. Looking around, Joachim couldn't see anything that had changed. No new fires, no new crumbling structures. He looked up at Darcie again who had begun to cry. She stared at the jungle, and so did the others. They didn't move. Joachim didn't know if it was because they were too scared or simply because they knew it wouldn't matter.

They came like an outbreak of wasps, like the time he and Ben stumbled into a hive when they were kids. Hissing, seething, buzzing creatures poured from the jungle and into the village. Their beady eyes glistened, and their feet kicked up sand as they charged.

With nowhere to run, the village became a scene of terror. He saw blood. He saw tears. He saw agony and fear and death. It was like one of the battles from the history books of Old Earth, except there were none of those tanks or guns. But the creatures didn't need those.

They attacked the villagers with no discrimination. Some took on the bigger adult men while others snatched children from the arms of their mothers and dragged them into the jungle. Within a minute, human corpses lay on the sand. The creatures even stopped to feed on their flesh but were careful to leave the carcasses spread out. Their tokens. Their territory.

Joachim searched for Darcie. He saw his mother using a bow to ward off the intruders. Trent and Rae both used knives, Rae managing to stab the ones that tried to climb on top of him. He scanned the faces of the poor villagers, his heart racing. None of them were hers.

"Trent. Help me!"

He shot his head around, finding Darcie on the opposite side of the beach. She held their baby close to her chest, pursued by two of the demons. Though she managed to keep running from them, they closed in on her. They closed in on his child.

Before Joachim could push himself to move, the sound of a whistle resounded over the beach. The creatures stopped their pursuit, retreating back to the jungle and dragging those they were in the middle of killing with them. A figure emerged from the path.

Zupay's looked around at the fallen village, and his nostrils sifted through the smells of burning and ripped flesh.

"Give them to me."

The villagers stared at him. What did he want? They didn't know. But Joachim knew. He knew too well. He didn't have them.

"Give me what I need, and no one else will die."

"What do you want Zupay?" Alena's voice was shaky, and blood covered her face. Some of it was her own.

"Give me the ingredients for the immortality potion," Zupay yelled, "and the child! Give them to us, and I will end this."

"The ingredients aren't here. They still have seven days," Trent bellowed.

"I need the ingredients and the child right now!"

"What child, Zupay?" Alena croaked.

"The child born to the only remaining woman from the tribe I willed you to murder." His eyes shot to Darcie. "Give it to me."

Heat built in Joachim's face. He could see Darcie crying, calling out to the village for protection. Many of the men yelled at him, but many others remained silent. None moved. Trent crossed the beach and stood in front of her.

"You cannot have her," he said. "She's not yours to take."

"Then you will die defending her."

"Please, Zupay," Alena cried. "The ingredients will be here soon. We had ten days. There is still time. You cannot harm us until it has been ten days. There was a contract in blood."

"I know the ingredients are hidden here in the village." Zupay said. "You have lied to me. The contract means nothing. You have until the count of ten."

"But, Zupay—"

"You had ten days."

"We don't—"

"Nine. Eight."

"Please, just—"

"Seven days. Seven days."

The villagers fled like a family of boars smoked out from a bush. They tried to escape into the jungle only to be caught by Zupay's minions that waited just beyond the tree line. The creatures then appeared again from the jungle, readying themselves. Blood dripped from the flaps of skin over their mouths.

"Three. Two."

Zupay paused, lifting his arm.

"This is your last chance," he said. "Speak now or forever be silenced."

Joachim heard the crashing ocean waves through the quiet, accompanied by the sobs of villagers awaiting death. The creatures continued to hiss and sneer, ready for Zupay to authorize their attack. They waited for him to signal the time to eat.

"The era of humankind has indeed ended," Zupay said. "Turns out you're not invincible after all."

Alena stepped toward him, her hand outstretched.

"Zupay, please."

"Find the ingredients, and kill them all."

With the child already cooing in the demon leader's arms, he turned his back on the village and entered the jungle, the sounds of slaughter echoing through the trees.

ᘒ ᕱ ᑭ ᕴ ᘓ ᕳ ᘰ ᕸ ᘄ ᕲ

When Joachim awoke, he discovered that he had slept for eight hours. Dinnertime would now occupy most of the members of the High Council's army and the Great Druid's Road would be slightly less protected, masking their crossing. After a few pieces of dried meat and stale bread, Tilicea gave Joachim a bow and quiver of arrows she had crafted during his sleep. The travelers packed their belongings again and continued through the forest.

Most creatures had started their descent into slumber even though the crickets droned on still. Despite his renewed energy, Joachim didn't feel any more observant of the forest. He tried to concentrate, attempting to keep his ears tuned into the soundscape and his eyes ever-shifting, but he could not focus his mind. He thought about the dream. The attack. The slaughter. He thought of his newborn child in Zupay's arms.

After walking a half-hour, Joachim slowed and let Tilicea walk a little farther ahead. He eyed Baruch. In return, Baruch did the same and walked beside Joachim. He rustled a hand through his gray hair.

"Troubled sleep?" he asked.

"Nightmares, actually. Like nothing I've ever dreamt before. It was almost premonition-like."

"Bad dreams plague the best of us, Joachim," Baruch said.

"It was about Zupay," Joachim said. "He and his demons attacked the village. He said that he needed the ingredients and that he wouldn't respect the time limit of ten days. And there was Darcie and my child."

"Darcie is fine until we get the ingredients," he replied, "and so is your child. There is much time before it is born."

"He took it right from Darcie."

"I can see why this troubles you," Baruch said, now stopped and looking at him. "It must be hard fighting for something that you know very little about and now, to envision Zupay annihilating the village and kidnapping those closest to you. But you must distinguish which is reality and which is the delusion of your fear."

A child. Baruch, too, was concerned about a child. This one, however, was not in any dream. He was treating Joachim like he was one. The aggression of the hunter was building inside. So much for a sleep that would curb his irritation.

"But why must we continue to live this way?" Joachim demanded. "Why didn't we kill the creatures many years ago when we first discovered their strength?"

"Joachim, you know that wasn't possible, and it remains impossible."

Baruch's voice was raised, but only enough to signal to Joachim that he didn't enjoy the conversation. A rain began to fall, the clouds blocking out the remaining light and cooling the air. Tilicea walked in front of them still, not noticing their discussion, perhaps willingly.

"I wish I could offer you more comfort, Joachim. I wish I could tell you that these dreams will go away. I wish I could do those things, but frankly I would be lying to you. Joachim, you accepted this when you joined me. If you naively believed that this expedition would be like a typical hunt, like a glamorous occasion spent with your friends, you were seriously deceiving yourself.

"These dreams will stay as we get closer to Zupay's goal, and they might even persist if we survive. But you need to be stronger than your imagination. You need to know the difference between imagination and reality, and you must never let the lines blur between the two. If you do, Joachim, I may as well go on alone."

Baruch's words made his heart beat loud in his ears. Though he knew the old man said these things to caution him, he wished he wouldn't. Baruch strode away, and Joachim kicked a rock, bouncing it off a tree and into the bushes.

How could the man speak that way to him? As his companion and leader of the village, Baruch should have listened and supported him. Baruch shouldn't have made him feel so stupid. So weak. But the man didn't care, and something inside Joachim didn't expect him to.

Baruch had authorized the slaughter of Darcie's people after all. He was ruthless. He was heartless. He was a murderer. Joachim could trust only himself.

"If you care, I saw Ben," he called after him. "He told me to beware the Great Druid's Road."

"Quiet, Joachim."

"No, I think you should listen to me."

"Silence," Baruch whispered.

He stopped. He could hear movement. The hunter counted, hearing a group of four individuals ahead. Only one of them was Tilicea, who continued to walk without noticing the commotion.

He saw three men from the Empress' army. The two on the side carried lit torches. The one in the middle, large and rigid, led the pack. Tilicea lowered her rucksack to the ground. Glancing back at Baruch and Joachim, she signaled them to stay back.

"Move," Baruch whispered.

Before Joachim could think, Baruch tackled him into the brush. Joachim threw his arms in front of his face as they crashed into the thorns. Through the branches, they watched as the men approached Tilicea.

"Who are you?" the one in the middle probed. The leader.

"My name is…" Tilicea started, acting meek and small, "my name is Elli, Elli Wolfe."

"A Wolfe, are you?" The leader snickered. The men who carried the torches did too. "My father used to work with you lot. You're all nothing but a bunch of ignorant fools who support the rebel movement. What might a Wolfe like you be doing in these forests? Thought you could travel to Zerna and pickpocket some precious metal?"

"I was—"

"Tie her up, and take her with us," the man to his left said, the one with the hooked nose.

"Take me with you?" Tilicea asked.

"Shut up, you unworthy pig." the leader bellowed.

"But—"

"Nobody speaks to Theron unless he beckons you to speak." The shorter, fat man to the right said, lurching forward.

The hooked-nose man rummaged through his rucksack while Theron grabbed Tilicea. From the sack, they took some rope and tied her wrists together.

"Let's take her to Ionia," Theron said. "We can set her up for deportation to Guluki tomorrow morning."

The army men dragged her away, her cries awakening the birds in the trees. In a final glance to Baruch and Joachim, she signaled them to follow her with a jerk of her head.

CHAPTER FOURTEEN

THE ARMY MEN AND THE FORTRESS

They waited in the bushes until the footsteps could no longer be heard. The forest resumed its drone of humming crickets and blowing leaves, safe to do so now that the army men had left, and Baruch stood. The rain stopped, and dusk approached like an unwanted visitor. The third night began. Joachim felt more hopeless than ever.

"What are we going to do?" Joachim asked.

"We have to go after them," Baruch said.

"And how are we going to do that?"

"You're a hunter, Joachim. Let's not forget."

"We only have the rest of tonight and then six days, Baruch," Joachim said. Visions of his dream and the village flashed in his mind. "Won't she use the runestones to get herself out?"

"They'll likely look through her pockets, assume she has stolen the runestones, and then confiscate them," Baruch explained. "Besides, they're taking her to Ionia. Tilicea said that the Great Druid's grave is near the fortress there."

Joachim closed his eyes. His head spun.

"Relax, hunter," Baruch said. "If we're going to find Tilicea at Ionia, you need to focus on using your tracking skills and clear your mind of all else. Don't preoccupy yourself with the time limit. Doing so will only delay us further. Besides, we're very close to the first ingredient."

He knew Baruch was right. The more he dwelled on things he couldn't control, the farther he got from achieving his goal. The only way he could save Darcie and the rest of his village was if he could remove them from his mind for a little while and concentrate. Only then could he save his child.

He focused on the forest. It was impossible to see anything in the dark. The stars above were very little help, and they disappeared whenever a cloud masked the sky or he and Baruch travelled beneath a tree.

"Which way did they go?"

"That way." Baruch pointed ahead of them, a little to the right.

Just what Joachim thought.

"Do we have any lanterns?"

"Tilicea's left us her rucksack." It sat on the ground in front of them. "I'll check."

Baruch retrieved a lantern and a tin of oil. He placed the can into the glass enclosure and lit the wick with a match. The tiny flame illuminated a small distance around them. It was big enough to let them see where they were going, but small enough to hide anyone lurking in the shadows. Anyone who might attack them.

"Here you go." He gave it to Joachim and threw the pack around his shoulders. "I'll keep guard. If you hear anything, let me know."

Joachim examined the endless lines of trees. There was no path to follow to Ionia, just the Great Druid's road ahead that they would have to cross. He walked slowly in case he could find something to help them. He heard Baruch shuffling behind him but nothing else to complement the crickets—not even the wind. Soon, Joachim heard something else.

"I hear people up there," he said. "Hold the lantern. I'm going."

Without venturing too far, he came to the Great Druid's Road. At first he didn't see anyone, but as he went closer, he saw them: men from the High Council's army.

Atop two large animals, they patrolled the road. They held the reigns with one hand and lanterns with the other, scanning the path and surrounding trees. Across their backs they had a bow and case of arrows, and they had swords in the scabbards around their waists.

Joachim looked from the riders to their animals. The animals were much taller than he, their heads probably able to reach the roof of a dwelling. They were entirely covered in hair, wispy and tangled and long. They had two large tusks on either side of their trunks. Their ears and tails swung with each stride, and their eyes shone in the lantern's firelight.

He couldn't help but think that they looked like the hairy elephants he had read about in Baruch's library.

"She begged me not to," one of the men riding said. "I just laughed. She was completely helpless to my will. That was the second woman I had that evening."

"I remember my first," the second man said. "We had just raided her village. She claimed I murdered her children. I promised she'd be blessed with a new one soon, one not tainted with the blood of rebel scum."

They laughed so loud it echoed through the trees, silencing the crickets. Joachim couldn't believe what he heard. Those helpless women: who knew how many others there were in Zalm? He thought of Darcie. He shuddered to think what they would do to her.

Or what they might do to Tilicea.

The guards and their beasts continued down the path, not noticing him as they passed by. When he couldn't see them any longer, Joachim went back to Baruch. The man stood with the lantern out, still waiting.

"Is it safe to cross?"

"I don't know," Joachim said. "I saw two men guarding the road. They rode these enormous creatures."

"Mammoths," Baruch said. "They existed in our world many eons ago, but were extinct long before the Great Death."

Joachim had never heard of such creatures before. Then again, Joachim probably hadn't even studied half the creatures said to have existed on Old Earth. Baruch said that their world had changed much since them, but he found it strange they still lived in Zalm. It was like being visited by something from the past, something long since dead. It was exhilarating.

"The men spoke of their rape victims, Baruch."

The man looked solemnly at him and took a breath.

"Go find them again, Joachim." Baruch moved toward him. "I'll put out the lantern."

"Find who? The army men?"

"Yes."

Joachim stared at him. He blew out the lantern.

"Why?"

"We're going to need a way to get into Ionia," Baruch said. "Two strangers entering the fortress in an attempt to save an oracle woman aren't going to be well received."

"So what do you think we should do?"

"I'll wait at the road, concealed in the trees," he started. "That way, you can pursue them. Once you have found them, take them out with arrows. We'll steal their clothing."

Joachim nearly laughed out loud, but not because what the man said was funny. His laugh was one of surprise, disgust even.

"You're kidding."

"Do you have a better idea?"

Baruch waited, but Joachim didn't know what to say. He couldn't believe that the man who led his village, the man who Joachim had admired since youth, proposed to kill another human with so little thought. He thought about Darcie's village. Had Baruch decided that quickly to kill them too?

Despite that, he found himself considering it—willing almost. Before he could think again, he moved through the woodland.

"Let's go."

He took the bow and an arrow from behind, one that Tilicea carved him, and led them both to the spot where the Great Druid's Road cut a line through the trees. He looked to both sides and listened for a long while. He couldn't hear anyone close on the path, no one for at least a mile.

"I'll wait here," Baruch said.

He looked one more time at the old man, turned, and sprinted. The gravel of the path felt hard and painful underneath the thin lining of his shoes. Even though the soles of his feet were tough from years of hunting, he would get blisters and cuts from this night, he knew.

He ran for a couple minutes before he could see the light of the army men's lanterns. Then he dipped into the forest, running alongside the path. His movements were fast but deliberate, soundless and lethal. They wouldn't hear him coming.

He was the hunter.

He slowed, watching his prey from behind. He readied his arrow.

Joachim had never killed a human before, hunting only animals to feed the village. Though he knew that his prey could speak, had family, and had a soul, he thought of them as no different. They were animals, the both of them. They had no doubt raped many women and probably killed many innocents. Besides, how many lives had they ruined of those they spared?

In that moment, he convinced himself he had more reason to kill than Baruch did all those years ago. This was better than that. *He* was better than that.

The first arrow left his bow, hitting the man on the left mammoth in the back of his head. Instantly, he fell from his beast and crashed onto the path. Just as the second army man turned and raised his weapon, Joachim released the second arrow.

It pierced him between the eyes.

The mammoths fled, leaving the two dead army men alone on the Great Druid's Road. As he removed the heavy clothing from the two men, he didn't even cry. Sometimes when he killed an animal during a hunt, the remaining warmth of the animal's body would bring a tear to his eye, knowing that he had cut a life short.

This time though, he didn't feel sadness. He felt rage. There was rage for what he had done, for killing another human being who had done nothing to him, but there was rage, too, for their deeds. He knew their victims would rejoice if they knew. He thought of Darcie.

He would have done the same for her.

With the clothing, he went back to Baruch. He spotted the man leaning against a tree, a small glow coming from a pipe.

"It is done."

"Good," Baruch said. "Let's put on their clothing."

They did so in silence, the garments too large for both of them. Baruch extinguished his pipe and placed it in the rucksack.

"Are you ready to track?"

"Yes," Joachim said.

They crossed the road. Joachim could see a parting in the trees on the other side where the three men hauled Tilicea. They followed an unwavering trail through the forest. He soon realized Tilicea had purposely marked the path with rips of clothing and damage to the plant life. That or the army men's confidence resulted in carelessness. Either way, this made tracking fairly easy.

Hours went on, and the forest remained asleep. A gentle breeze danced through the trees and blew the leaves, but the night was clear. Just as he started to get used to the sounds, Joachim heard a humming up ahead, a sound that was not a breeze or cricket song.

"Listen," Baruch said.

"I hear it."

"It sounds like a waterfall."

He was right. Joachim stopped and closed his eyes, filtering out the other sounds of the forest. He could hear it clearly, water swelling and flowing, then falling and crashing onto rocks.

"It's close to us," he said.

Joachim took them through a mass of trees. On one of the branches, he found a splatter of blood. He didn't tell Baruch. He didn't want the man to worry. He just hoped it was from one of the men and not Tilicea herself.

They squeezed through the tiny space between the tree trunks, and he wondered how the men managed to do so, especially with a struggling captive. On the other side, Joachim saw tall bushes.

He squinted and tried to see beyond them. The waterfall roared, and he could see mist rising behind the greenery. It was at the other end of a canyon that was at least a hundred feet across. It took water from a river and plunged it down into the earth, deep into darkness. The walls of stone amplified the sound and the haze masked a fortress.

The fortress at Ionia.

Nelda let the leaves settle to the bottom of her cup before taking a sip of the tea. The city beyond the window of her quarters had fallen quiet, and only the torch light from her troops patrolling the streets shone through the darkness.

She'd be surprised if any rebels attempted to disrupt her city on this night. If they did, she'd given one command: don't hesitate to kill.

As the liquid in the glass touched her mouth, the herbs inside made her lips tingle. She swallowed, and the tingling moved in a wave across her chest. She sat back in her chair, closed her eyes, and let the herbs relax her. They were the finest poppies grown in her private gardens just north of Zostrava and known for their calming properties. She felt them clearing her mind of the numbers of troops and the maps of occupation and the countless letters she had signed to the generals of the High Council's army.

With a knock at the door, she put the cup down on the desk.

"Enter."

Valeska and Panthea came into her office and curtsied. Behind them, a short man entered also, holding a scroll in his hand and bowing.

"We've received news from Guluki." His eyes were serious.

"What news?"

"There's been an uprising," he said.

She took another sip of her tea. "There are uprisings all the time. Certainly, it's nothing the guards can't handle."

"She used runestones."

Nelda coughed on a sip. Any reference to her sister made her want to smash something.

"Do what you must with her," Nelda said dismissively. "I have little time for her nonsense."

"She escaped last night, my Empress. The guards were able to squash the rest of the uprising, but they were unable to find her anywhere near the prison."

The man unrolled the scroll and handed it to Panthea who placed it in her hand.

"And she took the two prisoners from the other world with her."

Nelda stared at the scroll, the scribbles of ink indicating just what her confidant had told her.

"Find them." She could hear her voice rising. "Find them and bring them to me so we can dispose of this problem. And bring me more tea!"

CHAPTER FIFTEEN

THE KIDNAPPING

The fortress is over there," Joachim said. "Beside the waterfall."

Joachim gazed out across the canyon and saw the blurry outline of a building. He thought it would be bigger, perhaps as big as Guluki, but it wasn't even half the size. Giving it the title of *fortress* might even be a little misleading.

"I see it," Baruch said.

"How do we get across?"

"There's a bridge," Baruch said. "It starts over there."

He pointed. Joachim saw its mouth mounted to the dirt, its narrow path barely big enough for a wagon or carriage. After the first few meters, the rest of the bridge disappeared into the misty blur of the waterfall's haze.

"The fortress will be guarded," Baruch said. "Even if it isn't, I doubt we will be able to enter through the main gates."

"We're wearing their uniform," Joachim said. "Couldn't we just walk right in?"

"But we don't have their accent. They'd know."

"Then what should we do?"

Baruch dug through his pockets and pulled something from

them. He took out a small rock and handed it to Joachim. He realized that it was one of Tilicea's runestones.

"Where did you get this?"

"It was in Tilicea's rucksack," Baruch said.

"Do you think she knew?"

"Well, she is an oracle."

Joachim felt its texture with his fingertips. On its face, there was dot carved into the stone. It glowed red.

"What does it do?"

"It's the same stone used by Tilicea's people at Guluki. It starts fire."

"So we're going to light the fortress on fire?" Joachim asked. "With Tilicea inside?"

Baruch took the stone from his palm.

"Of course not," he said. "But we can use it for a distraction."

Joachim remembered how the rebels had set fires in Guluki, magical infernos that seemed to catch to stone. He couldn't see any shrubbery near the fortress from where they stood. Even if there was, he knew the mist soaked everything. He didn't doubt that they could start a fire.

They would use the runestone to draw the army men out.

"Weapons drawn." Baruch pulled a dagger from his pack. "I'll lead."

Joachim readied his bow, and they approached the bridge. With each step, coolness sprinkled onto his face. It felt nice on his skin, cleaning the filth from the days in the prison and in the forest. He breathed it in, the mist rushing into his nose and soothing the dryness inside. Even as it went deeper, he could feel it in his throat and pushing into the expanse of his lungs. He felt fresher—more alert somehow.

On the bridge, the wood moaned and creaked. It swayed at their smallest movements. Though he tried to keep his bow drawn, he clung to the suspension rope. The bridge no longer seemed like the best route. The void of darkness and mist seemed endless below.

"Watch your step," Baruch said. "There's a plank missing here."

Joachim stepped over the gap. He wondered how long he would fall before meeting his watery end.

"The other side is near." Baruch stopped.

Joachim could see where the bridge clawed back onto the earth.

"I don't see anyone there," Baruch said. "I'll light fires and draw them out. In the commotion, sneak into the fortress and look for Tilicea."

"Where will I find her?"

"The lowest level, most likely," Baruch said. "The Council has a soft spot for dungeons and torture chambers. Don't speak to anyone, Joachim. The clothing we stole will be enough to shield you, but your voice will give you away."

Baruch led them to the end of the bridge. Still no one greeted them. The waterfall roared close now, and the ground shuddered, much of the clearing in front of the fortress soaked.

"I'll hide in those shrubs over there," Baruch said. "Once you've taken Tilicea from the fortress, go across the bridge back to the other side. Don't try to find me. I'll meet you there. For now, wait behind that tree until I light the fires and men come outside."

Joachim looked to where Baruch pointed. He turned back to Baruch, but he was already walking toward the bushes on the far side of the clearing. Joachim strapped his bow around his back and returned the arrow to his quiver. He too went to his hiding spot, using the tree trunk to mask him from the fortress. He could feel the void behind him, mist exploding upward from the canyon just a few feet from the tree.

It would just take one small slip.

He saw a light. It started slow and travelled across the clearing. He first thought it was a lantern, but it hovered too high from the ground. It was like an orb of light, like an overgrown firefly. He watched it glide across the clearing, passing the main doors of the fortress. It stopped and hovered.

With a loud bang, the ball of light slammed into the ground.

Firefly indeed.

The area burst into flames, burning the dirt and stone beneath. The fire was small, but within moments the flames became an inferno, burning at least two dwellings worth of ground.

Calls echoed from the fortress as the main gates opened. Army men poured out. They kicked dirt onto the fire, but it grew still, their efforts only fuelling its fury. More men came with pails and sheets of fabric. Even their water and beating did nothing to tame the blaze.

Magical fire.

Soon the flames consumed the entire right side of the clearing, and the men buzzed around. Some ran with the intent to put out the fire, others fled across the bridge or to the trees where Baruch hid. Joachim knew he didn't have any more time to wait. He emerged from behind the tree.

He sprinted across the clearing toward the gates, trying to look as disoriented as the other men. He felt the fire's heat on his face. He sweated underneath the army man's uniform.

"You there," a man called to him. "Go get another pail. We need to control this before it reaches the fortress."

He nodded obediently and tried to hide his flushed face. He continued into the fortress without anyone stopping him. It wasn't until he found himself surrounded by the fortress walls that he realized he had no idea how to get to the dungeons.

A stampede of mammoths pushed past him and nearly toppled him over in their flight. A group of men followed, their whips snapping at the beasts, but they wouldn't stop. The creatures fled the fire, and they were right to. Joachim could see the flames over the fortress walls.

He found the main entrance and entered the foyer. It looked much rougher than Nelda's palace—more worn, more disturbing.

Firelight shimmered off the dark stone walls. There was a staircase in front of him. A flight led down.

He descended the steps. They curved around a corner and let him out on a landing that opened to a long corridor. Torches along the wall went down as far as Joachim could see. Nobody else was down there with him.

He ran. No other path branched off the hallway, and he still couldn't see an end to it. At last, a sign overhead pointed toward something to the right. He found a closed door. Strange writing that he could not understand marked the bronze plate on the wood. Could it be a torture chamber? Would he find Tilicea inside marred with cuts and bruises or bound by her limbs like Darcie? He pushed it open.

He was unable to see anything in the darkness.

"Tilicea," he whispered. "Tilicea, are you here?"

No one answered. He opened the door fully, letting the light from the torches flow in. It was a supply chamber. He was saving Tilicea from a supply chamber.

He closed the door, and something brushed past him. Turning to see what it was, a hand clasped over his mouth. He struggled, swinging around and pinning the person down to the floor. Lifting his head, he gazed into green eyes.

"Tilicea?"

"Yes, it's me."

Joachim helped her to her feet.

"I'm sorry, I didn't realize," he said.

"It's alright." She brushed herself off. "What's going on up there?"

"Baruch set a fire in the clearing. I came in here to find you and bring you back."

Joachim saw cuts on her face and arms. It looked like a bruise was forming around her left eye. Though he didn't expect anything less from monsters who raped, he was surprised. He wanted to give them all black eyes.

"Are you okay?"

"Yes," she said. "Standard practices of the High Council's army, that's all."

"How did you escape?"

"They hadn't locked me in a cell yet," she said. "Just as they were preparing to, I used a knife I had stolen from the torture chamber to get away."

She presented a knife from the pocket of her torn cloak. It was stained with freshly spilt blood. No black eyes needed, apparently.

Joachim pulled her down the corridor.

"Wait," she said.

She brought him back to the supply chamber and began stuffing her pockets. Joachim did so also, filling each one with dried meats and vegetables. When he could fill his pockets no more, he looked up at her.

"That's enough," she said.

They sprinted down the corridor back toward the staircase. Ahead they could hear tumult on the steps. Light reflected on the wall rounding the corner. Someone came to join them.

Tilicea grabbed the knife from her pocket and Joachim readied an arrow in his bow. A large man entered the corridor from the stairs and stared at them. It was Theron, the same man who took Tilicea to the fortress.

"What do you think you're doing?" he called.

Joachim stopped. Blood poured from the brute's nose, and his face was blackened with ash and soot from the fire. He held a pail in his hand.

"I should have known the fire had something to do with you, Wolfe," he snarled, walking toward them. "You dirty lot are like bad omens, sympathizing with the old ways of dark magic. And who is this fellow with you? Some lover to help you spread your diseased bloodline?"

Before he could speak again, Joachim released the arrow that was in his bow. It struck the man in the shoulder. He cried out and fell.

Joachim took Tilicea's hand, and they ran down the corridor, passing the brute as he writhed in pain. They ascended the steps back to the foyer. The doors to the fortress grounds stood open, revealing the panic. Revealing the fire.

The flames consumed parts of the fortress walls. The men carried pails of water out, but there were less of them now than there had been. Tilicea and Joachim ran toward the gates. The mammoths were not in any of their pens.

Outside, the mist of the waterfall fell just as heavy as before, but the fire continued on. Army men with runestones spewed water onto the flames. Though it contained the fire better than the pails did, it threatened to consume the fortress at any moment. No one noticed Joachim and the prophetess scampering to the bridge.

"Where's Baruch?" Tilicea asked.

"He'll meet us on the other side," Joachim said.

"Stop them!"

A voice bellowed across the clearing. Joachim bolted around and saw Theron, his shoulder bleeding, but the arrow removed from his flesh. He yelled again to the men around him, pointing to Tilicea and him.

"Those are the prisoners," he yelled. "They're trying to escape!"

They all stopped, only the fire moving with gusts of the wind. Those who didn't use runestones to put out the flames lowered their pails and started to rush toward them followed by Theron who attempted to keep up. They each drew weapons from their scabbards.

"We have to move," Joachim said.

Passing the tree he hid behind while he waited for Baruch to light the fires, they came to the bridge. He hesitated. The bridge swayed and disappeared into the mist, but he couldn't delay. He could hear the army men drawing nearer. They were like the creatures of the jungle: grunting and calling and ready for blood. They would be on them soon.

As soon as Joachim and Tilicea started across, the bridge swung. They tried to move as quickly as they could, but every jerk made it harder to keep balance. Their movement became even slower as they realized the wood was slick with mist. The waterfall thundered.

The army men only made travel worse across the bridge. The men poured onto the thin passage, and the wood jutted back and forth with their pursuit. Joachim pushed farther, but the weight of the other men caused the bridge to sink, pulling them into the void below. Soon the weight would be too much.

"There it is," Tilicea cried. "I see the other side."

The bridge groaned. There were at least forty men on it, each moving toward them with their weapons drawn. Joachim could see the face of the cliff below him, the bridge bringing him closer to safety.

Joachim fell forward. He half-expected to continue falling and to become consumed in the darkness, but he could feel wood from where it impacted him in the stomach. A plank of wood had broken. Before he could stand, Tilicea's hands pulled at him.

"They're coming!"

With another groan, the bridge shuddered, and Tilicea toppled onto him. He tried to pull his leg from the gap in the wood, but the bridge shook too much to get a hold. The shuddering intensified. The men clambered closer. The posts on land holding them suspended were moving. The weight eased them out of the soil.

"We have to get off this bridge!" Joachim yelled. "The men are going to pull us down."

"Then come on!"

Tilicea grabbed him again. He finally got his foot out from between the planks and was able to stand, holding onto the suspension rope. Behind, he could see the men just ten feet from them, moving ever closer.

With a leap, Tilicea and Joachim launched themselves onto sturdy land.

"Cut the ropes of the bridge," Tilicea said.

She frantically sliced at them, fraying the line and making the bridge sag on one side. Joachim pulled a dagger from his pocket and did the same, but the army men were too close to them.

"There's no time. We have to run."

Tilicea stood, but as she turned, one caught hold of her cloak. Joachim grabbed her arm. He tried to wrench her away, but he heard a *snap*. It was cracking wood, like Ben's clothesline pulled too tight the day he told Joachim of the creature's attack. The bridge split in half. Pieces of it flew up all around them. The other men fell down into the darkness with the rest of the bridge, their cries echoing and then drowned out by the waterfall.

With the bridge, he felt Tilicea slip over the edge too. The army man still held onto her legs, flailing wildly. Joachim felt himself losing hold. The mud made it hard to steady himself. There were only a few more feet before all three of them fell over the cliff.

"Let go of her!"

Joachim tried to strike the man with his knife. He could see the edge and feel the cool wind on his face. He tried to pull again, but he couldn't. He closed his eyes. He had to make a choice. He knew that if he didn't let go, all three of them would fall. Tilicea or Darcie.

Something whizzed past his ear. The man holding Tilicea went limp. Joachim opened his eyes as a second arrow flew past him. When it hit the man, he let go of Tilicea and tumbled into the darkness.

"Let me help you."

Baruch appeared behind him. He laid his bow on the ground, grabbed Joachim by the shoulders, and they pulled Tilicea onto land. They sat in silence, the flickering of fire still visible on the other side of the canyon.

"I thought you were going to let me fall," Tilicea said.

Joachim laughed. "I thought about it, but I realized that we didn't know where to find any of the ingredients."

She laughed too. Before long they all did, even Baruch. Soon they were wheezing and clutching their stomachs and gasping for breath. But their laughs weren't ones of those who enjoyed the situation they found themselves in. They were of those who had just escaped death—snorts of dizzying relief, cackles of madness. Laughter of those who, for a moment, thought they'd never laugh again.

When they finished, Tilicea stood. The darkness dissipated, and the mist glowed with the first rays of dawn.

"The Great Druid's grave is not far from here," she said. "Let's go before the High Council realizes there has been trouble at Ionia."

CHAPTER SIXTEEN

BOATS ON THE HORIZON

They returned from Zupay's colony in the middle of the night. The sun had long set, and they all went to their houses for rest, vowing to continue their work in the morning. Though he went to his, Rae didn't sleep. He lay awake gazing at the stars through the window beside his bed.

Sometimes he wept, sometimes he felt so angry he wanted to destroy everything in his home. Whenever he closed his eyes, even if only for a little while, he saw visions of the demons' terrible feast of his father's flesh.

Finally he fell asleep just as the rays of sunlight bathed the beach. When he awoke, he had slept most of the day, and it was late afternoon. He put on a fresh pair of shorts and a tunic and went out to the rest of the village.

Outside, villagers prepared for supper. They gathered grains to boil and washed the vegetables. He passed Trent's dwelling, the man's snores echoing from inside. He saw the infirmary across from where he stood. He should have time for a short visit before Trent woke.

He crept inside. The woman in the bed stirred. He put his hand on her arm and gazed down at her.

"Ben?"

"No, Mom, it's me. It's Rae."

Ophelia opened her eyes and smiled. Rae smiled back, touching the skin of her cheek. Her face looked pale, and her skin was dry. Around her eyes he could see the puffy remains of tears. She sat up in bed, the blanket falling off her. Underneath her clothing, she had grown thin. Though it had only been a couple days, it was apparent she hadn't eaten.

"Rae," she said. "Where have you been?"

"I've been doing work for the village, Mom." He spoke softly. "How have you been?"

"What sort of work?" she asked.

"Just the regular chores: collecting wood for the fires, tending to the gardens," Rae lied. "What about you? How are you?"

Ophelia sighed, looking down at the fraying seam of her shirt. She played with it in her fingers, a placid look invading her face. She then looked to the window. The rays of sunshine fingered through the shades.

"Is it warm out?" Ophelia asked.

"Yes."

Ophelia swung her legs around and stood on the floor. She stumbled, finding her balance. She looked up at him, her eyes wide and grin childlike. His mother grabbed his hand and started pulling him out the door.

"Where are we going?" Rae asked, trying to slow her.

"Follow me."

"What about Jolyne? Won't she notice you're gone?"

She brought him out of the infirmary and into the rest of the village. They walked through the dwellings and into the jungle, following the path that would lead them to the water. Within moments, the obstructing branches opened to endless miles of blue. The sun warmed his face. With the sand underneath his toes, Ophelia took him to the right. From behind the curve in the treeline, Rae saw that she led him to the Black Rocks at the edge of the beach.

He didn't want to go.

She walked on, her feet clapping on the surface of the stones as she hopped along to the water. Rae didn't join her. He stood still, numb to her voice and the ocean breeze. Why was she acting this way? Why did she bring him here?

"Come," she called out to him.

He hesitated. Though he didn't understand why his mother seemed so odd, so apparently unaffected by the tragedy that surrounded the village, he chose to ignore it. He decided he wouldn't tell her about what he was doing at Zupay's village and the hopelessness he felt. He would enjoy these few moments of calm. He knew it might be their last if they failed.

"Rae, come here." She beckoned.

He stepped out onto the rocks. In spots, the surfaces felt warm with the sunlight, and the splashes of water cleaned the filth from his feet. He sat down beside Ophelia and dipped them in the cool seawater. She looked at him.

"This is where Ben asked me to be his wife," Ophelia said. "He said he always loved these rocks."

She took his hand again, squeezing his knuckles between her fingers.

"You look a lot like him. Did I ever tell you that?"

The words made his chest burn and his eyes water. He didn't want to cry in front of her. He didn't want her to become upset too.

"Yes," he said. "You have before."

She looked back out to sea.

"I saw something on the water yesterday," she said. "When I came here after dinner."

"Something on the ocean?" Rae asked.

"Yes. It was just there, where the sky meets the water." She pointed. "It looked like a boat."

"It could have been anything, Mom. It could have been a bird or a trick of the light."

"No," she said. "It looked the way they used to describe them to me as a little girl. I could see giant sails, three of them. It travelled right across the horizon."

The memories of the stories his father recited came back to him. They were just that now, like the man who told them—stories without good endings.

"Baruch says he's never seen anyone who travels these waters, not in his entire life. There aren't any other villages like ours. No one else who survived the Great Death."

She grinned.

"That's not what Ben says. Wait until he gets back; he'll tell you all about it."

He stared at her. He couldn't speak. She laughed, but Rae didn't have any idea what was funny. Did she not know that he was dead? How could she not? She had fallen into fever and dismay afterward. That's what Jolyne told him. She continued to laugh a laugh so obscure, so juvenile that it made him shiver. He had never seen his mother act this way before. It frightened him.

"Rae?"

A voice called from the up the beach. Rae turned to see who it was as Ophelia leapt to her feet. She hopped along the rocks, and he stood to follow her. Trent greeted her as she jumped onto the sand and hugged him.

"They need you at the kitchens, Ophelia," Trent said. "We'll meet you up there."

She nodded and curtsied, giggling as she ran back up the beach and toward the village. Trent's smile faded as Rae approached him.

"What's happened to her?" Rae demanded. "Why is she acting like a little girl? Why doesn't she know that he's dead?"

"She does. They told her. She's just suffering from some form of neurosis."

"Neurosis?"

"She acts as if nothing happened even when prompted," Trent said. "It's like she reverts to being a child whenever she can't handle the stress of it. It's a way she's developed to deal with the grief."

"Well, maybe she should learn like the rest of us."

Rae wiped a tear from his cheek. He didn't want to cry. He was done crying. He was an adult now and a hunter. Hunters didn't cry.

"Jolyne says she'll get better," Trent said. "And while we're working to stop Zupay, it's better that she remains in her care."

Rae didn't look at him. He felt like destroying something, like going back to his dwelling and burning it to the ground. Above else, he felt like getting away from the village. He wanted to run far into the jungle, far enough away that no one could find him. Better yet, he wanted to build a boat and disappear into the horizon.

"Let's go help with supper," Trent said. "After, we'll discuss what we need to do next at Zupay's colony."

At supper, the villagers sat silently. Besides the occasional giggle from Ophelia, the others were quiet. He didn't like the looks they gave her now. They looked at her like a nuisance. In fact, they looked at her as if she would need to be punished soon before she caused any trouble. They looked at her as if she had lost her mind.

And maybe she has, Rae thought.

Even once dinner ended, no one spoke. The villagers were tense, glancing around whenever there was a change in the wind or a rustling in the bushes. Even the children felt it, refusing to leave the table once they had finished, afraid to leave their parents' side. None of that mattered to Rae. He used the silence to calm himself and to ready himself for the events to come.

As the other villagers cleared the table and prepared for a night in their dwellings, Rae and Trent met Tabitha at her home.

"Fear is in the air," Trent said as they entered. "The villagers are terrified to breathe too loudly, and it doesn't help that we're so secretive about what we're doing out in the jungle."

"We have to be," Tabitha said. "We can't risk compromising our plan. If we do, all of the village will certainly perish."

They sat down at her table. Tabitha lit a pipe, took a few drags, and passed it to Trent. The smell stung Rae's nostrils.

"Are you all right?" she asked him.

"Yeah. It just smells, that's all."

"And back at the village?"

Rae looked at her, digging his nails into the grooves of the wood.

"I'm fine."

"Okay." She took the pipe from Trent and inhaled again. "I propose we do our attack in the early hours of morning."

"That would work," Trent said. "If we leave here just after midnight, we can be there before the sun comes up. We'll drop the poison in the well and be on our way home before the sun rises."

"And then they can drink the water first thing in the morning."

"Exactly," Trent said.

"What are we going to poison them with?" Rae asked.

"Ah." Tabitha smiled. "One moment."

Handing the pipe to Trent, she stood from the table and entered a second room. She returned with a sealed pail in her hand and plopped it on the table triumphantly.

"What is it?" Rae asked.

"Smell."

She lifted the lid on the pail. Rae didn't need to lean forward to smell what was inside. It reminded him of the time he found dead rats in Baruch's library, their bodies rotting in piles of their own feces. Trent plugged his nose. Dinner started to churn in Rae's stomach.

"What is that?" he managed to ask.

"Water hemlock," she said. "I picked it and mashed it this morning."

"And it'll work?"

"Oh, yes." She put the lid back on the pail. Between the pipe smoke and the smell of the plant, he felt nauseated. "People used it in executions in ancient times."

"Won't they smell it too?"

"It's possible," Tabitha said. "But not likely. Something tells me they're immune to bad smells."

"Sounds like we're set then," Trent said. "Let's go get some rest and then meet at midnight."

He gave the pipe back to Tabitha. She took another drag and sat down at the table. Trent led Rae to the door.

"You can stay in my dwelling for a while," he said. "There's plenty of room. Unless you're too old for company now that you're a hunter."

Rae snorted. The man grinned. "I think I'll choose my own bed, thanks," Rae said.

"Alright."

Trent pushed open the door. Leaves swayed in the fading sunlight, slower now that the breeze had died down, almost like they prepared for slumber. Rae walked a few steps, but noises that didn't sound like a sleeping jungle filled the air. Rae heard screams through the trees.

On the path that led toward the village, someone ran toward them.

"Trent!"

The man came closer. Rae recognized him as one of the men that had hunted with his father.

"What's going on?" Trent asked.

"It's Ophelia. She's having a nervous fit."

Before the man could lead them, they ran. Rae's legs pushed hard below him. They turned the corner onto the path that led to the village fire pit and dining table.

"No! Leave me alone!"

Ophelia held a knife out in front of her, swinging it at a second man who tried to calm her. Her nightgown was filthy, and tears streamed down her face.

"Get away from me."

"What happened to her?" Trent asked the man who led them.

She looked around madly.

"She was helping clean the dishes," the man said. "She dropped a plate and cut her hand on one of the shards. When we tried to help her, she panicked and grabbed the knife."

"Ophelia." Trent walked forward, his arms outstretched. "It's me. It's Trent. Put down the knife."

"Don't touch me!" she screamed. "Stay away from me, demon!"

"Go find Jolyne at the infirmary," Trent said to the man. "Maybe she can calm her down."

The man ran across the clearing, careful to avoid Ophelia. Trent and two other villagers started to close in on her. Rae watched from behind. He wanted to help them stop her, but he didn't know what to do. He could see others watching from the windows of their homes. One mother shut her blinds, shielding her young son from the scene. Rae didn't recognize the look in his mother's eyes.

"I said get away!"

Swinging the knife, she broke into a fit of screams, each one piercing Rae's ears.

"Mom!"

He stepped forward. The men watched him but kept their arms toward Ophelia.

"Mom, it's me. It's Rae."

She stood still. "Rae?"

"Yes," he said. "Put down the knife. These people are your friends."

"Oh, Rae." She dropped the knife and held him. "I thought I'd lost you."

"No, I'm here." His voice sounded foreign even to himself. He couldn't lift his arms to hug her.

He saw Jolyne arrive behind them, her old face stern but her gaze soft. Her hair was cut short.

Ophelia let him go, but held his hand.

"Is she okay?" Jolyne asked.

"Yes," he croaked.

"Bring her to the infirmary, then. We're going to put her to bed."

She led them across the village grounds, the three other men following. As they passed, the people from the windows stared. He held his head up, but he couldn't stop from trembling. Ophelia looked up at the stars.

"We'll give her a sedative," Jolyne said once they had arrived, cleaned up Ophelia, and settled her into bed. "Just to make sure she'll last through the night."

She put a capsule into his hand.

"There's water on the nightstand."

"Thank you, Jolyne."

She left the room, closing the door behind her. The village outside had fallen quiet again. Only the crickets hummed through the darkness. Rae pulled the covers over his mother, walked to the window, and drew the shade.

"Leave it open," Ophelia said. "I want to watch the stars."

"It's time to sleep now." He pulled them closed. "Swallow this."

He crossed the room and put the capsule in her palm. He was careful not to put it in the one that had been cut in the cookhouse and then bandaged. He picked up the mug of water and waited for her to swallow.

"But—"

"Just do it."

The smile faded as she put the medicine in her mouth and swallowed a mouthful of water. He put the mug back on the nightstand and turned.

"Goodnight, Mom."

"Wait."

He turned back. She held her hand out to him.

"Can you stay with me until I fall asleep?"

He took the chair and sat down beside the bed, staring at the far wall. She slipped her hand under his. He could feel her watching him, but he refused to meet her gaze. She had angered and humiliated him. Worse, her condition added to the hopelessness he felt. Even if Rae could stop Zupay's creatures from crushing the village, nothing in his life would be joyful ever again.

"Rae?"

"Yes, Mom?"

"I want you to tell me when he comes back," she said. "Promise you'll wake me once Ben returns."

He swallowed down a sob. It waited in his throat. "I will."

"He'll come from the ocean, you know."

Her grip relaxed on his hand, and her speech was quiet. The pill was working.

She closed her eyes. "In one of those boats on the horizon."

CHAPTER SEVENTEEN

THE EYE OF THE DRUID

Though the woods filled with daylight, the clouds kept the forest from warming. The wind picked up as they travelled, and Joachim's cloak did little to keep it out. Patters of rain eliminated the morning fog, but as the morning drew on, every one of the travelers was soaked. Joachim wondered how long it would be before the contents of his rucksack became soaked also.

"The willow tree is just beyond those trees," Tilicea said when they stopped for breakfast.

"And the Druid's grave is there?" Baruch asked.

"Yes," she said. "At the roots of the willow tree, there's a cave. We must follow the cave to the end. There we'll find his grave. Remove the lid, and find his eyes. As soon as we get one, we can head south across Minerva's Pass to the Cliffs of the Gods for the harpy egg."

"You will be joining us?" Baruch asked. "I thought you would only take us this far before you go to help your people."

"Considering that you saved me from those men at Ionia, it's only fair that I help you finish this journey. Besides," her voice lightened. "With all the trouble you two have made during your short visit to Zalm, you'll be lucky to make it home even with my help."

"Thank you, Tilicea." Baruch smiled.

"Yes," Joachim said. "Thank you."

He thought he should sound more sincere than he did. He should trust Tilicea and be grateful she would continue to guide them, but he couldn't shake his uneasiness. Tilicea smiled in return.

"Why do they call him the Great Druid?" Joachim asked.

Maybe he could distract them from his half-hearted smile.

Tilicea ate the remainder of her bread and wiped her hands on her cloak. She took a sip of water.

"He is a symbol of an age long passed," she said. "He made the magic of runestones available to all citizens, from those in the Council to those who were poor. He was our last monarch. Before the High Council took over, the Great Druid was the leader of Zalm. He ascended the throne in a long line of other druids who preached magical equality and strived to unite our world."

"What happened to them?" Joachim asked. "Why were they replaced by the High Council?"

"A rebellion," she said. "The rich decided they didn't want magic available to all. They said not all were worthy. They overthrew the Great Druid and established the High Council, one that heavily regulated magic. They told the people how to live, how to think, and made it hard for them to become as profitable and powerful as they, erasing the freedoms people once held."

"Why is his grave out in the open then?" Joachim asked. "Wouldn't that just encourage a return to the way things were before?"

Tilicea shook her head. "It's hard to identify with something you know nothing about. Education is controlled by the Council, and only the most powerful are taught about the Age of the Druids. To regular people, the druids were lost many years ago. They are nothing but a legend now, one perpetuated by a mysterious, rarely-visited grave."

"That must have been very long ago," Baruch said.

"Yes, many years. I might even guess a thousand. The Council likes to skew the past and make their own history important. The exact dates of the revolution are not known, not even to those who know most about it."

"If the Druid died that long ago, how are we supposed to salvage his eye?" Joachim asked.

"The eyes of the Great Druid were not human eyes," Tilicea said as she stood. "Having lost his sight in his youth, he had fake ones made for him. They were said to be made of gold and blessed with a magic that made it possible for him to see. Let's go find him."

Joachim and Baruch stood. Joachim brushed the water from his hair and pulled up his hood. As another gust of wind pushed through his cloak, he was relieved he would soon enter a shelter of some sort, even if it was a cave where he would find a grave. At least he could let his things dry, if for only a short while.

Tilicea led them to a clearing. Tall grasses came up to his waist and swayed in the breeze. In the center of the clearing stood a willow tree. It was taller than the rest of the forest, and its long branches swept across the tops of the grasses. Mud squished beneath Joachim's feet and soaked into his shoes.

Coming closer to the tree, he smelled sweetness. It reminded Joachim of the honey they made at the village in the springtime just before the harsh summer sun or the syrup from the taps in the trees. On the branches of the willow tree, tiny yellow flowers dotted the leaves.

They parted the branches like curtains and exposed a small clearing.

"The entrance to the cave is just around the other side," Tilicea said.

The dirt under their feet was dry, and the branches concealed an area of at least three feet from the tree trunk. The sweet smell was even stronger there, and the rain water didn't leak into the shelter:

the branches created a roof. The coolness persisted though, perhaps even more.

Joachim saw exposed tree roots on the ground. Underneath, there wasn't any dirt. Tilicea took off her pack, leaned it against the tree, and then knelt beside the opening.

She parted the roots, careful not to tear them. Though they were thick with age, and it was practically a monsoon outside, they looked brittle and dry. Pulling them wide, she pushed her legs into the opening. She slipped down and disappeared into the ground.

"It's dark down here," she called to them. "Grab the lantern from my pack."

Joachim opened the rucksack and pulled it out. He lit a match and brought it to the wick, the flame glowing in the darkness. He passed it down to her. Underneath, Joachim saw the passageway was not very wide. Tilicea's head was not that far from the surface.

"Come," she said. "The grave is just down here."

Baruch lowered himself to Tilicea. Joachim then widened the roots again and swung his legs over, taking a last breath and dropping into the cave.

So much for the flowers. The air in the cave was warm and reeked of sour mildew. The passageway was narrow, and there wasn't enough room to spread his arms out to either side. The mud walls breathed as the roots of the willow tree pulled water from the ground. Joachim followed the dim light down the passageway, the groans of earth and the blackness making him feel surrounded. Confined.

He stepped out into the clearing with Tilicea and Baruch and saw they were covered in mud. He noticed that he was too, filth caking his arms and legs and staining his cloak.

The tomb wasn't very big, perhaps slightly smaller than a room in his dwelling back at his village. Roots from the willow tree layered the ceiling, some dangling down toward the ground. On the far wall, Joachim saw a stone plaque with words he couldn't read written on it.

"Where's the body?" he asked.

"That plaque indicates the Druid's grave is here," Tilicea said. "We have to dig."

Joachim rolled his eyes. "Of course."

Getting on his knees, he pulled mounds of dirt from the ground and threw them away. The other two did the same, staining any clean spots left on their bodies. Before long they cleared mud almost a foot down. Joachim could taste it in his mouth and feel it in his hair. With another pull, his fingernails raked against something solid.

"I feel it," he said. "I can feel the stone of the coffin."

He pushed his hand back and forth, trying to clear the face of the stone. No use. He hadn't been this dirty since Ben pushed him into marsh on one of their hunts. And Joachim was used to getting dirty.

"There's still too much," Baruch said. "Keep digging."

They dug until they exposed the entire expanse of stone to the dim light of the lantern. There was nothing on its surface, and the coffin itself looked rather small, perhaps fitting a body only three-quarters his size.

"Move over," Joachim told the others. "I'll pull off the lid."

He couldn't find the lip of the stone through the mud, his fingers caressing the side of the coffin. When he did though, it came off easily and was surprisingly light. He placed it on the ground beside him.

"A long time it has been, indeed," Baruch noted.

Inside the coffin, it was hard to know whether its contents were the decay of a human being or the same dirt that surrounded it. Tilicea lifted the lantern and shone it down on the grave. Through the dirt Joachim could see fragments of bone and some teeth where a head would be. Just above those teeth he saw something else. Two tiny globes glimmered in the light.

"His eyes," Tilicea said.

From the pocket of her filthy cloak she pulled out a small sack and handed it to Joachim.

"Take one of them, and put it in here."

He glared down at the spheres. Each was tiny, small enough to fit into someone's eye socket. The insides looked a little foggy, but rather transparent. He wondered how terrifying someone would look with those things for eyes. They'd look hollow and blank, and their eyes would definitely glow in the firelight. They'd have fire inside.

Joachim took one in his hand. When he grasped it, the lantern flame flickered out and thrust the cave into a bout of darkness. He dropped the sphere back onto the ground.

"Stop playing with the lantern," he said. "I dropped it."

"We didn't touch it," Tilicea said.

Joachim looked at them. They stood above him, but neither of them held the lantern in their hands. It sat on the dirt beside him.

"What happened to the light then?" he asked.

"I saw it too," Baruch said. "Maybe it was the wind."

Joachim narrowed his eyes. "The wind? Down here?"

Baruch shrugged. Tilicea looked around the cave, and Joachim took a breath. He was filthy and smelly and frustrated. He just wanted to get the damn Druid's glass eyeball and get out of there. He grabbed it again.

When it touched the flesh of his hand, the flame in the lantern flickered again. This time, he held it tightly. The entire cave sat in complete darkness. Through it, Joachim saw a man in front of him. His face was long, and his cheeks were plump. The glow in his eyes made Joachim fall back.

"I'm sorry, my dearest Druid. The newly established High Council of Zalm no longer finds your presence necessary."

The lantern light flicked back, but the image remained imprinted in Joachim's eyes. He stumbled, falling into the mud. He could feel it under his clothes now. Or was that the echo of the phantom voice settling under his skin?

"Did you hear that?" he asked.

"Yes," Tilicea said. "It must be a vision triggered by your touch."

Joachim placed the globe into the sack and drew the strings to close it inside.

"I experienced it too," Baruch said.

"Ancient peoples thought the eyes were the window to the soul, much like the prophecy says," Tilicea explained. "It is quite possible that we saw and heard one of the last memories this soul has of the world of the living."

"Well, here, take it." Joachim thrust the sack at Tilicea. "I've had quite enough of that. Let's get out of this place."

Joachim pulled himself out of the ditch and put the stone lid back on the coffin. Taking one last look around, he began down the passageway that led out of the tomb. The others followed. After pulling himself back through the willow tree roots, he helped them to the surface also.

They parted the curtain of leaves and embarked on the forest again. They travelled farther away from the Druid's grave, but Joachim couldn't remove the set of glowing eyeballs or the vision of that strange man from his mind.

Fire inside.

Ꭹ Ꮧ ᚷ Ꭸ Ꮳ Ꮤ Ꮧ Ꮝ 8 Ꮼ

Though Nelda had just changed into her night robes, she didn't go to her bedchamber. She descended the steps to the lower levels of the castle, the floors where no one could enter unless they received special permission from her or another member of the High Council.

She passed the guards, waving a hand at them as she pushed the door leading to one of the most secret rooms. There she kept all the prophecies that Tilicea had made over the years. They were prophecies she found foolish and perhaps useless, but prophecies she feared nonetheless. Prophecies worth keeping.

She searched for a specific one, one that had haunted her waking life and her dreams since she discovered her sister had escaped Guluki. It was with *their* help after all, those fools from the other world. Their presence in Zalm meant nothing but trouble.

Finding a catalogue aptly named *Prophecies for this Era*, Nelda sat on a pillowed chair and opened the enormous volume. There must have been at least one thousand pages to the book, each with several prophecies scrawled out on scrap pieces of paper pasted onto it. How was she ever going to find the one she was thinking of?

She closed the book again, examining the spine and the pages. She noticed that the page marker was in, the string denoting a certain page. She flung the book open to that page, scanned the prophecies, and smiled. Though she despised her sister, she did always know exactly what Nelda wanted.

She settled back in the chair and read the prophecy aloud several times, letting the words sink in. The words told of two travelers who would come from beyond the Unknown and would speak of terror and destruction in the other world. What it said next made her palms sweat.

After the liberation of a prison, which was obviously Guluki, it talked about the disruption of the slumber of the Great One as well as a visit to an indigenous species of their world. The Great One? Nelda stopped reading. Who could that be? Besides herself or anyone on the High Council, she could think of no one else living or dead who could be powerful enough to be regarded that way. Lastly, the prophecy spoke of an uprising.

Nelda snorted. Silly prophecy. That's all it was. That's all they ever were. So many of them had passed without fulfillment, why should this one be any different? Yes, it did have a few coincidences, but she planned to stop the rest of it. She had so many army men tracking and looking for her sister, the old man, and the young fool. They would definitely be captured within the next day.

She closed the book. There was a knock at the door.

"It is I, the High Empress, in this chamber. No need for alarm."

"Your Highness?" The voice was quiet. "May I come in?"

"Most definitely not," she bellowed, recognizing the voice. "Wait. I'll be out in a minute."

Standing, she looked around the room again. The endless shelves of prophecies sickened her. She wondered how someone could devote their life to something so trivial, so meaningless—so stupid. Even still, she took the book with her. Perhaps there would be clues to her sister's whereabouts. It weighed nearly as much as a small child. But that's all that Tilicea was, she thought. A child. A stupid, worthless child not even her mother wanted.

She opened the door. The man shrank back. It was one of her confidants, an aide who received news from her generals and relayed it back to her and the Council at Zostrava. She hoped he brought her good reports, for both her and his sake.

"What is it?"

"A messenger sent word from the army."

She stared at him and the scroll in his hand.

"And?"

"They came upon them," he said. "The travelers and the prophetess. They were taken in at Ionia."

"Excellent," Nelda said.

She began up the stairs.

"There's more, my Empress."

"Then say it, idiot!"

"They escaped," he squeaked.

She descended the steps and gripped his collar. "Then find them. If the generals are incapable of executing the most obvious actions, then they will be replaced," she hissed. "Tell them that! If they continue to aggravate me with such morsels of information, I will come down there and find them myself!"

"They burned down the fortress," the man said. "And trackers found they had visited the willow tree. They dug up and looted the Great Druid's grave."

Her eyes widened. In the silence, the confidant held out the scroll to her, scrunched in his nervous grip. She took it from his hands and read the two short paragraphs of text. She trembled as each word settled, meshing with the ominous words of Tilicea's prophecy. The Great One. The Great Druid. How could this be? Out of all the prophecies to come true, why this one?

Or perhaps Tilicea had written the other prophecies as distractions for the only one to be fully realized.

That deceitful whore.

Nelda pushed past her confidant and ascended the stairs back to her office, the book of prophecies still tight under one arm and the scroll in hand. In her office, she found Panthea and Valeska, their faces drained of color. Nelda slammed the book down on her desk, the ink bottles falling and splattering on the floor. The confidant came in behind her.

"What should I tell them?"

"Tell who?"

"Tell the messenger to relay to the army generals, my Queen."

"What more is there to say?" she barked. "Tell them to find the three travelers and knock them unconscious if need be. I want them in these palace walls as soon as they are captured."

The man bowed and scurried out of the doorway. Valeska and Panthea remained, holding a tea set and setting it down on her desk.

"Get out of here," she screamed. "All of you!"

With the scroll still her in grip, she crushed it and tossed the paper onto the ground. In an outbreak of shrieks, she took the pot of tea from a side table and threw it also, smashing the porcelain and spilling the poppy tea on the mahogany floor. As Valeska and Panthea closed the door and walked down the hallway to their rooms, they could hear the destruction from the chamber growing louder and louder.

The Empress wrecked her chamber long into the night.

CHAPTER EIGHTEEN

CONTAMINATION

When Ophelia finally fell asleep, Rae let go of her hand and crept out of the infirmary. He crossed the village, most people now asleep. Those who weren't sat around the fire pit and watched the remaining embers glow in the night. Rae knew that those men stayed awake as guards in case Zupay's creatures attacked.

They looked up at him as he passed, only nodding. Rae continued to the path, followed it for a few moments, then turned onto the one that led to Tabitha's home. She sat just outside her dwelling, a lit pipe in her hands. Spicy herbs.

"Am I late?" Rae asked.

"No." She took a drag.

"Where's Trent?"

"He went back to his dwelling to get more daggers."

He nodded and looked at the dark trees surrounding Tabitha's home. She looked out also, smoking her pipe rather quickly. The jungle was quiet. Not even the crickets dared to sing. There was no breeze to move the branches above them, and he could see past them. Stars and an almost-full moon lit the night.

"Are you alright?" Tabitha asked. "I mean, with your mom and all?"

"I will be," he said. "I just want all of this to be done. I want our village to be normal again."

"Well, I can promise you that things will never again be the normal we know."

Rae looked down. "That's what I'm afraid of."

She cleared her throat. "It will be better, my child. We've reached a point now where either our lives will change or we will all die. We win no matter the outcome."

"That doesn't exactly make me excited," Rae said.

"It should," Tabitha said. "Because I don't plan on dying just yet."

She laughed. It was dense and throaty and infectious. Rae smiled, though he tried not to. He'd smiled in the past few days, sure, but he knew those were different. Those were smiles to mask fear and anger. Maybe this smile was for hope. Maybe this was for the village Tabitha envisioned.

"Besides," Tabitha said. "If we succeed in our work, we will know a new normal, one without the threat of creatures and their half-brained leader."

She ruffled his hair. "So how about that?"

He laughed. "Well, I don't plan on dying either," Rae said.

"There you go," Tabitha said. "And look who comes."

Trent walked up the path, three scabbards in his arms.

"Are we ready?" he asked.

"I think so," Tabitha said. "Come inside."

They entered her home. The pail of hemlock and jar of invisibility ointment sat on the table. Tabitha emptied the ashes of her pipe into a garbage bin and grabbed her rucksack from a chair.

"Let's apply the invisibility ointment," she began. "After we travel through the jungle, we will dump the hemlock into the water and warn Darcie not to drink it. If we make good time, we should be out of their village at least an hour before the morning light."

"You make it sound easy," Trent said.

"Whatever helps us get it done and back to the village."

"How will we know if it worked?" Rae asked.

"We will go back tomorrow evening," Tabitha said. "After supper. By then, any creature that drank the water will be dead."

"Hopefully that will be all of them," Trent said.

"That's unlikely," Tabitha replied. "The hemlock is fast-acting, leaving the body in convulsions within a half hour. We can hope for at least half the colony before they realize the sickness comes from the water. Hopefully Zupay will be one of those."

Rae's heart leapt at that idea. He wanted nothing more than to see that terrible *thing* die. Better, he wanted to kill it himself, strangle it with his bare hands and then spread its organs along the grass and tree trunks like it had done to his father.

"Questions?" Tabitha asked.

Trent and Rae shook their heads.

"Excellent," she said. "Let's head into the jungle."

ㄅ ㄑ ㄨ ㄐ ㄈ ㄗ ㄈ ⅋ 8 ㄣ

They walked most of the night, the air quiet and warm. Though they stopped a few times because Trent heard something off in the distance, nothing else slowed them. For a while it seemed as if they were the only living things in the jungle. As Rae saw the glow of Zupay's colony, he remembered they were not.

"Dawn will be here within the next two hours," Tabitha said. "We need to move fast and be out of here before any of the creatures realize what we've done. Do you still have the pail, Trent?"

"Yes."

Rae saw the pail floating beside him. He could smell the plants from beyond the plastic covering. He couldn't tell whether his stomach stirred because of the stench or because of what they were about to do.

"Let's just do it," he said.

The pail led them toward the light, the glow brightening as they approached. They crept through the trees. Though the colony was fully lit, Rae didn't see any of the creatures. Rae hoped they were all asleep in the trees.

The three snuck just outside the grasp of the light. They passed Zupay's cave, snores ringing through the stone, and reached the path that led to Darcie's cage and the well. Rae tried to move as quietly and smoothly as he could, but his legs were shaky and each step sloppy and uncertain. When they reached the clearing, they went to the back of the cage.

The bonds had been taken off Darcie, and she lay on the ground, her legs curled up to her bulging belly.

"Darcie?" Tabitha whispered. "Wake up."

The woman's breath quieted but she didn't stir.

"Darcie, it's me, Tabitha. I've come from the village with Trent and Rae."

She opened her eyes. She didn't recognize any of them. And how could she? They were invisible. She sat up, rubbed her eyes, and looked around the clearing before settling in the direction of their voices again.

"Is it really you, Trent?" she whispered. "Have you really come?"

A cool breeze pushed through the trees, and Rae eyed the path that led to Zupay's cave. Though he couldn't see any movement, he felt them all around him. He felt like they were watching.

"Yes."

"Why can't I see any of you?"

"We're wearing an invisibility ointment to hide ourselves from the creatures," he explained.

Darcie's eyes were critical.

"Then how do I know it's you?" Darcie asked. "What if you're some dirty trick from Zupay?"

"Because I remember a time when you were a little girl," Tabitha said. "You wandered to my home from the main village. Most other children were terrified to come close, afraid I was some sort of sorceress."

Darcie leaned forward, her fingers grasping the spokes of the cage.

"But I discovered that you weren't." Darcie smiled. "You taught me how to skin jackalopes."

"And you wailed the entire time."

Darcie snorted. "Yes, I did." She sighed. "Tabitha, where's Joachim?"

"He's gone away for a while," Tabitha said softly. "But just for a short while. He went in search of ingredients for a potion Zupay wants. Once he's returned with them, Zupay will let you come back to the village."

"Where is he going to find those ingredients?" Darcie asked, furrowing her brow.

Another breeze blew. The trees around the clearing swayed. Rae thought he could see something move in the branches. As he stared, he thought his eyes must be confused in the dim light. He hoped they were.

"We haven't the time to explain everything to you, my child," Tabitha said. "Just be sure we are working very hard to ensure the safety of the village and to get you back."

"Then why have you come if you plan to wait until Joachim returns?" she asked.

"We've come to start our own plan," Tabitha said. "We've brought a pail of hemlock to dump in the well over there. When the creatures drink it, they will die. Hopefully enough of them will, and a second attack will go smoothly against Zupay's weakened colony. But you must make sure not to drink any of the water.

"We've brought you safe water in these canteens." Tabitha pushed two into the cage. "Hide them and ration them carefully."

"I understand," Darcie said.

Trent picked up the pail. "Rae, come with me."

Rae followed the pail across the clearing to the well. In the trees, he heard something. He tried to imagine it was just crickets or night animals, but as he listened he realized it sounded like a person walking through leaves.

"Trent, stop," he said. "Listen."

"I hear it too," Trent said. "Let's just do this and get out of here."

They came to the well. There was a bucket at the top of the pulley underneath a roof made of bamboo and palm tree leaves. Rae looked down into it. He took the pail from Trent.

"Wait," Trent said. "I hear it again."

"What is it?"

"I don't know, but it sounds close."

Rae listened again: the same rustle through the fallen leaves. Whatever approached them murmured a strange hum that resonated through the trees. Rae tried to pinpoint where the noise was coming from, but he couldn't. Maybe it was the creatures. Maybe they'd awoken early.

The silhouette of a human stumbled into the clearing from their left. Rae's eyes widened.

"Mom?"

"Ophelia!"

Trent left the well. At first Rae saw nothing, just his mother wandering farther and singing softly. She seemed unafraid of where she was and completely unaware of the danger of this place. Perhaps she had no idea that she stood in Zupay's colony at all.

Ophelia stopped and swayed on the spot. Through the quiet of the night Rae could hear another voice muttering to her, a much deeper voice. He prayed that Trent could talk to her, but even if he could, how could they bring her back to the village safely?

Ophelia looked around. She flailed her arms as if pushing something away, something that held onto her. Rae put the pail down on the ground and ran toward her, just as her cry pierced the night air.

"Be gone, demon!"

Rae grabbed her arm. He found that Trent already had a good

hold of the other one. She screamed out again, her hands held down by invisible grips.

"Mom, it' me," he tried to whisper. "It's Rae."

"Let me go, you horrid creatures!" she shrieked. "Let me go and show yourselves. I will not be fooled by your lies!"

"No, really, it's me." He squeezed her. "I need you to be quiet or the real demons will come. Listen to me, I'm your son."

"My son is back at the village," she cried. "I left him at my bedside."

"Then how did you get here?" Rae asked, his grip slipping.

"Ben brought me here, but now I know that was a trap. All of this is nothing but a trap. I won't let you take me!"

She kicked her legs out, and Trent went down beside him. With another scream, Ophelia pushed him off of her, and he toppled to the ground. She started again across the clearing, passing the cage where Darcie watched them. Before she reached the trees, she tripped.

Rae ran toward her. A pang of pain shot through his leg. He looked down and saw that his knee was badly bruised and beginning to swell. Beside him, he noticed many marks on Trent's body, bleeding from their struggle with Ophelia. It wasn't until Tabitha's figure darted toward the cage, her bare breasts pale in the starlight, that Rae realized what had happened. His chest filled with fear.

He heard the snarling of awakened creatures, and Rae realized that they were no longer invisible.

"I can see you," he called.

"We have to run," Trent said.

They came to Ophelia and Tabitha. A root held down Ophelia's ankle. Tabitha tore the plant off and brought her to her feet. Rae heard the creatures tearing up the path.

"Did you get the hemlock into the well?" Tabitha asked.

"No," Rae said. "She came before I could."

Ophelia looked up at him and blinked. She smiled. "Rae, how

nice that I should find you here. I just spoke with your father."

"Move, now," Trent said.

They went toward the jungle just as creatures came into the clearing. They poured in from the path, hundreds at a time. Though his leg burned with pain, he pushed himself to keep up with the others. They ran into the trees. Ophelia began to sing.

"They're coming!" Rae cried.

The creatures passed the cage and gathered speed. Hundreds ran toward them now. The villagers climbed over the trunks of fallen trees, each movement burning the muscle of Rae's leg. The creatures, too, approached the jungle as they crossed the clearing. Their hissing and laughing rang through the trees, loud like screeching birds—loud like sirens.

"Split up." Trent said.

Tabitha dragged Ophelia to the left, and soon they disappeared into the darkness. Trent continued straight ahead, and Rae followed him, breaking from his trail after a few strides. He dodged the trees and ran for as long as he could. He couldn't hear creatures behind him, but he didn't dare to slow. The cries of two women echoed over the jungle.

Tabitha and his mother had been caught.

He stopped running when he reached a river. It enveloped him, the tiny clearing surrounded only by the water and the trees where he came from. He couldn't see anything in the jungle except the glow of the Zupay's colony in the distance. The moonlight shone down on the ripples of water beside him. Now that he stood still, the burning in his leg became so intense that he collapsed.

Shaking and breathing heavily, he heard nothing in the jungle, nothing but the whistles of wind through branches. Maybe they had lost him. What now? He couldn't go back the way he came. He couldn't return to the colony, and going the other way led farther from his own village and into the unknown.

His feet ached. He took his dagger from the scabbard at his

waist and held it out in front of him. He could hear something in the trees. He could hear *Them*. They watched him.

A creature tore through the leaves and jumped on top of him. Before he could react, he fell to the ground, and the dagger flew from his hand. The creature hissed at him, gripped his arm, and called out into the night.

He struggled to push it from him, its teeth gnawing at his skin. He could feel slobber on his arm, teeth breaking skin. With a push, he tossed the demon off his chest. The creature hurtled through the air and landed with a splash. Rae sat up. He had thrown the creature into the water. It screeched and struggled, clawing at the surface.

It couldn't swim.

After a few moments it stopped moving and succumbed to the water. Its limp body floated face down in the river. Soon the current would drag it away. It'd be lost at sea by the midday heat.

Before he could stand, two more creatures threw him to the dirt. He felt his head strike a stone. His mind dizzied, and his eyes became blurry.

He lay still, the demons crawling over him like rats on scraps. But he wasn't scraps.

He'd be the meal.

"Take him with the others," a voice said.

The trees were spinning. The creatures lifted him from the ground, one gripping his injured knee. He looked up at the one standing on two legs, unlike the others. He muttered more words to his minions, inaudible sound that caught in Rae's ears. The creature smiled, and the jungle faded away. It was Zupay.

Chapter Nineteen

The Other Village

The sun broke through the trees and shone on Rae's face, the glow waking him. He opened his eyes but didn't move from his spot. His entire body ached, but his leg was the worst. Flexing his muscles made it burn, and even when he relaxed, the pain didn't go away. The breeze fingered through the leaves of palm trees above him, and Rae remembered that he hadn't fallen asleep in his bed.

He sat up. There were five cages. In the one directly beside him, he saw his mother on the ground. Darcie was in the one beside her, and Trent was right across from him. All were asleep except for Tabitha in the cage to his left. She watched him.

"Are you all right?" she asked.

"Yes," he said. "It's just my leg. How long have I been asleep?"

"A couple hours," she said. "We were captured just before sunrise. Judging by the sun, it's almost ten in the morning."

"And they all slept?" Rae motioned to the others.

"They were all unconscious when they brought us into the cage. Ophelia and I were captured first; she howled like a dying animal as they dragged her and knocked her out. I pretended to be knocked out too, but truthfully, I wish I had actually been."

Rae looked at his mother. There was a gash on her left temple.
"What's the plan now?"

"There is no plan," Tabitha said. "They found the hemlock. They took all of our weapons, and Zupay has decided to keep us here until we awaken so we can vouch for our freedom."

"Freedom?"

"It's a joke," she said. "There's no way he'll let us out of here alive, especially since we interfered with Darcie's captivity. Any plan we think of now is futile."

Rae shook his head. He didn't want to hear it, didn't want to think it was really over, that they had really lost. But Tabitha's face was bloody, and she nursed what looked to be a badly injured arm. Trent didn't look much better, and he was still unconscious.

"So that's it? We just give up?"

"If you have any ideas, enlighten me." He sensed the venom in her voice. "I'm as upset as you are, my boy, but unless we can break out of these cages and get to my pack, we're stuck here."

There was no plan. He had no plan he could execute from captivity, and they hadn't told the other villagers of their task, so no one would come. They were alone. Just them and the creatures.

He studied the cage. The bamboo was linked together with thick rope, and he found it impossible to see where the door could be. Looking at the spot where the cage met the ground, it seemed as if someone had driven the columns of wood into the ground, making a sturdy foundation. How were the creatures able to do this so well in such a short amount of time? There had been only one cage when they first arrived with the hemlock.

Tabitha cleared her throat. Rae looked up and saw three creatures coming up the path. The one in the middle walked on two legs, while the others walked on four. They wore a small piece of fabric over their torsos, but majority of their pale green skin was exposed. The creature in the middle held a pipe in his hand.

Coming closer, the two creatures on four legs sprinted. They ran toward the cages and leapt on top of them, awaking the three remaining villagers. Trent rubbed his eyes and looked around, a dark expression on his face. Darcie merely stirred, seemingly unaffected by them. Ophelia began to scream and tried to pry the bamboo of her cage open.

"Calm down, you silly woman," the creature who walked on two legs said.

She gazed at him then buried her face into her hands, sobbing. Rae didn't try to console her. This was her fault. If she hadn't come to the colony, Rae would be back at the village, waiting for the poison to set in.

The creature blew pipe smoke through his sharp teeth and came to the side of Rae's cage. The other two creatures came to the ground.

"I haven't met you before," the demon said. "But you do look vaguely familiar. My name is Zupay."

It took everything in him not to speak. If he did, he feared he would say things that would only get him and his fellow villagers into more trouble. Or he'd jab Zupay's pipe into his eye.

"You're a quiet one." Zupay smirked. "I can't say the same for your father."

A tear fell down his cheek. The creature moved on, peering into Darcie's cage, but saying nothing. He then walked to Ophelia's, his tiny feet pattering on the dirt.

"Good morning," he snickered.

He stuck a finger into the cage, waving it at her. She cried out and squirmed, pushing herself to the other side of the cage.

"Leave her alone, Zupay," Trent said.

The creature's head snapped toward the man's cage.

"You're brave now?" he asked. "You didn't seem that way when we last met. You cowered like a pathetic child. Now look at you. You've orchestrated some elaborate plan to kill me and my colony. Hemlock, was it?"

Trent didn't speak.

"You'll be lucky if I don't take that poison back to a well in *your* village and watch as each person drinks and dies a slow death."

Rae's heart fell at the creature's words. He could see the same despair in Trent's face. Tabitha burst into tears.

"Well, what's stopping you?"

Rae looked to the cage to his right. Darcie sat up now and stared at the creature, her eyes narrow.

"Why don't you just kill us all?" she taunted.

He took a long drag of his pipe. "That wouldn't be very humane of me, now would it? Besides, I have a deal with the leader of your village, and I'm a creature of my word."

"Are you now?" Darcie snorted. "That didn't stop you before."

He crossed the grass to Darcie's cage. She remained upright, glaring at him.

"Don't mock me, or I may change my mind."

"Your words mean nothing, Zupay," Darcie said. "You always just do what you want, and when you get those ingredients for your potion, there will be no way to stop you, not even with contracts or promises. Besides, this is your second village, isn't it?"

The words made him stop. Zupay smiled. Darcie's eyes were so heavy on him that Rae could barely stand to look at her. Trent looked at her, and Tabitha stopped crying.

Like Rae, the others had no idea what she was talking about.

"Second village?" Trent asked. "What does that mean?"

"Ask him," Darcie said, tears in her eyes. "Ask him what he did to my village—to my people!"

Zupay took a drag from his pipe, a wild look in his eyes. "I didn't do anything. It was not my hand. No doubt Baruch explained it all to you, about how he slaughtered your old village and took in the remaining survivors."

"Baruch did what?" Trent asked.

"He never told me anything. I found out on my own," Darcie said.

"Then surely you know he is to blame," Zupay said. "He

could have sacrificed himself and Joachim's father to save both villages instead of taking the deal. He chose blood. He chose to kill your people."

"That was not a fair choice!" Darcie yelled.

Zupay dumped the remainder of his pipe on the ground and waved his two creatures toward him.

"Life isn't fair, Darcie," he said. "But I will not kill you this day. My decency and loyalty to Baruch restricts me from annihilating your entire village at this moment, something I should have done after the half-witted attempt of your friends. Just hope that your husband and the old man can make it back in time."

$$\text{チ} \text{ʑ} \text{ㄨ} \text{ゑ} \text{ㄷ} \text{Ꭷ} \text{ㄷ} \text{ミ} \text{ठ} \text{↩}$$

A thousand questions swirled in Rae's head. What were Darcie and Zupay talking about? What did they mean when they said Baruch slaughtered another village? Who were *her people*?

Though the others had dozed off in the sun, Darcie remained awake and faced the other way, crying. He tried to ignore her, studying the cage and the jungle, but he couldn't stop the thoughts from surfacing. He could no longer let himself theorize about it. He had to know.

"What happened to them?" Rae asked. "Your people?"

Darcie didn't turn around.

"I doesn't matter, Rae," she said. "It's over now."

"Maybe if you talk about it, you'll feel better. You don't have to face it alone."

She turned to him. Although her eyes were puffy, and her face was red, she smiled.

"It's not that," she said. "I don't feel alone. The village is my home, and I love everyone in it."

"Then what is it?"

"I don't want to taint it for you," she said. "I don't want you to think less of Baruch or any of the other elders in our village.

Besides, I don't know everything that happened. Like I told Zupay, I found out by myself."

"I could fill in the gaps if you'd like."

Rae looked over and saw Tabitha sitting up in her cage. She had fashioned covering for her torso and breasts from the wide leaves of the tree beside her, her original clothing taken away with her rucksack. She didn't look up at Darcie.

"You were there?" Darcie asked.

"We all were," she replied. "All the elders in the village: myself, Baruch, Alena. Though I never authorized the attack, I am ashamed of it all the same. I should have never let it happen."

"There was no other way, Tabitha. You did what you had to do—"

"What happened?" Rae snapped. "I need to know. Now that it's been revealed, there's no way to hide it again. Besides, our village has been ravaged by lies: lies about our safety, lies about what we've been doing, and now lies about our fellow villagers. We deserve the truth."

Tabitha shook her head. Darcie looked at her but not angrily. She looked at the woman sympathetically, the woman who had somehow allowed the murder of Darcie's village. Rae didn't understand.

"It was a long time ago," Darcie said. "I was just a child. My family and I lived in another village, one that had never made contact with any other survivors of the Great Death or Zupay and his demons."

"Where was your village?" Rae asked.

"I don't know," Darcie said. "I don't remember."

"Near the caves," Tabitha said. "If you keep moving in the direction we travelled to get to Zupay's colony, you'd find it. Our people had never hunted there before. We thought that anything this way was Zupay's territory."

"There were only twenty of us," Darcie said. "Many had died without bearing any children. Many had mysteriously disappeared into the jungle. We lived very differently than we live now—in trees, much like Zupay's creatures do."

"Zupay had been feeding on them for a long time," Tabitha said. "They had no idea. Joachim's father, Joel, had been captured by Zupay and his creatures. Killings had happened in our village for many weeks prior, and he threatened to kill Joel if we didn't adhere to his will."

Rae couldn't believe what he was hearing. The deal they made with Zupay, the deal that ultimately ended in failure and Joel's death, was responsible for the slaughter of Darcie's village. Zupay was right. Baruch had killed innocent people.

He swallowed hard. "Why didn't you die?"

Darcie wiped her eyes. "We had gone to the ocean," she said, "my family and I. We were bathing. When we returned, they were all dead. Only evidence of a struggle and the wreckage of our village remained."

"Then how did you fail?" Rae asked, looking back at Tabitha. "Why was Joachim's father killed anyway?"

"Zupay discovered there were survivors," Tabitha said. "Before we could explain, it was done. He killed Joel."

Tabitha's head sank. Rae turned back to Darcie.

"What did you do?" he asked.

"The only thing we could do," Darcie replied. "We took to the jungle. I remember living as a nomad for a while, hunting and gathering food. We lived like that for almost a year until we met Baruch.

"A band of hunters found us and took us back to their village. I had never seen anything like it: it was the most spectacular place I had ever been. And there were books. Baruch taught me how to read. He taught us how to live again. We had found a new home.

"I never knew," she said, unable to stop the tears now. "I discovered the truth in my adulthood. When I found out, it nearly broke me. It was a cruel irony, really: I grew up to love the man whose father my village died to save. I never even told Joachim."

"How did you find out?" Rae asked.

"I found a journal in Baruch's home," she said. "My parents had just died, and I was the last living member of my family. I snuck into looking for the key to the workshop, to the library. He had left on a hunt and forgotten to give it to me. The very first entry was about what had happened to my people. I married Joachim two months later."

She cried again. Tabitha sat at the edge of her cage and cried also. Trent had awakened, too, and listened to the story. His hand was over his mouth. Even Ophelia was awake, though she paid no attention to them. She found dead bugs in the bottom of her cage and proceeded to eat them.

Rae just stared. The words overwhelmed him. He couldn't believe what had been done to Darcie. Furthermore, he couldn't believe what the village had done. He was furious with Baruch.

In fact, he hated him.

CHAPTER TWENTY

KNOTS

They spent the entire day in silence. The only noise was from the creatures that came every couple hours to bring dried meats and water. Rae refused to eat, terrified that the water might be laced with hemlock and afraid of what kind of meat the creatures had hunted for him to eat. Darcie had no problem. She gulped down the water and only stopped once to spit out a shard of bone in the meat. She had stopped crying, and the others had stopped asking questions. It was done now. They knew the truth.

The more he watched her, the more it hurt him. The people he had trusted, the leader of their own village, had done something so terrible, so unimaginably horrid that he felt ashamed to live with them. How could Baruch look at her after what he had done? How could Baruch live with himself?

He couldn't believe how subdued Darcie had been about it, how quiet she had kept after all these years. It must have been hard to hide the secret from everyone else in the village and to hide herself. Even if it was for good reason, the deeds were unacceptable. Baruch and the other villagers had killed a group of other humans. They had taken all those in her old life away.

As he gazed at her, she looked up at him. Before he could look away, she smiled at him. He couldn't find it in him to do the same back. He wanted to cry.

"What's the matter?" she asked.

"It's just—" he stuttered. "I just…"

She looked down. "It's best to just let it go."

"How can I?" His voice was louder than he intended it to be.

Her eyes flickered up to the sky, and he could tell that she held back tears. He felt bad for reminding her of it again.

"Because I can," she said. "I have forgiven Baruch. I have forgiven them all."

"But why?" he asked. "Look what they did to you. Look at what they did to your family. Aren't you mad?"

"Yes," Darcie croaked. "And I was for a very long time. I couldn't talk to Baruch. I couldn't be around him. But I never hated him. I still don't. I can't blame him for what he did. He did what he needed to do for his village. It's easier to do something terrible when you can't see the faces of those you're affecting. He fought for the faces he could see—his fellow villagers. And I'm not convinced I wouldn't have done the same."

His mouth fell open. He couldn't stand to hear her say it.

"What do you mean?"

"What if it were the other way around?" Darcie asked. "What if Zupay had taken my husband? My child? Would I not do anything to get them back? Would I not kill another? If you could get your father back, wouldn't you do anything?"

He inhaled, the air like dirt in his lungs. He closed his eyes, and he felt the crying come again. His stomach was in knots. It wasn't the fact that she mentioned his father that made Rae so distraught. It was that she was right.

He would do anything.

"And that is why I forgive them," Darcie said. "That is why I stayed in the village. And you should think the same. The last thing we need is for Zupay to wedge us all apart. We must stand together as a village regardless of what happened in the past. He's divided us before, but now we have to stand together as humans."

Rae sat up. Darcie's words settled in, and he found that he didn't hate Baruch. In fact, he found it hard to stay mad. It must have torn the elder apart to do what he did and then face his village again. Face Darcie again.

The setting sun dimmed the sky, and the air cooled as the creatures brought another meal. They pushed the food through the columns of wood, hissing and sneering as they passed. The creatures left and the others sat up to eat but Rae didn't, staring at the bamboo top of his cage. A thought came to him, bursting across his mind like a shooting star.

"The food is safe," Tabitha said. "We've eaten all the food and water they've brought, and we're still living. Eat."

Rae looked down at his food.

"What's the matter with you?" she asked. Trent eyed them.

"We're getting out of here tonight," Rae said. "I've found a way to escape."

"How?"

"Look at how the cage has been constructed," Rae started. "The creatures have driven the bamboo into the ground, and the seal there is strong. I should have realized this before, but I just noticed it now."

"So digging isn't an option," Darcie said. "I already knew that."

"Yes," Rae said. "I'm not sure how, but the wood is so far into the ground that the cage wasn't constructed by the creatures above-ground. They somehow had the cages spring up from underneath."

"That would explain how they appeared so quickly," Tabitha said. "They had four new cages ready as soon as we were all captured."

"But how does this help us?" Trent asked.

"Tabitha, do you remember how they got us into these cages?" Rae asked.

"Vaguely. It was dark," she said. "And they put a blindfold on me."

"Think about it," Rae said. "What did you feel?"

She thought for a moment, taking a sip of her water. "Well, they lifted me up somehow, and when they removed the blindfold, I was inside the cage."

Rae smiled and pointed up. Tabitha and Trent stood to get a closer look. The roof overhead was made of bamboo like the rest of the cage. However, instead of being secured by the dirt like the bottom of the cage, the creatures had used rope to hold the roof onto the columns.

Trent laughed as he examined it.

"We have to climb up and over," Rae said.

Tabitha eyed it. "What about the rope? We have nothing to cut it with."

"When my father was alive, he was passionate about two things." Ophelia moved closer to Rae as he spoke. "The first was hunting. He promised to take me with him one day and teach me his ways. That was until he passed."

"And the second?" Tabitha prompted.

"He was an expert at knots," Rae said. "That was one skill he did manage to teach me. He would spend hours showing me how to tie them properly and then how to disassemble them without using a knife. He put tests all over the village. They were my favorite pastime when he went out on hunts. It distracted me from how badly I wanted to be out there with him."

He looked up at the roof again. "I doubt these creatures could tie knots half as well as my father."

Tabitha let a smile grace her lips for the first time all day.

"Good job, Rae," she said. "We'll wait until night when all the creatures have gone to sleep."

The sun continued to set as they sat in an anxious silence. Rae examined the knots that held the roof to the cage. There were only four knots, one on each corner, and they didn't seem too complex. Finally darkness crept over the surrounding jungle and the five cages, sluggish and cautious, knowing it was awaited. The sound of bustling creatures ceased in the trees of Zupay's colony.

They didn't move yet. The silence cloaked them. Above, stars and a full moon lit the sky. The moon was just bright enough to illuminate everyone's faces. Rae stood and examined the knots once again. The moon was just bright enough to help him.

"Okay," he whispered. "Here I go."

He gripped the bamboo and wedged his foot between two pieces. He looked up. The cage was only about ten feet tall, he reasoned. He had scaled bigger tree trunks when his father was alive. He would make the man proud, even in his death.

He pulled himself up with his arms, his feet lifting off the ground and gliding between the bamboo. He reached the first line of rope that held the structure together at about four feet. He swung his legs through and placed his feet down on the rope. It was strong enough to hold him.

There was another line of rope in another couple feet. If he pulled himself up to that one, he would be right under the roof of the cage, even if a little squished. He heaved himself up, crooking his neck and steadying himself. He could feel the roof pressing down on the back of his head. Rae fingered the knots of rope that secured the roof on the cage.

"Can you get it off?" Darcie asked.

"Yes," he replied. "It's actually a very simple knot. I don't think Zupay expected us to climb over the top."

He pulled at a section of the rope in the center of the knot. The rest slacked. He pulled again, this time a groan signalling strain on the wood. He grabbed a second piece of the rope and took it through the opening he made. The wood resisted again, but the rope came through fairly easily. He slipped the rope around the first piece he still held.

With a small tug, the wood relaxed, and the rope fell away. Next he moved to the other corner, repeating the process there. He did the same for the final two knots. As the last one unraveled, he pushed the roof off the cage, and it tumbled onto the ground. He laughed aloud.

"You did it," Trent whispered.

He inhaled the night air. Somehow it felt fresher in his lungs. He stretched his body, able to come completely out of the cage's hold. He climbed over the side and landed on the dirt.

"Come get the rest of us," Tabitha said. "We'll need to get back to the village and prepare."

Rae had already climbed on Darcie's cage and was pulling at the knots. "Prepare?"

"Yes," Tabitha said. "Once Zupay has found out that we've all escaped, he will take out his anger on the village."

ﾌ ⚹ Ⴟ ⚵ Ⴆ ⲿ Ⲥ ⯎ Ȣ ↭

Zupay strolled down the path that led from his cave to the cages, the freshly lit contents of his pipe beckoning him. The sun had just started to rise, and its rays illuminated the trees around the colony. He hadn't heard anything from the captives the previous night, not even the agonized cries of the crazed woman. Two creatures appeared beside him from the jungle and followed him. He waved them forward toward the clearing. The captives would enjoy another wake up from his demons. He took a drag from his pipe.

He came around the bend and exhaled. It caught, burning his throat and making his eyes water. He coughed and gaped. The smoke was still ashy in his mouth. His heart thumped loudly, but it wasn't from the herbs in his pipe. The two creatures came back to him, hissing.

Five roofs sat on the ground beside their empty cages.

"Go to their village," he said. "Go to their village, and hold every one of them captive there. Kill those who resist."

They scurried off, but before they were out of sight he called one of them back. The creature seethed as he waited for Zupay to speak. The leader took a long drag of his pipe.

"Have the females start birthing new young," he said. "I want a new generation ready to feed by morning."

CHAPTER TWENTY-ONE

THROUGH THE FLASHES OF LIGHT

Tilicea, Joachim, and Baruch travelled the rest of the day, making it almost to the north end of the Erebian Mountains before stopping for the night. Though they tried to stay awake in case the High Council's army pursued them, they all fell asleep. Joachim managed to get a few hours, a slumber that was restless and dreamless, hardly a sleep at all. He woke up before daylight and sat up, watching the forest. Only Baruch and Tilicea stirred.

He dug through his rucksack of goods stolen from the fortress at Ionia and took out a morsel of bread. He chewed on it while he waited for the other two to wake. Tilicea was first, and she disappeared behind some trees soon after, returning just as Baruch sat up and rubbed his eyes.

"It seems I have slept late," Baruch said. The dawn had just arrived. "But good morning nonetheless."

"Morning," Tilicea said.

Joachim didn't say anything.

"What's the plan for today, Tilicea?" Baruch asked.

"We'll travel along the mountain range until we reach Minerva's Pass. There we can cross the western plains until we reach the

Cliffs of the Gods. We should arrive tomorrow evening if we only rest for a couple hours tonight."

"Tomorrow evening," Joachim repeated. "Then that leaves us four days to get the final ingredient and back to our world."

Tilicea looked at him and frowned. "It's not my fault you have been given a time limit, Mr. Joachim. I'm doing the best I can to get you where you need to be, and I'm sacrificing the revolution of my people to help you."

"We could find one a transportation rune," Joachim said, his voice low. "And then we could leave you to more *important* business."

"Joachim." Baruch glared at him.

"If you'd like to take the chance, go ahead," Tilicea said, surprisingly calm. Patronizing. "But when the High Council finds you and tries you as a fugitive, it will delay your task even further, and I may not be able to rescue you in time."

Joachim tossed the remainder of his bread onto the ground.

"Let's just go," he muttered.

"Fine." Tilicea stood. "And I will ask that you not throw food onto the ground. A hunter should know better than to be careless with rations. There may be someone else who'd like to eat it."

ツ ㇀ メ ㇰ ㇀ ㇰ ㇰ 8 ㇰ

"Elli Wolfe was my nursemaid as a little girl," Tilicea said. "She raised me, really. I used her name as a disguise. If the army men knew it was Tilicea Shorciman who they had captured, they would have sent me back to Zostrava to my sister."

They travelled most of the day through the forest. The mountains constantly watched over them to their south. Their peaks loomed over the tips of the trees whenever there was a valley. Baruch and Tilicea spoke of trivial things, and Joachim ignored them. He still felt hostility toward the woman and their journey, however unjustified he was. Joachim only listened now that she spoke of the alias she used at Ionia.

"You weren't raised by your mother like Nelda?" Baruch asked.

"No," she said. "It has long been decided that the eldest girl is the heir to the throne. Since Nelda was born first, she was raised as such, learning the ways of royalty and the High Council from my mother. On the other hand, I was placed in the care of Elli. She raised me from when I was an infant until I was almost seventeen years old."

"I'm sorry," Baruch said. "It must have been terrible to be cast away from your family."

Tilicea laughed. "No, it wasn't really. Elli was my family. She taught me many things I would not have learned in a life of royalty: history and languages, how to sow patches onto clothing, how to cook. She taught me how to take care of myself. Above all, she told me the truth."

"The truth?" Baruch asked.

"Yes," Tilicea said. "I started writing prophecies at an early age, the images and words coming to me in dreams. Though my mother, the High Empress at the time, thought they were nonsense, Elli encouraged me to embrace them. She later had me using my gift to help others.

"You see, my family was in the small percentage of people who held all of Zalm's wealth and power. Elli was not; she was part of a lower class and knew nothing of such riches. She was granted special privilege to care for royalty after many years of hard work for the High Council, and that's how I fell under her care. I was in a special position, one that placed me in a limbo of sorts between the two worlds."

"And that started your ideas of rebellion," Baruch noted.

"In a way, yes," Tilicea said. "Elli would take me out to Zostrava and its surrounding villages on day trips without my mother knowing. She never forced the idea on me, but she didn't need to. Before long I was appalled with the way others lived in poverty while the rest of my family embraced exotic luxuries and excess. The High Council slept in expensive furs in expansive rooms while children froze to death in alleys not far from the castle. In those experiences and in the stories Elli told me of oppression, I formulated my own opinion of the world."

"What happened to her?" Joachim asked.

"They hung her," she said, a solemn look coming over her face. "My mother discovered I was defiant of the High Council and traced it back to my upbringing with Elli. I was seventeen when she died."

"I'm sorry," Baruch said.

Joachim felt it too.

"I ran away and disappeared for many years, living under different names," she said. "No one knew who I was, and I gathered a following in the lower classes of Zalm. I didn't surface for twelve years, returning only when I decided to warn my sister of the prophecies I'd seen. She confiscated my prophecies and threw me into Guluki like I knew she would. I was to wait for you two to come along."

"How long did you wait?" Joachim asked.

"Not long at all," she said. "I was able to pinpoint your arrival when the southern cities started to revolt. The torching of Minua harbour occurred but a month and a half ago."

"And what do your prophecies say about Baruch and me?" Joachim asked. "Will we succeed in gathering the ingredients and saving our village?"

"I wish I knew," Tilicea said. "I don't often get to choose what I see and what I can predict. The prophecies come to me in dreams or in the hallucinations I receive when I smoke the herbs, and I have no choice but to experience them. Otherwise the gods will tell me when to enter a trance like the one I entered at the Zalmish Sea."

"So, you don't know?" Joachim felt himself descending into a foul mood again.

"Just because prophecy doesn't explicitly explain something to me, that doesn't equate failure," she said. "If there was no chance of your success, the gods wouldn't have placed me here to guide you. I believe in your success more than you know."

Joachim looked away from her, his mind finding the darkness of hopelessness and despair. How could he be so foolish as to come on this journey? Why did he think he could save his entire village by getting farther away from it? He should have stayed and fought. He could have used the ten days Zupay gave to prepare for war.

Now the sun set on their fifth day. They were halfway through Zupay's time limit and not even halfway done the task. He could feel time slipping away, dragging him farther and farther from saving those he loved—farther and farther away from Darcie. He had to shut that image away before it drove tears from eyes.

"A fight for what is right is never futile, Mr. Joachim, even if you should fail," Tilicea said. He realized that they all had stopped. "You made a choice to do what was best to try to protect your village. The fact that you could do that in such trying circumstances demonstrates great courage by itself. Don't let yourself down by giving up."

She stared at him until he met her eye. He didn't want to look up, but once he did, he felt the words impact him as if hearing them a second time. They rang through his ears like the repeated rush and retreat of sea waves on a summer afternoon. If he gave up now, he would never get to see his wife ever again. The journey had progressed too far for him to just walk away. Walking away now meant certain failure.

Even if he felt unsure and completely alone, he remembered the people he did it for: Darcie, his child, his mother. In fact, the more he thought about it, the more reasons he thought of. He did it for all of them: for Trent and Rae and his dearest friend Ben. He did it for the village. He wouldn't let them down.

He wiped a tear from his cheek. "I know," he said. "I know what I have to do, but it's just that it doesn't seem fair. I don't mean to be so unreasonable."

Tilicea smiled. "It's quite all right. Sometimes what the world asks of us isn't fair. We just need to trust that it will be worth the pain."

Joachim nodded, not feeling the resentment he held before. He knew none of this was her fault, and it wasn't right for him to blame her for it. Tilicea stepped forward and embraced him.

When she let go, she gazed up at the stars.

"We'll stop for a little while," she said. "Minerva's Pass is only about ten miles from here. I want to cross it during the darkest hours of night to keep the High Council's army men from finding us. We'll start again just before midnight."

Good, he thought. He could feel sleep calling for him again.

The sky above Joachim rumbled. He could smell rain in the air, carried by the gentle breeze. A flash of lightning illuminated the forest. In the brief lapse in the darkness, he could see where he was running. He dodged tree trunks and scurried around bushes. He thought he could hear someone calling to him in a breath of wind.

He ran still, his feet pulling him forward. From a gathering of trees in front of him, he could see a glow that was not from the lightning. Who could be out here in the middle of this storm? Would Tilicea and Baruch be waiting for him at the light? Why was he running in the first place?

Those questions dissipated in another pull of wind, and he continued toward the glow. The sky grumbled again like his empty, upset stomach, and a light rain waved through the trees. It was close. He could see it just ahead, just beyond the curtains of the willow tree. He slowed.

Through the leaves he could see them. Six men wore long cloaks and stood in a circle around an altar. There, a man lay on his stomach. His arms and legs were bound, and he squirmed as a seventh man held him down. On the ground, Joachim could saw a scythe resting on the side of the altar beside an executioner.

"This is not necessary, Silvia," the man on the altar cried out.

Joachim had not seen the woman before, but he did now as she strode to the altar. She wore long emerald robes and a tall pointed hat on her head that masked locks of her bright red hair.

"You will address me as High Empress Rhea Silvia," the woman said. "I don't care if it's the moment before your death."

"And what will you tell people once you've killed me? What will you say happened to their leader?"

"Their hatred toward you fueled our ability to usurp you," she said. "This is what they wanted."

"What about the prophecies?"

The man on the altar looked at the woman. Joachim's palms sweat when he saw his features. The man's face was long, and in the torches that lit the clearing Joachim could see his wide eyes. They shimmered gold. Fire inside.

"Which ones?" The Empress laughed. "You've predicted so many futures. It's hard to be sure which one is real."

"The oppression of Zalm at the hands of this High Council," the man said. "Soon the common man will know nothing of the sacred magic. Worst of all, when the visitors come from the other world, there will be violence like no age before."

"Oh, move along, old man," the Empress said. "This world is no longer yours. We have grown weary of your predictions that paralyze the productivity of the working men and women of this nation. We won't support a ruling class of fools who derive their decisions from ancient mysticism."

"Without us you will suck this world dry. Who will receive word from the gods and teach Zalm to live according to their guidance?"

"Well, firstly, we won't live by such archaic ideas," she said. "You know as well as I those gods are nothing but fable, a way to keep a society from thinking. You yourself have a hard time proving they're even there."

"It's easy not to hear the truth when you've plugged your ears."

"My ears are open," the Empress said. "And from now on, we will listen to reason."

She signalled the men with the cloaks to move forward. They held down the man while the executioner picked up the scythe. She watched him.

"I'm sorry, Druid," Rhea Silvia said. "The newly established High Council of Zalm no longer finds your presence necessary."

Joachim blocked his eyes as they swung down the scythe. The woman's laughter filled the night, soon indistinguishable from the crashes of thunder.

$$\mathcal{J} \, \mathfrak{t} \, \mathcal{X} \, \mathfrak{z} \, \mathfrak{E} \, \mathfrak{z} \, \mathfrak{E} \, \mathfrak{z} \, \mathfrak{z} \, \mathfrak{z}$$

Joachim pulled his cloak up around him even though the rain penetrated the fabric. The other two didn't stir, somehow unaware of the storm that tore through their slumber. He gazed out at the forest. Through flashes of light, he thought he could still see images from his dream, images of the life draining from the Great Druid's eyes.

Images of the fire inside.

CHAPTER TWENTY-TWO

THE NEST

B y the time Tilicea and Baruch woke up, the rain had stopped and silence had taken over. Joachim stood and shook the grogginess from his head. He tried to wring the rainwater from his cloak, but the dampness still made him shiver when he put it back on. He decided to carry it alongside him. The night air felt warmer than the fabric on his skin.

They walked along the foot of the Erebian Mountains without speaking. He looked out at the forest, through the gnarled branches and masking leaves and wandering shadows. He tried to recall the events of the strange dream. Though he knew it was just that, he couldn't help but feel it was plausible, that it might be real. Had he actually witnessed the last moments of the Great Druid's life in his dreams? How could that be possible? If it was, what did the memory wish to tell him?

"Minerva's Pass is just up ahead," Tilicea said. "We'll avoid the path and keep in the trees. We should be on the other side by the morning."

Tilicea led them south. The mountains seemed to turn that way also, remaining constantly to their left, companions on a journey that seemed to stretch out endlessly. The trees grew denser, and

Joachim could hear distant sounds of movement.

"What is that noise?"

"The army men are guarding the path," Tilicea said. "Since the uprising in Minua and the Plains, the High Empress has kept a heavy patrol on travel between the two regions of Zalm."

"Won't they patrol the surrounding forest?" Joachim asked.

"Maybe," she said, "but it's not likely. When I was in Guluki, I heard some guards talking about patrol duty in the pass. They described strange apparitions and disappearances in this forest, and many of the men were afraid to even come here."

"Should we be worried about seeing such... apparitions?" Baruch asked.

"No." Tilicea laughed. "Though magic has been outlawed in Zalm, old superstitions and fears remain. I reckon the things that the guards see are just tricks of the dim light or the result of their lack of sleep. Besides, I'm certain our hunter over here would detect any menacing creatures before they could harm us."

She smiled at Joachim. He nodded in return, though he hoped he wouldn't have to experience a meeting with such creatures. He had enough of his own creatures to deal with back at the village.

"And what about the disappearances?" Baruch persisted.

"People disappear from the army all the time," Tilicea said. "Perhaps the army men who disappeared sympathized with my people all along and found a way to join them once they reached Minerva's Pass. Perhaps they themselves were my people who lived in the north and were forced into service by the High Council. I doubt any of the disappearances would be suspicious to us. Fear can be a good deterrent for the minds of the wicked."

They journeyed through the Pass much of the night, accompanied only by the occasional sound of voices or carts along the path. Even then they weren't much company, just sounds of those who didn't know the travelers were there, sounds of those they needed to avoid. They stopped a few times to be sure, but no army man threatened to discover them. Perhaps fear was a good shield after all.

As the sun rose on their sixth day in Zalm, the mountains beside them disappeared, though reluctantly. Tilicea pulled a water canteen out of her rucksack and took a long gulp.

"We've made it through," she said, offering the water to Baruch. "Now we need to cross the path a little bit farther south and make our way to the Cliffs of the Gods. We should reach there by nightfall."

"And what will we do once we get there?" Joachim asked.

"We need to steal an egg from the harpy nests," Tilicea said.

Joachim shrugged. "Sounds simple enough."

"Not as simple as you would think," Tilicea said. "Harpies are notoriously territorial creatures. In old times they would assault nearby villages in large swarms, snatching up all the villagers' food and sometimes even their children."

"Their children?"

"Yes," Tilicea said. "Harpies are no ordinary bird. They have the torsos of women and the legs and wings of a large bird. Some of them are the size of you and me."

"Well, it should be a good challenge then," Baruch said.

Joachim glared at him.

ㄢ ㄨ ㄨ ㄨ ㄈ ㆍ ㄈ ㄙ ㄨ

They travelled through the forest for the remainder of the morning and crossed the Empress' Highway in the intensity of the afternoon sun. Unlike Minerva's Pass, no army men guarded the path, and the travellers disappeared into the forest on the other side without coming across anyone.

For the second half of the day they crossed immense plains. They were flat and treeless, and their travel was easy. But Joachim was anxious. With nothing to shield them, nothing stopped the High Council from spotting them. Joachim was used to hunting in little more than shorts, but he couldn't shake the feeling of nakedness. There was nowhere to hide.

The plains were endless. The mountains that sprang up in front of them never seemed to get any closer. By the end of the afternoon, the sun had not only dried him, but made him sweat. They stopped for a couple mouthfuls of supper but continued on long after the sunlight diminished. As Tilicea lit torches, they embarked on an expanse of forest. The Cliffs of the Gods lay just on the other side of the trees.

Before long, Joachim could hear the calls of the harpies piercing the night air. They were sharp and shrill, and though they seemed close, Tilicea said they still had more to travel yet. She was right, of course. The calls only became more deafening as they drew closer.

Just when Joachim started to believe that the harpies didn't exist at all, just echoes of mysterious screeches, Tilicea stopped.

"We'll need a plan," she said. "We can't just walk into their colony and steal one of their unborn."

"A distraction?" Baruch suggested.

"That could work," she said. "But whoever it is will need to run quickly. The creatures have wings, after all."

He felt their eyes on him.

"Fine," Joachim said. "What do you want me to do?"

Joachim found himself once again in the forest. He ran through the trees before he glimpsed the nests on the cliffs above him. Before long, he spotted the harpies through the branches, their silhouettes barely visible in the dim light. Most of the creatures sat perched atop their nests, hollering out to the jungle. Others flew circles and scanned the forest below.

Claws gripped the side of the cliff, and stalky legs held up feathered torsos and wings. Long, tangled hair cascaded down their fronts and their wide eyes protruded from their ugly faces. They gnashed their teeth between each shriek.

Coming to the rock wall, Joachim took two stones. Back in the clearing to his right, Baruch and Tilicea placed their lanterns on the ground and readied themselves to climb.

"Hey!" Joachim clapped the stones together. "Look down here, you stupid birds."

A harpy saw him and cocked her head to the side. It was like her face had been smashed against rocks or pulled through branches. He tried to anger her, hooting and waving his arms, but she just turned away.

Joachim called again, but the birds didn't pay any attention. They just squawked—a noise of mild irritation, of warning. But he didn't need to be warned. He *wanted* to annoy them. He felt the weight of one of the stones in his hand.

"I'm over here."

He threw the stone at the harpies. They moved out of the way, some lifting their wings to avoid it, but they didn't come to him. They hissed at him now, their eyes wide. He was making a nuisance.

"I said I'm over here!"

He threw the second stone. It clocked a harpy on the head, the ugly one with the mashed up face. She gazed down at him and hissed again. Others joined her. They waddled over to the edge of the cliff and spread their wings. Then they were in the air.

They dipped through branches and descended toward him. He ran in no particular direction, and very soon could hear their fluttering and screeching behind him. He dashed in between the trees, zigzagging to try to slow them. Tilicea said the harpies would only pursue him until they became weary. They were fat, lazy birds, she said. He didn't need long, just enough time for Baruch and the prophetess to snatch an egg. Joachim just hoped they would tire quickly.

He rounded a group of shrubs and came to a river. He hesitated but knew he had no choice but to cross. He went into the water, the ripples blurring the reflection of the moon on the surface. At its deepest point, the water came to Joachim's waist, slowing him. He pulled himself out at the other side. The harpies didn't slow.

As Joachim came to a large rock, he ran into a long expanse of clearing. At the other end he could see the wall of the cliff again. He scanned the forest, the moonlight his only illumination, trying to gauge where he was in relation to the nest. He slowed as the rock face drew nearer. He would pull tight against the cliff and turn again. Hopefully that would be enough to stall them.

But then he stopped. There was no more fluttering.

Joachim surveyed the trees. Perhaps they flew higher to avoid hitting the cliff. Perhaps they now sat in the branches and waited for him to go back out into the forest. He let his breathing slow and waited but found himself alone. He couldn't spot the harpies anywhere.

He pushed himself away from the cliff. His first steps were cautious until he was sure they'd gone. Stupid birds, he thought. How could they be capable of snatching children when they couldn't even be bothered to protect their nests? Joachim went back into the trees to where Tilicea and Baruch would return with the harpy egg.

As he turned, something knocked him from his feet. He found his face down in the dirt, something pushing and pulling at the fabric of his tunic. He twisted onto his back and saw the harpies had returned, biting and pecking at him.

One flew up above the trees. It plummeted down again and collided with his stomach. The impact knocked the breath from him, making him dizzy and nauseous. Another ascended, readying herself to dive down at him again. It was the one with the ugly face who looked like she'd gotten into a fight with a rabid boar. He rolled out of the way just as she nosedived.

On his stomach again, he threw his arm around him to reach for his knife. He grasped it in his sweaty fingers, but the impact of a third bird hit him hard in the back and knocked the hilt from his hand. He swung onto his back again. Yet another ascended above the trees and prepared to free fall at him. Tilicea wasn't kidding when she said they were notoriously territorial. And he was right in their territory. They'd pummel him until he was broken. Until he was dead.

He grabbed the knife just as the harpy dove at him. Though she tried to slow, she couldn't stop herself. The expanse of the dagger plunged into the bird's stomach. It stared at him with wide eyes as it whimpered, falling on top of him and squirming. It limped away, her cries echoing through the trees.

He regretted this immediately. The hunter knew he'd made the wrong choice. When confronted with a group of angry predators, wounding one of them was not to be done. It would only anger the rest, lead them to become more violent.

But this did the opposite. The rest of the birds deserted the forest. He stood up but didn't move. What if this calmness was another trick of the harpy assault?

"Joachim!"

He located Tilicea not far to his left. He felt his vision piqued and sharpened, the sound of her voice clearer. He ran toward her, each stride deliberate and crisp. Through his journey in Zalm he'd almost forgotten how electrifying a real hunt could be. And he was the hunter.

"Were you successful?" he asked as he came to them at the foot of the cliff.

"Yes," Tilicea said.

She had a little dirt on her cloak but otherwise looked fine. Baruch had bruises and cuts all over his face and arms. He smiled under weary eyes.

"Baruch had a little trouble, though," she said.

"The wretches returned to their nest right as I snatched one of the eggs," Baruch said. "They dove at me and pecked at my back and face."

"I had to use the fire runestone to scare them off," Tilicea said. "But we got what we came for."

She held the egg out to him. It was smaller than Joachim thought it would be. The outside shell was colored brown with blotches of darker spots. He held it in his hand. It felt surprisingly light.

"We picked the youngest looking one to avoid it hatching," Tilicea said.

"It'll hatch?"

"Probably not," she replied. "After a few nights out in the cold, it will probably die. The egg needs to be constantly kept warm. A lot of them die anyway, even with their mothers incubating them."

The longer Joachim held it, the worse he felt. It was still warm in his hand. In a different situation, he would have left the harpy egg alone, let it have an opportunity for life like everyone else. But Joachim couldn't afford mercy in this case. Zupay didn't care about who needed to die to get what he wanted. In fact, he only cared about one thing, and without it, Darcie was dead.

Joachim placed the egg on the ground. Tilicea eyed him, but Baruch came to his side. He, too, knew what had to be done. Whenever the hunters killed an animal, one who had done nothing to them but was needed for meat nonetheless, they gave thanks. The people of Old Earth called it prayer, but the hunters didn't pray to anything at all. They just remembered.

The elder and the hunter bowed their heads, knelt before the egg, and closed their eyes.

Thank you, Joachim thought, *thank you for your sacrifice.*

ꑂ ꑊ ꑆ ꑋ ꑌ ꑍ ꑎ ꑏ ꑐ ꑑ

Tilicea tended to Baruch wounds, his gasps resonating in the trees each time the cleansing ointment touched his flesh. Joachim did the same to his arms and face, though his wounds weren't as numerous as the old man's. After Tilicea finished with Baruch, she did the spots that Joachim couldn't reach. Each touch of ointment made him gasp too.

"We'll sleep for the rest of the night," Tilicea said once she finished treating them.

"Where will we go in morning?" Baruch asked. "Where can we find the water nymphs?"

"There's a colony of them at the Deadman's Bluffs," Tilicea said, "and I suspect they will be just as welcoming. In fact, I'll bet they'll be more resistant than the harpies were."

"How long will it take to get there?" Joachim asked.

"If we leave by first light, we can be there by sundown," she replied. "And once we harvest the blood, we can get you back home."

They lit a fire and ate some of their stale bread and meat. Joachim settled into a level spot surrounded by bushes and a large stone. Through a gap in the trees, the stars looked down on him as he dreamt of the place Tilicea mentioned, a place he'd lately only been able to find in sleep. It somehow felt closer to him now.

Home.

CHAPTER TWENTY-THREE

A LEADER'S WRATH

Rae and the others travelled through the jungle until the birds announced the arrival of dawn. The journey had been long, stalled by Darcie's need for breaks and Ophelia's outbursts of madness. Even when they moved for a long period of time, their travel was slow, and they listened to the night as they went in case the creatures were after them. In the twilight of a dawn that seemed reluctant to come, Zupay's former prisoners broke into the clearing at Baruch's library.

"Trent."

There were two men at Alena's side, and they strode the path that led to the rest of the village. They held bows and had quivers slung on their shoulders.

"And Darcie!"

Her eyes went wide, and she ran. When she reached the woman, she clung and sobbed into her shoulder. Before long, Darcie cried too. Alena then examined her, a smile stretching across her cheeks.

"Oh, you're showing, my dear. How marvelous," Alena said. "And if you're here, that means Baruch and Joachim have returned, and Zupay has let you go free. I was getting worried. I was just assembling a party of men to go look for you all in the jungle."

Darcie held the woman's hand and looked down.

"Not quite," Trent said. "Our plan to poison Zupay's water supply was unsuccessful because Ophelia followed us into the jungle. We were captured by the creatures and placed in confinement. Only Rae's knowledge of knots helped us escape."

Though he felt proud that something his father had taught him was useful, Rae felt ashamed as Alena looked over at his mother. Ophelia sat on the ground, blowing the seeds of dying dandelions into the air and humming to herself.

"We must prepare for battle then." The smile disappeared from Alena's face. "I will inform the rest of the village of what has happened. We have no time to lose. Zupay is coming."

$$ \mathcal{Y} \; \mathcal{L} \; \mathcal{X} \; \mathcal{Y} \; \mathcal{C} \; \mathcal{A} \; \mathcal{C} \; \mathcal{S} \; \mathcal{S} \; \mathcal{S} $$

"I'll take care of her," Darcie said. "I'll keep her here while you help the rest of the village prepare."

Rae looked from the woman to his mother. She had fallen asleep on the couch of their home and snored softly. He had just finished unpacking his rucksack and scarfing down some dried meat and bread. After a long gulp of water, he nodded.

"Thank you," he said. "But I can look after her for a while if you'd like to return to your dwelling to rest."

"No. I had enough resting in Zupay's village. Now I want to help fight him so we can return to our peaceful lives."

She placed a hand on her belly. Though a layer of dirt covered her bruised and torn skin, her eyes still shone a radiant light blue. She sat down at the table.

"Tabitha said to meet her at her dwelling once you were ready," Darcie said.

Rae watched his mother. He knew he needed to get back to the others as fast as he could, but he couldn't bring himself to leave

Ophelia. It wasn't that he feared something would happen to her once he was gone. He feared that Ophelia would get in the way, that she'd ruin their efforts. Again.

"She'll be all right," Darcie said. "Everything will be all right."

The words set in, but the voices inside screamed. How could everything ever be all right again? His father was dead and would never come back. His mother was scarred and may as well be gone too. He would live the rest of his days without real parents. That would never change, and that would never be all right.

He left his dwelling, crossed the village, and he reconsidered. Villagers gathered weapons, flurrying through the dwellings with a new urgency in their movements. Only one thing would make Rae's life all right again.

The feeling of Zupay's fresh blood on his fingers.

"I have hunters patrolling the forest a mile from the village."

Alena's voice rang through the trees. Rae rounded the corner to Tabitha's dwelling.

"They are to set off a flare at the creature's approach and fight off as many as they can before they reach the village."

Rae came to the dwelling. Though Alena and Tabitha stood, Trent sat on a chair on the porch, his head in his hands.

"And what from there?" Tabitha asked. "What will we do once they get to us?"

"We have two options," Alena said. "We don't have time to do both, so whichever we choose, we have to follow through if we wish to survive this attack."

"What are they?" Trent asked.

"We build rafts and head out into the sea," Alena said. "We would travel just far enough to be out of sight once the creatures arrive. Since they can't swim, they will think we deserted the village and will set off again into the jungle looking for us. That will give us time for a counterattack on their colony. The other option is rather blunt. We stay and fight. We overcome them with force."

"I like the first option," Trent said. "It would give us ample time to refine our plan."

"No," Rae said. "I like the second option."

"There's too much of a risk, Rae," Trent said. "These people in the village aren't fighters. After our wall of hunters in the jungle falls, our strength is diminished. How could we possibly defend ourselves?"

"And what about the boats?" Rae countered. "How do we know we'll have enough time to build them? How do we know they'll leave when they realize we aren't here?"

"I agree with Rae," Tabitha said. "I'd much rather prepare for a battle than focus on a plan we won't have time to complete. Besides, how can we build enough boats for the entire village? I think that would be rather ambitious. I think we should stay and fight. All or nothing."

Rae looked at Trent. The man took a breath.

"Fine," Trent said. "All or nothing."

He stood from the chair and descended the steps of the porch. Tabitha walked around her cabin and brought an array of weapons. Rae took a bow, a quiver full of arrows, and a dagger.

"Right then," Alena said, holding a bow also. "Let's go address the village."

They followed her back down the path. Though many villagers still gathered weapons, most stood around. Alena cleared her throat.

"As many of you know, our village is under attack." Her voice was strong. "Zupay's demons are angered after our attempt to poison and weaken their village, and now that these brave villagers have returned, the attack could come at any moment."

"We should flee," one of the villagers said, holding his wife close to him. "We won't win against these creatures."

"We cannot flee. We have nowhere to go where they won't find us. We have to stay and fight."

"What about Joachim and Baruch?" another man asked.

"That contract means nothing now," Alena said. "But this time, we have broken it. We have no choice but to stay and face them."

The man opened his mouth to speak again, but no words came out. The other villagers were speechless too. Some cried.

"All those unwilling to defend our village are welcome to leave now and seek safety elsewhere," Tabitha said, standing beside Alena. "But we cannot run from this anymore. All we have done since the founding of our village is run from Zupay and his creatures. We can do that no longer. The time has come for us to be free."

Rae looked at the villagers, at the ones who cried and those who remained hardened. Suddenly, the man who spoke first raised his fist in the air.

"Then I will fight," he said.

"And so will I," the second man said, raising his fist also.

The words echoed through the crowd as fists rose above them. Before long, every person there, whether man or woman, young or old, had sworn to fight against Zupay and for the freedom of their village. For the freedom of humans.

"I want the adults preparing for battle," Alena said, quieting the crowd. "Those who are hunters should be prepared as if this were a hunt. I want those who cannot fight to take the children below fourteen into hiding at the Black Rocks by the ocean."

Suddenly, an explosion echoed through the jungle. The embers of the flare fell through the sky.

"That's the alarm!" Alena yelled. "They're coming."

Two injured villagers and an elderly woman gathered the children and fled down the path to the beach. Darcie and Ophelia emerged from Rae's dwelling and followed them toward the Black Rocks. The villagers who remained drew their weapons and spread out. Rae followed Trent, Alena, and Tabitha just behind the fire pit. They stood beside the flames, their weapons ready. The fire was warm on his face.

There was silence. Not even birds murmured in the trees of the jungle. Animals hid in the creatures' presence, someone once said. Rae listened but couldn't hear them in the distance. No cry of battle, no clamour of weapons. Only the sound of sea breeze as it played with the leaves on the trees.

Then he heard it: the rustling of beings running through the jungle, their impact as they fell to the ground, the cries of man and demon alike. He could do nothing but listen and wait for battle. Listen and wait for Them.

The first creature trickled through. It scurried along the path toward the inner dwellings and approached the fire pit. Tabitha lifted her bow, took an arrow from her quiver, and aimed. Slicing the air, it struck Zupay's creature in the head, and within a second, it lay motionless on the ground, dark green oozing from the wound.

The rest of Them came in a flood through the village, like when a tropical storm washed ashore. Villagers held strong as the creatures moved into the village, but They were like a tsunami pushing through the coastline trees—powerful and destructive and relentless. Though Rae missed the majority of shots with his bow, he managed to take two down before they came on the clearing of the fire pit. All too soon the creatures engulfed the village.

Rae's quiver was empty. He watched his last arrow pierce the chest of a creature, and he pulled his dagger from his scabbard as another approached him. He swung his blade through the air and slashed it across the throat.

The villagers fought hard. Rae was beside Tabitha and Trent, killing any who came to him. Alena weaved in and out of the battle, barking orders and replenishing arrows to the fighters. Though bodies of both humans and creatures cluttered the ground, the villagers outnumbered Them. It was as if the hemlock had worked somehow.

Rae stabbed another in the abdomen and noticed no more creatures remained. The village fell quiet. The tsunami had relented.

"That's all?" a villager cried.

"We've won," another said.

"No," Alena shouted, putting more arrows into Rae's quiver. "That was just the first wave."

She was right. Like a swarm of bees, the villagers could hear the creatures buzzing in the jungle. Their feet pattered on the ground and echoed through the trees. Rae wiped the sweat and blood from his palms. Then They poured into this village again, perhaps three times more numerous than before.

Arrows soared through the air like the typhoon's rain. They struck down the first line of demons, but still They came. As the villagers readied their second arrows, the creatures approached dangerously close. Rae shot another just a few feet in front of him. He drew his dagger again. They were too close for arrows.

A creature hurled itself at him, and he stabbed it in the stomach. He slashed the legs of a second one as it sprang past him to Trent, and it writhed in the sand. He looked up from his kill. The creatures easily outnumbered the humans, and They still came from the jungle.

"There's too many of them!" He heard Tabitha yell nearby. "We have to retreat."

"There's nowhere to go!" Alena yelled back.

Rae turned to her. She drew her knife also and plunged it into a creature. They swarmed like flies, some even making it to the path that led to the Black Rocks.

A creature dove on him and toppled him onto the sand. It dug its claws into his shoulder, and Rae felt blood leaking onto his tunic. The demon bit at him, its sharp teeth threatening to burrow into his face. Rae managed to push it from him.

He pulled himself up, but another latched onto his legs. The first creature rejoined and pushed his chest down again. A sharp pain ignited in his thigh, and through the blur of struggle, he saw the second creature had bit him. He tried to call out, but he couldn't pull air into his lungs. He swung his knife around, but it found only the empty air.

Why wasn't anyone helping him? Did anyone even notice they were on him? A worse thought came to him: maybe the other villagers were overcome with the creatures too. Maybe the creatures smothered them like they did him. He struggled to push the demons from him, but his attempts did nothing to stop them. Rae felt another grab onto the arm that held his dagger.

Immobile and unable to get a breath, he could feel the jungle fading. He'd die like his father before him, glorious but gone all the same. And who would miss him now? He had nothing left, no one to care.

At least he was a hunter.

The creature hurled off his chest, and he let in a painful inhale of air. His eyes were blurred, and he struggled to sit up. A figure pulled the second from his lower body and tossed it away. Struggling to find his dagger, he felt around in the sand. When he found it, he drove the blade into the third and pried it off of him. Suddenly free, he looked up at the person who had helped him.

"Mom?"

Ophelia stood over him, dirt and blood covering her face and hands. Before he could go to her, she jerked forward as if impacted by something. She looked at him and smiled. Her eyes glazed over, and her smile faded.

"I love you, Rae," she said. "You make your father and me so proud."

Blood leaked through the front of her dress, and she fell forward, kneeling. Rae saw an arrow planted in her back just below the shoulder blade. He could feel his vision blurring again, but this time with tears. He went to her and held her hand, her head in his lap.

"That's quite enough," came a voice.

Zupay stood in front of him, a bow in his hand. The struggle had ended, and creatures pinned down the remaining villagers. They snarled and laughed in the presence of their master.

"The battle has ended," he said, "and you have lost. Drop your weapons at once. You are now under the rule of my colony. They outnumber you, and our females are birthing more as we speak."

Two demons came from Zupay's side and pried his mother's limp body from Rae. Though he resisted them, They pinned him to the ground. Beside him, Tabitha struggled with the creatures too. He saw Trent and Alena restrained also. They dragged Ophelia into the trees.

Zupay strode forward and sniffed the air.

"Anyone who resists our presence in this insignificant village will see a swift death," he said. "Any questions?"

CHAPTER TWENTY-FOUR

OCCUPATION

Outside Rae's dwelling, crickets whined in the afternoon sun. Every now and then creatures pattered past. Zupay sent the villagers who survived to confinement in their homes and forbid them from coming out. If they did, he promised death. They were powerless now. The leader of the demon colony possessed complete control.

Rae didn't bother looking out of the window any longer. The sound of the creatures' teeth gnashing on fresh meat made him sick. He paced and wept, tumbling through cycles of numbness and agony as each hour cascaded into the next.

Zupay made sure to separate the five villagers who had been in captivity the evening before. Rae was alone. The one other person he could share his home with was now dead. He replayed the scene over and over in his mind, watching the color drain from his mother's face. He would never forgive himself for how insensitive he had been to her. He spent her last days resenting and blaming her. He'd never be able to tell her how much he loved her.

He wished he could turn it all back. He wished he could rewind time and take his mother and leave the village. He could have taken off into the sea after those boats on the horizon that she had been so insistent on. He could have escaped into the jungle and run away, far away. If he had, she would still be alive.

But how could he abandon the village? They were his family as much as she was. And what would his father think of him if in fact he lived on in some place beyond the living world? He knew his father would never desert his village. He would have never deserted his home and the people he loved.

Rae hated himself. He couldn't leave the village, and it hurt him that he even thought to try. The other villagers would never abandon him, and his parents wouldn't think to abandon them either. Not even his mom. They would fight beside them as fellow villagers, as family. And they did. Even Ophelia did, and she died to show him that.

Rae would do the same. He would do it in his parents' honor.

He wiped the tears from his eyes, went to the window, and pulled open the thin curtain just a bit. The creatures had finished eating, and entrails carpeted the sand. Rae drew the curtain closed again. He couldn't bear the sight. He swallowed hard and pushed the tears from his eyes. He braced himself against the sill and watched out of the tiniest slit between the window's edge and the fabric.

The creatures strode across the village in small groups. They sniffed the ground, their noses leading them around like wild dogs. Whenever they found something of value, they either destroyed it or ate it.

He opened the curtain wider, not enough to be seen but just enough so he could hope to spot Zupay. He needed to find a way out of his dwelling and into one where he could join the others. He needed their help to formulate a plan, a way to either drive Zupay out or escape him.

If Baruch and Mr. Joachim did indeed return, Zupay would not honor the contract. The villagers had rebelled against him and tried to kill his colony. Twice. Their only hope now was to reach Baruch and Joachim before they arrived with the ingredients to Zupay's potion and find a way to exploit the leader.

After this night, they only had three days at most before Mr. Joachim and Baruch returned and the village faced total annihilation.

He saw Zupay on the other side of the window. The leader walked along the path from the Black Rocks to the fire pit. He had two companions at his side. Rae inched open the glass pane.

"Every villager has been accounted for," he said to them. "I want you to tell the others to keep watch over the dwellings. No villager is to leave. You will patrol in four hour shifts. Those not guarding can sleep with me near the workshop in the jungle."

The two creatures at their leader's side called out to the others. They passed the fire pit as other creatures joined them. They travelled toward Baruch's workshop.

When Zupay left, Rae surveyed the village. Only one third of the demons patrolled. The area was practically vacant compared to the occupation before. Judging by the sky, he knew it must be around eight o'clock in the evening. He had four hours until midnight. He had four hours until a fresh shift of demons came to watch over them.

He had to break out of his dwelling and get to Tabitha or Trent. Trent's dwelling stood just beyond the fire pit. If only he could somehow sneak there.

There was a soft knock at his door. At first, he wondered whether he had actually heard it or if it was just a trick of his anxiety. The knocker persisted, and Rae moved to the door, his ear against the wood.

"Who is it?" he whispered.

"It's me," the voice said. "It's Tabitha."

He was silent. How was this possible?

"How did you get here?" he asked. "Zupay instructed the demons to kill anyone they saw leaving their dwelling."

"Don't be silly, my dear boy. Zupay's creatures didn't see me."

His heart leapt at the realization. They had managed to sneak into Zupay's village before without being detected. The answer to their escape lay in the tools they had already used.

Rae opened the door slightly, exposing the porch. He noticed an ankle bracelet hovering just an inch off the ground.

"Let me in quickly," Tabitha said. "There aren't any demons around here."

He swung open the door just long enough to see the red bracelet enter his home, and then closed it. He heard Tabitha shuffle around and then the clunk of something heavy placed on the table. She exhaled loudly.

"Could you get me some water?" she asked.

He moved to the jug of water on the counter and filled a mug. Placing it on the table, it lifted into the air, and Tabitha took several long, loud gulps. The mug glided back onto the table.

"What's the plan?" Rae asked.

"We're going to get you in this invisibility ointment and then find Trent," she said. "From there I hope he'll know what to do."

"I think I have an idea."

"Good," Tabitha said. "You can share when we get there. Now take the pail, and get a move on. I want to be far away from the village before anyone realizes we're gone."

He felt the pail thud against his arm. He fumbled to find its invisible handle.

𝄞 ⚡ ✗ ⚡ ☾ ⚡ ☾ ⚳ 𝄇 ⚴

They knocked on the door to Trent's dwelling, but it remained quiet inside. They heard him stir, but he didn't speak. Tabitha knocked again. This time, he peeked out of a tiny rip in the curtain of the window nearby, eyeing the entrance.

"Who's there?"

"It's us," Tabitha whispered. "We're wearing the invisibility ointment. Let us in."

The door opened slowly, and the two poured inside. He closed the door behind them.

"What are you doing here?" He turned to them, his face red.

"We've come here to escape," Tabitha said. "Put on some invisibility ointment. We can discuss our plan in the jungle."

Trent sat down on a chair and shook his head.

"I'm not going anywhere," he said. "And neither are the two of you."

"What?" Rae saw Tabitha's bracelet move to Trent as she spoke.

"We've failed to stop Zupay two times already," he said. "It cannot be done. The best thing to do is to let him assume control and wait for Baruch to return. Once the ingredients come through, Zupay will leave the village."

"Oh, how can you be so naïve?" Tabitha hissed. "Do you really think Zupay will leave?"

"Do we have any other choice?" Trent looked up. His eyes were distant. "If we stage another attack against him, we will all be killed. Us and our fellow villagers."

"Staying here means certain death, and you know it, Trent," Tabitha said. "At least if we can escape we have a chance."

Trent shrugged. He looked now like a man who had given up, a man defeated. He shifted uncomfortably on the chair and didn't look up from the ground.

"I have a plan, Trent," Rae said finally. "You don't have to come with me. Neither of you do. With the invisibility ointment I can do it myself. I just need you to listen to me and give me advice, if you can. Will you, Trent?"

"You're not going anywhere, Rae." The man looked up, his eyes dark. "I swore to your father that I wouldn't let anything happen to you. You will stay here until Baruch and Joachim return."

"No, I won't."

Rae's voice was louder than he intended, but he could feel the power of his words coursing through his veins. His face became warm, and his whole body tingled. He wished Trent and Tabitha could see the determination on his face. He would have looked fierce, eyes set like a hunter.

"I've spent the past two plans doing what I was told, fearful to do anything otherwise because I didn't want to ruin our chances," he said. "But I know I can help. I can save this village. I know this because I already escaped the demons once. If I hadn't known how to tie knots, if my father hadn't taught me how to, we would still be trapped there. My father wouldn't have wanted me to stand by and watch as his village lay at the hands of Zupay."

Tears came to Trent's eyes, and he hurried to wipe them. He took a breath, shaky and deep.

"What's your plan then?"

"We need to reach Baruch and Mr. Joachim before Zupay does," Rae said. "That way we can tell them what's happened and find a way to exploit Zupay into sparing our village."

"And how do you propose he'll do that?' Trent asked. "I think we're beyond being spared. Once Zupay obtains the ingredients from them he'll kill us all. We broke the contract by rising against him. He'll see that we pay."

"Then we'll have to delay them while we think of another plan," Rae said.

"This won't work, it's too unstructured," Trent said. "Face it, Rae. There's nothing else we can do."

"We owe it to them. We can't let them walk into the situation blind. If we do, they'll hand over the ingredients with no resistance for sure."

"Zupay has spoken a lot about females birthing back at the colony," Tabitha said. "If we could make it to them, we could cut off their ability to continually repopulate and make it easier to defeat them."

"The caves to Zalm and Zupay's colony are too far from each other and the village," Trent said. "We don't know when they'll be back. If we're busy trying to kill the creatures again, we might miss Joachim and Baruch. They could be on their way back already."

"Then we can split up," Rae said. "I'll go to the colony while you two go to the caves."

"By yourself?" Trent asked.

"I'll bring weapons with me," Rae said, "and a supply of the invisibility ointment."

"But what will you do once you get there?" Trent asked. "How will you stop them?"

"Hemlock," Tabitha said. "I still have some in my dwelling. He can put it in the well. Birthing mothers will need lots of water to sustain themselves. If Rae can get it in their water supply, I don't doubt all of them will be dead within a day."

"No," Trent said. "It's too dangerous for you to undertake on your own, Rae."

"But if we don't try we're dead anyway."

Trent raked his face with his hands.

"Baruch and Mr. Joachim would want us to," Rae said. "To try, at least. And so would my father."

Trent looked at the spot where Rae stood. His face was serious, but after a moment, he smiled bleakly.

"You're just like him, you know," he said. "Your father never knew when to give up."

CHAPTER TWENTY-FIVE

DEADMAN'S BLUFF

Joachim had slept poorly. He'd spent the entire night wide awake, listening to Baruch's snores. The following morning, their journey across the Southern Plains seemed to drag on and on, each step forward more arduous than the last. The mountains remained a presence to their right, guiding them farther and farther south but never bringing them to their destination. The sun rose high and already started to descend when Tilicea stopped them.

"The Deadman's Bluffs are about an hour from here," she said. "We'll have to make sure to be cautious. The Undines can be a dangerous people and have driven many men mad. Or worse: they've brought many to death."

Though he heard her warning, the haze of exhaustion blunted the words. He'd heard that before, that something was extremely dangerous, and he needed to take extreme care. Whether it was from the lack of sleep or not, the words seemed almost meaningless now.

"How long will we need?" Joachim asked.

"We should be able to harvest the blood by morning and then we can move to Ithra's Keep."

"Ithra's Keep?" Baruch asked.

"Yes," she replied. "It is the stronghold of the rebels, of my people. There I can allow you to use a transportation runestone that will take you to the cave and bring you back to your world."

She took a package from her rucksack and uncovered some bread. She passed it to Baruch and Joachim. He ate slowly. Each chew made his jaw ache. He looked around at the plains and realized that they ended soon, giving way to another forest. In the trees, he thought he could see the silhouette of a person.

"Are you ready?"

Baruch's voice brought him out of the daze.

"Yeah."

He hadn't actually eaten very much of the bread in his hand. He stood, positioned the rucksack on his shoulders, and ate the bread as quickly as he could. They travelled toward the trees. He could no longer see anything that resembled a human there. It was just his eyes, just a trick of his fatigue.

They moved with little slowing them except for Joachim's aching muscles. The mountains were still at their side, but soon the forest shielded them from view. The air was quiet, and as the darkness fell on them Tilicea lit a lantern. Though he could feel sleep creeping in on him, he kept pace with Baruch and Tilicea. Soon, his legs felt numb, and he could feel his eyes threatening to close.

He stumbled over a rock, and the rucksack on his back shifted. Before falling forward, he clung to the trunk of a tree. The world blurred, and his head spun. He looked up. He couldn't see anyone with him. He scanned the trees, suddenly finding himself wide awake. The hunter stirred, grasping each sight and scanning, but the glow of the lantern was gone. He couldn't see his two companions anywhere.

"Hello?"

No one replied. He called out once more, but Tilicea and Baruch didn't answer. Where were they? Had he been so dazed that he'd wandered away from them? Or had they left him?

Maybe they hadn't left at all. Maybe someone had stopped them.

He thought he heard something behind him. He shot around. He tried to open his ears to the forest, but he couldn't focus. He had to pull the hunter out of slumber. It was like dragging a child back to the table and forcing them to finish their vegetables. Perhaps it was his child. But he didn't have a child yet. Maybe it was him.

The hunter confirmed the air was silent and empty and still. He shivered.

He started forward again. He could hear the sound of the ocean humming over the trees. He must be getting close to the Bluffs. Maybe Tilicea and Baruch were there. Maybe they were waiting for him. He could hear something else also. It sounded like the voice of a woman.

Joachim examined the trees, and the singing stopped. Goosebumps rose on his skin, and a chill climbed his back. The hunter could do nothing now. He was too tired to focus, and he couldn't decide whether he had actually heard a woman's voice at all.

Just before he decided to move again, he heard it behind him. The giggle came faintly, barely audible over the roar of the ocean. He sprang around and saw a woman. She ran, nude, into the forest.

He followed her, weaving through the trees. Who was she? Her long hair flowed behind her, and Joachim thought he could smell the sweet scent of flowers. But where was she going? And why was he following her?

Perhaps she could lead him to Tilicea and Baruch.

Though he tried to keep up, he lost her. Slowing, he found himself completely disoriented. He didn't know which way the Bluffs were, and he couldn't hear the ocean's song resonating over the trees. He did, however, hear a different one.

It came low. The voice sang in a language he couldn't understand, but it didn't matter. The song was the most beautiful he had ever heard and took him to the days when Darcie would sing to him. He closed his eyes, the singing rising in volume and pitch. Within a moment it enveloped him, the sweetness making his body and his heart writhe in pleasure.

"*Come to me.*"

His mind leapt at the words. It was Darcie. She was there with him, there in the forest. He opened his eyes and looked for her, for the voice that would lead him to her. He went in the direction of her call. The majestic harmony resonated, pulsing through him with every step, with each honeyed note.

She sat on a rock, her legs curled up beside her. Her flowing hair covered her breasts, and she toyed with the locks of hair. Her blue eyes pierced the darkness, and she smiled at him coyly, beckoning him forward.

"I've been waiting for you," she said. "It has been such a hard wait."

He couldn't believe what he saw. He knew it was completely illogical that Darcie was there with him in some desolate forest in southern Zalm. What was worse, he had no idea where his friends were. Even if this was her, she should come with him to find them.

He opened his mouth to speak, but before he could, she stood. She glided toward him, the curves of her naked body calling to him. She touched his face, her lips just an inch from his. She smelled like heaven, and his body screamed for her. It didn't matter where the others were. He needed to have her now.

Darcie brushed past him and held him by the arm.

"Follow me." Her voice was breathy.

She pulled him through the trees, again singing beautifully. Each note intoxicated him, wrapping him in haziness. The forest leapt to life. Flowers opened as they ran past, and their scents showered them. Underfoot, he felt the ground had changed also. Joachim no longer felt the soft earth and fallen leaves. The ground had become hardened stone.

The Bluffs were near.

The trees cleared, and dirt stretched out in front of them. They kicked up loose soil as they ran. Darcie's hair blew in the breeze, and the tips graced his cheeks. The need for her kept his heart racing, his feet sprinting.

At last they reached the end. Joachim peered over the edge of the Bluffs, Darcie's hand firmly in his. The ocean roared and crashed white waves on the rocks below. Darcie's singing stopped.

"Jump with me," she said.

"Jump?"

"Yes." Her voice was sweet. She smiled shyly at him.

"But…" He looked down again.

"We can be together there, my love. We can be free."

She came forward, and her breath enticed him with the scent of honey. She opened her eyes wide and touched his face. Her fingers made his back arch, tingling shooting up his spine and forcing him to draw a breath. She brought her lips to his but pulled away as he came in for a kiss.

"Let's go home, my love." She gazed out to the sea. "Jump with me."

He wanted to, but he could feel something in his stomach—in his chest. It was a rushing feeling, like he was falling, but there was madness to it. There was screaming. Muffled, as if smothered with a pillow, but it was there.

He gazed out again. Darcie's song filled his ears. He'd spent so much time searching and wanting so badly to be with her. He couldn't let her go now. He was so close after being so far, and he never wanted to leave her again. He closed his eyes. She was right.

He was going home.

Suddenly, hands pulled him back. He found himself on the ground in a tangle of limbs. He tore his eyes open, looking for his love. Her voice no longer echoed in his ears, and he couldn't see her over the body that pinned him to the ground.

He threw the body from him and saw that he recognized the man. His mind was too hazy to recall him at first, but hands shook him. He gazed into Baruch's eyes.

"Joachim, help me!"

He looked over to where the voice came from. On the ground, he could see her. Darcie's hair lay in a mess, and her arms flailed to push the person off her. He saw that Tilicea held a knife to her throat.

"No!" He screamed.

He clawed Baruch's hands off of him and dove toward them. Grabbing Tilicea by the arm, he dragged her off Darcie. As he turned to the woman he loved, a hand grabbed his shoulder and pulled him back down. Before he could realize what had happened, Tilicea pinned him down, his cheek scraping against the dirt.

Baruch bounded forward and grabbed Darcie. He drew a knife from his scabbard.

"My love, save me!"

"Baruch!" Joachim yelled, tears streaming from his face. "Don't do this."

But the man drove the knife into her chest. Joachim screamed out, feeling as if his own heart had been stabbed. He tossed Tilicea from him and pushed Baruch away from the woman he loved. Holding Darcie in his lap, he cried.

$$\mathcal{G} \, \natural \, \mathcal{X} \, \natural \, \mathcal{C} \, \mathcal{d} \, \mathcal{C} \, \mathcal{S} \, 8 \, \leftrightsquigarrow$$

"Joachim, open your eyes."

The fog cleared from his head, and he found himself with tears on his cheeks. Though he didn't remember why at first, he remembered Darcie had been killed, and there been a struggle. He looked around. Tilicea and Baruch sat near him, both covered in dirt and blood. Something heavy lay in his lap.

He looked down at it. The naked body was covered in blood from a wound on the right side of the chest. The woman's skin was pale blue, and she was incredibly thin. He cleared dark hair from the woman's face. Her teeth were pointed and sharp. Fierce eyes stared back up at him.

The woman hadn't been Darcie at all.

"What happened?" He pushed himself from the body.

"I told you that the Undines were dangerous," Tilicea said. "But luckily, your foolishness led us to kill one without too much struggle."

"How did it trick me?"

"The Undines have that effect on men," she laughed. "They have the ability to take the shape of a beautiful woman and then use a seductive magic to enchant them. This one was trying to bring you back to her colony in the sea."

"And what would she have done with me there?"

"It is believed they use their magic to feed," she said. "But it doesn't matter. You wouldn't have survived the fall. Even if you did, you would drown before you could find out. That is why they call this place Deadman's Bluffs."

She took something from her rucksack and came toward the body. Joachim watched as she took her dagger and pried open the Undine's wound. With the blade, she guided the blood into the flask from her rucksack. When she finished, she corked the bottle and gave it to Joachim.

"You still have the eye and the egg in your pack, right?"

"Yes," he said.

He took the vial from her and opened his rucksack. On top of the food and extra clothing were two spheres covered in cloth. The first was tiny and held the Eye of the Druid. The second was larger and had become cold with the night air. He knew the baby harpy inside must have died during the journey. After ensuring the cork was tight, he placed the flask inside.

"And there you have it," Tilicea said. "We have collected all three ingredients for Zupay's potion. I will now bring you to my base at Ithra's Keep where you can return to the cave that will bring you to the other world."

"Thank you, Tilicea," Baruch said. "Without you, this journey might not have been possible."

She smiled at them, and Joachim found himself smiling back. Though he'd been suspicious and even condescending to the prophetess, he did feel now that he owed her a lot. Because of her help they had a chance to save their village.

He had a chance to save Darcie. The *real* Darcie.

CHAPTER TWENTY-SIX

ITHRA'S KEEP

The journey to Ithra's Keep from Deadman's Bluffs took much of the night. The only thing that kept Joachim going forward was the promise of sleep once they got to the Oracle's stronghold. She said they could take as long as they wanted to rest, and she would supply them with the lone transportation runestone she had there. Joachim wasn't sure whether he was more excited to sleep or to return to his village.

However, the more he thought about it, the more apprehensive he got. He feared even if they made it back to the village in time and handed over the ingredients, Zupay would betray their contract. He had done so before, after all, and that resulted in going to Zalm in the first place. He tried to clear his mind of those thoughts and watched the stars, but each constellation was a silhouette of Darcie.

The night drew on, and the air cooled considerably. Though he thought he was tired, he soon found the others were too. They moved slowly through the Southern Plains and took frequent breaks. It was almost morning before they saw the dim outline of a fortress in the distance.

As the sun rose on their eighth day in Zalm, they approached the gates of Ithra's Keep.

"She has returned," a voice from the lookout post said. "Open the gates! The Black Oracle has returned!"

The gate rose before them, the teeth of the gears clanking. Once it lifted, it exposed the bustle of soldiers inside the fortified walls and the wide tower of the Keep itself. The soldiers came to her, many bowing and kissing her hand.

The Keep looked to be nearly ten stories high but only as wide as to allow four or five rooms on each floor. Joachim wondered how it could house all the soldiers, but he saw more men pour out of the barracks along the outer wall.

As word passed about Tilicea's return, soldiers and maidens alike poked out of windows, waving and cheering at them. Unlike the soldiers of the High Council, the rebel army wore dark colors, the only brightness being the glimmer of firelight off their armor in the growing dawn.

Tilicea thanked each of them, blushing and even letting a few tears fall down her cheeks. Baruch and Joachim stayed in the background. Joachim watched how passionately the soldiers acted toward her, how emotional they got while talking to her. For the first time, the revolution Tilicea had spoken so strongly about seemed real. In the face of each soldier that approached her, he could see their struggle: a look that he'd found mirrored his own.

From the main door of the tower approached a man. He didn't dress like the rest of the soldiers, wearing a long cloak instead of armor and a uniform. His face, however, was that of an army man. His eyes were hard, and his cheeks were scarred. As he saw the prophetess, he smiled and embraced her.

"General Ares," Tilicea said. "It is wonderful to see you again."

"Same to you," he said. "To what do we owe this visit? I thought you said you would go to our stronghold on the Zalmish Sea after your time at Guluki."

"That was the plan," she replied. "But after doing the will of the gods, I found myself on the Southern Plains. My fellow travellers and I have decided to lodge here for the day, if your men will take us."

"Of course." The General looked behind her at Baruch and Joachim. "And while you're here, I can seek your advice and possible assistance. I have received troubling news from our men in the north."

"Most certainly," she said. "But first, let me introduce my friends, Baruch and Joachim. They have come to Zalm from beyond the reaches of the Unknown. Though their timing has not been ideal, we have been successful in our business. Once they've rested here, I will use the transportation runestone to return them to their home."

The General went past her and bowed to them. They lowered their heads in return.

"Any friend of Mistress Shorciman is a friend of mine," General Ares said. "We have several rooms where you can rest before you continue your journey. Let me take you inside the Keep."

After she had shown Baruch and Joachim rooms where they could sleep, Tilicea walked down the hall that ran through the center of the fourth floor of the Keep. Though it was the middle of the morning, they were high enough in the tower that it would be quiet. Only the distant humming of carts across the sand and the occasional yell of a soldier reached her.

She pushed open the wooden door to the room where she stayed whenever she came to the Keep. The bed was still neatly made just as she had left it, and there was the smell of lavender in the air. War weapons hung on the stone walls, relics of her father's days in Zalm. Though Ithra's Keep was the official residence of the High Empress' husband, much time had passed since one had lived there. Nelda had not taken a husband in her reign, and their father had long passed before her mother even gave up the throne.

It was not until Tilicea and her rebels captured the Keep several years ago that she saw the place where her father had lived. Each visit there, she discovered new possessions of his, new memories of a man she had scarcely known.

At the desk near the window that looked out at the Southern Plains, General Ares waited for her.

"I've missed you," he said.

"And I've missed you." She smiled. "You acted so formal out there, you convinced even me."

He chuckled. "Sometimes I doubt if I'm convincing anyone."

"Really?" she asked.

"You know how soldiers can get," he said. "They talk. I've even been asked about us before. And they tease me."

"Then I suppose we should let them talk," she said. "There's no sense in affirming their suspicions by fighting the rumours."

He took her in his arms. Before he kissed her, he looked into her eyes. It nearly brought her to tears. She had had her guard up for so long, she had been strong and away from people she knew for such a time that she had forgotten what it was like to be vulnerable. This time, she would let it happen. As she kissed him, she thought of nothing else. Not of her prophecies, not of her people, not of her war.

"How long will you be here?" he asked, relaxing his embrace.

"I don't know," she said. "The gods will me to ensure that Joachim and Baruch make it back to their world, back through the caves near Zostrava. After they leave I suppose I'll head north again."

"I don't suggest it," he said.

"Why not?"

"The High Council's troops have taken a heavy presence up there," he said. "I'm sure you've seen it. I've received word from my guerrilla troops they've begun preparing for invasion of the south. They have been gathering at Minerva's Pass since yesterday morning."

"Then this is it," she said. "This is the battle spoken about in the prophecies."

"Is it?"

"Yes. After I helped Baruch and Joachim from the other world, the gods indicated that the height of our struggle was near. I didn't expect it to happen so soon, but all the signs point to this."

"What will we do with your companions?" he asked. "If we don't get them to their world in time, they will find themselves in the midst of battle."

"I will transport them at the first rays of sunrise," she said. "If I bring them now, they will be compromised by their exhaustion. I'll let them rest and smuggle them out before the battle begins."

The General nodded. Tilicea looked at the letters left for her on her desk. They had been received from troop leaders outside the walls of the Keep. All from the past thirty-six hours spoke of one event: Nelda readied her army for a grand battle. She would come bursting through Minerva's Pass at any moment in hopes to recapture the south.

"Who will win, Tilicea?" General Ares asked. "Will we be successful?"

"I don't know," Tilicea said. "The gods have not said so. I doubt they even know. Perhaps there are too many variables."

"And what about you?" He looked up at her. "Do you think we will win, or will we once again fall to the High Council?"

Tilicea touched his face. Though she'd read only the first couple lines of each letter, she could sense the worry each messenger felt while writing them. She could sense the worry that General Ares felt. She offered him a tired smile.

"I wouldn't still fight this war if I thought we should fail," she said. "If I believed that, I would have remained in Guluki. Or I would have escaped into the wastelands of the Unknown to seek out those mythical kingdoms of child's fable. I would not have risked your life or the lives of my people if I believed we could never win our freedom back from Nelda."

He took her hand. Though his face was long and worn with fighting, he smiled. This smile, she knew, hoped for a better future. She smiled back. Perhaps, she thought, she could live the rest of her days in freedom with the man she loved, the man who had fought beside her for all these years.

"So, what should we do?" the General asked.

"Prepare for an invasion of Ithra's Keep," Tilicea said. "Only the location of our meeting is certain in this battle."

Nelda could see the Pass not too far in front of them. The sun began to set on the Empress' Highway, and the forest hummed with crickets. She could hear the huffing of the mammoths behind her and the calls of the army men who guided them.

Although trees still stood alongside the path, she could see that the mountains had turned inward and narrowed. She slowed her horse and took out her spyglass. Soldiers patrolled the Pass as she had instructed, and she could see a tent set up for her. She turned to her army, the men allowing their beasts to have a short rest.

"Mount your animals, men," she called to them. "We shall arrive at Minerva's Pass within the hour. You can rest yourselves and your animals once you arrive, but be aware that we will leave early to be at Ithra's Keep for sunrise."

Though they were tired, the High Council's army cheered. She pulled the reins on her beast and dug her heels into its sides. It lurched forward and galloped once again. Nelda smiled to herself.

Tilicea would pay for her insolence.

CHAPTER TWENTY-SEVEN

THE SON GOD

After Trent had covered himself in ointment, Tabitha gave Rae directions to get to Zupay's colony and a small jar of invisibility ointment for when his wore off. They opted to wait a couple hours before setting off to the caves and informed Alena and Darcie of their plan.

Tabitha told him the journey wouldn't be hard because they had travelled the same path many times over the past week. The body had a way of remembering, she said, much better than the mind. But she outlined the route anyway, noting where he would find landmarks to help him get to Zupay's colony.

Behind her dwelling they said goodbye to each other and promised to meet up at the caves that Joachim and Baruch would return from. Though he felt unsure, the caves were better than returning to the village. He feared what would happen after Zupay discovered they had escaped again.

Rae remained behind Tabitha's dwelling until the night's song drowned out their footsteps. He took the pail of hemlock in his hand and watched the trees. He couldn't run away from his plan now.

He entered the jungle. Tabitha told him to head away from the village following the direction of wind that blew that night. When he reached a group of pineapple bushes, he had to veer left and follow a river. Eventually the river would come to a colony of poisonous mushrooms. Tabitha specifically instructed him not to come near the mushrooms and just to follow them away from the river until he came to Zupay's colony. He knew what he had to do once he reached there.

For a while he followed the wind and kept searching for the pineapple bushes. In the dim light of his lantern he worried he would miss them. Occasionally, he stopped and examined the darkness of the path behind him, making sure he hadn't passed the marker. He also stopped whenever the wind became still. He didn't want to travel in the wrong direction and discover he did so only when the wind blew at his face instead of the back of his head.

He noted the moon had not moved much through the sky when he reached the pineapple bushes. Perhaps he hadn't travelled as long as he thought. Solitude always slowed the passage of time—or maybe it was the anxiety. The croak of a bullfrog made him jump. It was definitely the anxiety.

He picked a fruit from the bush and sat down on a rock. Skinning it with his dagger he watched the jungle. Though he didn't see anything that threatened him, he felt uneasy. He chewed and wondered if his father ever felt apprehensive on his hunts.

Rae found he had eaten the whole pineapple, though he hadn't intended to. He tried to remember the last time he had eaten and found he couldn't. Judging by the naked core in his hand and the pile of husk on the ground, it must have been a long while.

Peering left behind the bushes, he spotted a river. It flowed toward the ocean, he presumed. He stood and followed it upstream, keeping his eyes wide for the mushrooms.

He walked alongside the river, not stopping as frequently as he did during the first leg of his journey. Tabitha told him that he would see the mushrooms long before he approached. He even remembered catching a glimpse of them during a previous journey to Zupay's village. Despite that, he travelled for much longer than he did to find the pineapple bushes. The moon had moved three finger widths.

He spotted something in the distance and stopped. He thought it was just a trick of his eyes in the dim light, but he saw it again. It seemed as if something pulsated in the distance, its light reaching through the jungle like fingers, like it was drawing him in. He had seen it before.

Rae decided to move slowly and ducked behind branches and the trunks of trees. Though he knew it couldn't be Zupay's creatures, the light seemed too unusual for him not to be cautious. He looked again at the light and understood what it was.

He could see the outlines of mushrooms, giant mushrooms that pulsated in unison, their glow illuminating the entire area of the jungle. He just stared. How did he not know something this glorious was in the jungle? They must have sprung up after the Great Death the way Zupay and his creatures had, the apocalypse plunging them into rapid evolution. Furthermore, why had Tabitha instructed him to be weary of something so spectacular?

Deciding that Tabitha had been perhaps a bit too paranoid, he approached them. As he went closer they pulsed faster and seemingly with more luminescence. They knew he was there, and they liked him. He could tell. Each pulse made him feel calmer, braver even. It seemed that nothing could harm him in the jungle so long as the he had the light to grace his face and guide him. It was like the light of a god, like those ancient Egyptian deities he loved to read about in books. They would protect him.

He examined the stem of the mushroom more closely. When it wasn't overtaken with blinding light, blue and purple spots painted the mushroom's skin. Looking closer, he wondered how it was able to glow like that. And if it made him feel this good by just looking, how would he feel if he could touch?

Rae extended his arm and brought his finger to the stem.

An inch away, he stumbled back as if someone had pulled him, but no one had. He drew back because of what he saw on the ground inside the clearing created by the surrounding mushrooms. There were the innards of creatures smeared along the grass and up the fronts of the mushrooms. They continued to flare, each flash burning the vision into his mind.

He turned around and vomited.

In the mushrooms' hypnosis, he had forgotten Tabitha's warning. Even if the mushrooms didn't kill him, something else would. Perhaps while he stumbled around in an illuminated daze, creatures would come for him. He stopped himself before he could think of what those creatures would do with his insides. But he didn't need to think at all—just had to open his eyes.

The directions. He centered himself and tried to think. What did Tabitha instruct him to do once he reached the mushrooms? Though he recalled her voice, it was as if the mushrooms had fogged his mind and made him confused. He placed the pail of hemlock on the ground and thought.

Pineapple bushes. Follow the river to the giant mushrooms. Follow the mushrooms away from the river until Zupay's colony. He saw that the wall of pulsating glow extended far into the jungle. He cleared his mind, grabbed the pail again, and started to run.

He ran until his legs burned and his feet were raw. He saw another glow in the distance. This light, unlike the one that pulsed beside him, flickered in the breeze. The firelight of the colony.

Rae looked up at the sky. Judging by the movement of the moon, he had been away almost four hours. He took the jar from his pocket and smeared the ointment over his body. This gave him an extra couple hours of invisibility to complete his duty, get far away from the colony, and move toward the caves where he would meet up with Tabitha and Trent. He could only hope he'd be that successful.

He pictured his father in his mind. Holding on to that image, he moved toward Zupay's village. He stopped once, just once to make sure that nothing noticed he was there, but only the cooling breeze presented itself to him.

He could hear heavy breathing. He watched from behind the trees and saw hundreds of cracked shells littering the ground. He looked up at the trees to where the creatures slept. He couldn't see them, but he knew they were there. He crept to the stone wall just in front of Zupay's cave. The creatures were asleep in there too.

That was good, he knew, if the creatures had gone into the cave to birth. They wouldn't roam around the grounds and find him. He would be able to do his duty quickly.

He climbed the stone fence and crossed the opening of the cave, careful not to step on any of the eggshells. The trees closed in again, and he walked down the path that led to the clearing. When he arrived, there was no indication that there had been cages before. He scanned the vacant clearing and spotted the well on the other side.

He tore across the grass without trying to mask his footsteps. When he reached the rock of the well, he gazed down at it. His heart beat loud in his ears. He gripped the handle of the pail and balanced it on the wall.

Over the opening, a structure of bamboo suspended its own bucket down into the well. On the bamboo were the creatures' markings. Hieroglyphics. Well, not really. Even if they were, Rae would never know. He'd only ever read about them in the books from Baruch's library.

They reminded him of Amun-Ra, an Egyptian god from Old Earth. Though Rae was sure there were no gods, at least not anymore, he liked Amun-Ra. He was the champion of the troubled. He was the god of the sun. He was the hidden light.

And their names were similar.

Rae closed his eyes and let the hemlock fall into the water.

Before he could step away, he began to cry. He didn't cry about what he had to do or about how he had just condemned a colony of creatures to death. In fact, he didn't feel sympathetic toward the creatures at all. Rae cried for himself. He cried for the fact that he had made it and completed his duty. He cried because he had become the hunter he always wanted to be, though he hadn't done so in the truest sense of the word.

He cried because he knew he had made his father proud.

Wiping his tears, he chucked the bucket into the trees. He turned back toward the demon colony to begin the second part of his journey, but he heard a noise. What he saw before him made his limbs numb.

A creature the size of a boar, half the size of Zupay's other demons, wandered out into the clearing, its nose to the ground.

Rae stayed completely still. Maybe he could will the creature away. Maybe if he stayed there, the youngster would become bored and wander off. Rae quieted his breath and tried to slow his heart. The creature zigzagged through the clearing toward him. Rae gripped the stone of the well. The sharp rock under his palm dug into his skin.

The ointment that shields my smell, he thought.

He hadn't put any on when he left the village.

The creature lifted its head and looked at the well, merely three feet from Rae. It bared its teeth and growled lowly. Rae tried to remain still but the creature came nearer. He could see the drool dripping from its mouth and smell the foulness on its breath. His heartbeat rang in his ears.

The creature dove forward, clamping down on his leg and digging its teeth into the flesh. Rae tried to kick it off, but it clung hard. Rae took his knife and slashed across the creature's back. At the first impact of the blade, the creature scurried off of him, wading out two or three feet and hissing loudly.

Rae took this opportunity to run. He dashed around the well and stumbled to the other side. His leg burned. He glanced down at it. The red glimmered in the moonlight, not masked by the ointment. He couldn't see how big the gash was, but the amount of blood and the searing pain in his calf indicated his escape would be a slow one.

Suddenly a cry pierced the air. The creature that had attacked him faced the sky and called aloud. Rae kept to the trees. As its cry drew on, he could see something happening at the cave that lay just down the path away from the clearing.

The light in the cave flickered in the presence of shapes moving through it. The other demons were mobilizing and would come to the youngster's aid. They'd come for Rae.

Before he could think, the dagger was in Rae's hand, and he ran back across the clearing. When he came to the creature, he drove it into its head. Pulling the blade out, the creature fell over on its side, squirming and whimpering. He stabbed the blade again and again into the little beast, stopping only when its limbs ceased to twitch.

Amun-Ra. Champion of the troubled. Hidden light.

The Son God.

Though Rae didn't remember where to find the cave he would meet Tabitha and Trent at, he ran. They had said it would be in the same direction he had travelled to come to Zupay's colony, a direction that would pull him farther and farther into the jungle and away from his village. He wasn't sure his feet knew where they were taking him, but he was too terrified to stop.

The creatures would be on him if he did.

CHAPTER TWENTY-EIGHT

MISTRESS OF THE REBELS

The morning sent rays of the rising sun through the gap in the curtains. Tilicea had slept almost the full day they had arrived and much of the next night. She stirred and looked out of the window, narrowing her eyes in the light. She could feel the General's presence in her bed and her hand still entwined in his. She rolled over. General Ares slept, his heavy breaths indicating that perhaps he dreamt. About her, Tilicea wished.

He stirred.

"Good morning, my love," he said as he opened an eye.

"Good morning."

He sat up.

"How did you sleep?" His voice was hoarse.

Rough. Manly. She loved it.

"I slept well," she said. "And you?"

"The best I've slept in a long time." He embraced her. "Perhaps it had something to do with this bed not being so big and empty without you."

She kissed him. A breeze blew in from the window, parting the curtains and letting the light pour in. The air made her shiver as it graced her bare back. General Ares pulled her close to him.

"Mistress Shorciman."

The voice rang from beyond the chamber door. General Ares pulled away.

"Yes?" she called.

"I have news from the look-outs," the voice said.

She looked at the General and gave him a tiny smile, her fingers playing in the ridges of his hand.

"Okay," she said. "I'll be right out."

Joachim awoke to the sound of alarm bells. In the haze of his sleepiness, he rolled over. He had dreamt about Darcie all night, and now that the morning light bathed the Keep, he imagined he had slept beside her and awoke to the sound of the village's gulls. If only.

"Joachim, are you awake?"

Baruch's words tore open his eyes, and he remembered where he was. The room was large and had walls of stone, but the only furniture in it was a large bed and a desk beside the open window. Outside, he could hear people calling out and men clambering around the castle. Baruch stood at the doorway.

"Yes," he said. "How long have we been asleep?"

"Since yesterday."

"What's going on down there?" he asked.

"Tilicea and her rebels are preparing for battle," Baruch said. "The High Council is coming."

He sprang out of bed and pulled on his shirt. The tunic was worn and ripped with his days gathering the ingredients for Zupay's potion.

"We should go," Baruch said, "before the battle begins."

Joachim lowered the rucksack. He walked over to the window and parted the curtain. Beyond the grounds of the Keep, he could see a vast army, hundreds of men. They advanced across the

Southern Plains. Baruch was wrong. There was no time to escape. They needed to stay and fight.

"Where's Tilicea?" he asked.

"She's already on the grounds," Baruch said.

"Let's go find her."

"Why?" Baruch asked. "One of her aides has the transportation runestone waiting for us. We need to go back to the village."

"No," Joachim said, lowering his pack.

"What, then?"

"We should fight." He couldn't believe the words he spoke. "Tilicea has done so much for us and sacrificed her own objectives to do so. We still have a full day to reach Zupay."

"But we may die."

"We've been lucky so far," Joachim said. "It's the least we can do."

Baruch looked at him. It was the first time he had seen genuine terror in the old man's eyes. Killing a human was different than hunting an animal after all, and Joachim knew that. But that fact didn't make Empress Nelda's army any less malicious.

"We can't just leave Tilicea and her people," Joachim said. "She would have done the same for us."

In the hallway several soldiers ran by holding bows and long arrows. They descended the stairs, and their footsteps became part of the noisy chaos that consumed the Keep.

"Fine," Baruch said. "We fight. But at the first opportunity, we use Tilicea's runestone to get out of here. We shouldn't test our luck. We have been successful in Zupay's work so far."

Joachim rummaged through his rucksack. Besides the ingredients for the potion, there was nothing of importance in it. He made sure the harpy's egg and the eye of the Druid stayed wrapped tightly and that the vial of Undine blood was secure enough not to break. He put it back over his shoulder.

"You're taking it with you to battle?" Baruch asked.

"Where else would I put it? I don't trust anyone to watch it, and I don't trust leaving it in this room in case the whole keep bursts into flames. Besides, if I keep it on my back we'll be ready to leave as soon as the battle has ended."

The man shook his head. Joachim could tell he wasn't comfortable with their plan, but Joachim wouldn't change his mind.

"Why are you doing this?" Baruch asked. "Just two nights ago, you wanted nothing to do with Tilicea or Zalm."

"I was wrong," Joachim said. "I was unfair to her and wrong about everything. I only thought about my own problems, my own village. I didn't realize I wasn't the only person suffering. I didn't realize that sacrifice comes with great responsibility. I was sacrificing everything for Darcie but was being thoughtless and foolish along the way. It's time I fixed that."

Baruch threw his own rucksack over his shoulders.

"You're right," he said. "Let's go down. Our skill as hunters will be appreciated."

They left the room and crossed the hall, descending the stone steps to the atrium of the Keep. Soldiers carried weapons out onto the grounds while generals directed them. One of them Joachim recognized.

"General Ares," he called. "Do you know where we can find Tilicea?"

"She's atop the walls with the archers," he replied.

From a cart beside him, General Ares took two bows and two quivers of arrows. He handed them to Baruch and him.

"If you're going up there you're going to need these."

They thanked him and took the weapons out onto the grounds. Soldiers stood in wide lines in front of the gate, each armed and ready to fight. They passed them and came to the wooden stairs that took them up to the top of the Keep's walls.

All along the wall, soldiers stood with bows. Tilicea stood at the end of the row, her own bow drawn. They walked to her, careful not to knock into the soldiers as they passed.

"Your runestone waits for you to return to your village," she said. "Go down, and use it before the battle begins."

"No," Joachim said. "We're going to stay and fight."

"Why?"

"Because I was wrong," he said. "Your war is not pett, and I realize that now. I'm sorry for being so insensitive."

She looked at him. Before he could stop her, she hugged him, warm tears falling onto his tunic.

"Thank you," she said. "This means more to me than you will ever know."

"It's the least we can do," he said. "You helped us complete our journey after all."

"They advance!"

The soldier's voice rang out over the Keep, and they looked out on the plains. Below, Joachim saw the Empress' soldiers on horseback coming toward them and several lines of archers readying their bows.

"Prepare yourselves!" Tilicea yelled.

Joachim took an arrow from his quiver and strung it on his bow. Peering down the shaft, he pinpointed a soldier from the High Council's army. He waited for her word.

"Release the arrows!"

They soared through the sky like a flock of birds and rained down on the High Council's army, taking out many of the initial assailants. Scattered waves of arrows continued as rebels reloaded their bows and shot again, but the wall of Nelda's army approached still. Joachim loaded his bow and watched his shot strike another army man in the head. Not a boar—but might as well be.

He loaded his third arrow as the enemy's fire started to trickle down. It came slowly, and before long a few of the fellow rebels fell from their posts, crying out.

They launched many arrows, but Nelda's men continued

unwavering toward the Keep. Joachim knew they would attempt to breach the walls. Beneath them, Joachim heard the soldiers preparing to open the gates and pour out onto the battlefield.

In the swarms of enemy men below, Joachim saw something. He couldn't identify what it was, but at the sounds of the men around him, he realized that it was a catapult. He had only ever read about them in the books from Old Earth, but he knew the damage they could cause. The rock in its basket was alight with fire.

"Prepare for impact!" Tilicea yelled.

The rock sailed through the air toward the Keep. With the shudder of an earthquake, it collided, and Joachim nearly fell off his feet. Baruch struggled to stay up, Tilicea helping him. The rock impacted the wall on the far right side, and though he couldn't see it, he could there was smoke on the morning breeze.

"What do we do?" Baruch asked.

"Keep fighting," Tilicea said. "We have people with hydration runestones that can put out the fires. We must focus on our continued assault. The ground army will open the gates soon."

She took a runestone from her pocket and placed it on both Baruch and Joachim's arrows. Immediately, the tips glowed red and burst into flames. With the release of his fingers, Joachim's arrow tore through the sky and erupted on the chest of a High Council army man.

A second blast from the catapult took the watchtower on the left side. Though there were runestones, the flames seemed impartial to them and climbed inside until they poured out of the topmost window. The flames were blue. It was the magical fire like the one at Ionia. Tilicea yelled to get more hydration runestones on it.

They launched arrows for almost fifteen minutes, and the enemy army ceased to advance or use any more fire-rocks in their catapults. In fact Joachim thought they retreated. Perhaps Nelda had misjudged the force of the rebels and didn't adequately supply her own army with enough weapons or men.

"Are they pulling back?" he asked.

"Yes," Tilicea said. "But not because they believe we have won. It's part of Nelda's battle tactic. She'll send her army in waves with just enough time in between to give us a false sense of security. Each wave will become more and more intense."

"What should we do?"

"We should move to the ground and prepare for battle down below," she replied. "If she continues to use the catapult, it'll be safer for our archers to be away from her targets."

The archers descended the steps. Though some remained, most joined the rebels on the ground, waiting behind them at the gate. She handed Joachim and Baruch swords, wielding her own in the scabbard at her waist, and they joined the ground army. The world beyond the Keep had fallen quiet, and Joachim held his sword at his side.

At the signal of an archer atop the wall, Tilicea ordered the opening of the gates. Joachim could see nothing as he rushed forward. He could hear the cries of men, but he could only see the glow of the rebels' armour in the increasing sunlight. He could smell burning, and a wave of smoke blurred the battlefield. His sword shook in his grasp. He felt more terrified than he had on any hunt, and he hadn't even fought anyone yet. He could only hear clanking of metal.

He saw the first High Council soldier break through the rebels, and he didn't hesitate to use his sword. The blood of the man's stomach splattered onto the dirt. Joachim watched him fall—much like the army men on the mammoths in Minerva's Pass, so much unlike the boars he hunted on Earth. With another push forward, Joachim found himself on the plains, the stone of Ithra's Keep behind him. Flaming arrows flew from atop the walls, and many showered back.

Joachim struck the sword from an attacker, and in another swing brought him to the ground. Tilicea fought not too far in front of him, cries accompanying each dive of her sword. He found Baruch on top of a rock protected by three men with long blades and shooting more flaming arrows.

"Joachim!"

He could hear her voice through the chattering of blades. He stabbed another man and saw Tilicea's face covered in sweat and dirt. She came to him.

"Where's Baruch?" she asked.

"He found a rock," he replied. "He's shooting the arrows from there."

"Get him, and bring him with us," Tilicea said. "I'm taking a group of soldiers to find Nelda. Once we strike down the Empress, the High Council will have to retreat."

She pressed her back up against his, and as a pair they fought those of the High Council's army who approached them. Joachim brought them to the rock where Baruch shot his arrows. A crash and light erupted from the Keep behind them. Another flaming rock impacted from one of the catapults. It was good he had taken his rucksack with him.

"Baruch, we're going to find Nelda," Tilicea called. "If we can kill her, the battle will be stopped, and we will have won. I cannot stand any more bloodshed."

"Lead the way."

Baruch leapt down from the rock and pulled out his sword, the group of rebels still protecting him. Now six of them moved through the battle, slashing down Nelda's soldiers. The fire consumed almost the whole outer wall of the Keep and threatened to get inside despite the hydration runestones.

Their advance was slow, and they killed many High Council army men along the way, but soon they saw flashes of light ahead of them and the yells of a woman. Over the battle, Nelda perched high on a mammoth, launching green light from a runestone in her hand.

"There's a line of men protecting her," Tilicea said.

"How will we get close enough?" Baruch asked.

"I'll use my fire runestone to disperse them," she replied. "Kill as many as you can in the chaos. I will try to get to her."

"And what if you fail?" Joachim asked.

She looked away. Joachim could see the pain on her face, see the trembling lip and the welling tears. She steadied her sword. "Continue on, and kill her yourself."

Before he could question her, soldiers descended on them. He killed several of them, Baruch at his side. Magic from Nelda's runestones came close. He moved out of the way right as green light soared toward him. Tilicea steadied the runestone in her hand.

"Ready your bows!" She cried.

Just as Joachim cocked the bow and felt the wood strain, fire exploded before him. A wall of men ran toward them, some in flames themselves, and they escaped into the crowd. Joachim and Baruch shot as many as they could, and Tilicea's magical fire continued.

When all the army men were cleared, Joachim saw the High Empress. She glared at Tilicea from her beast and readied an arrow. Tilicea saw her and dodged it. She used the fire to burn the ground at the mammoth's feet. The animal kicked up and knocked the Empress from its back.

She landed hard, but managed to get to her feet and draw her sword. An army man came to her aid, but Baruch shot an arrow at him. The whole battlefield watched them. The rest of the fighting had ceased.

"Is this it then, Tilicea?" Nelda taunted. "Is this how it all shall end?"

"This is your doing, dear Empress," Tilicea said. "Isn't this what you wanted?"

"After all these years, you finally understand." She laughed at her. "Mother would have been so proud."

Nelda strode forward, and her sword met Tilicea's. The clanging of metal brought the plain into another outbreak of battle. Joachim used his sword also, striking down the High Council's army men. Rebel soldiers poured in toward them. Joachim kept fighting, often losing sight of the Tilicca and the Empress. When he did see them, it seemed one could not overtake the other. Sister against sister.

He came to another of the Council's soldiers. In the swordplay, the enemy's blade nicked his forearm. Immediately he dropped his sword, and the man's blade rested at his neck. The hardened expression on the man's face made him shiver. It was like the face of the jungle sun—harsh and dry and unforgiving. He fell to his knees.

Perhaps this was it. It was the risk he knew about, but he didn't regret his choice to fight. It was all for freedom.

He prepared for the blade's fury, but the man's limp body fell beside him. Baruch stood there with fresh blood on his sword. Joachim thanked him and took up his sword. The battle had fallen quiet again. Rebel and army man alike watched the sisters. Tilicea stood over Nelda, the blade of her sword at the Empress' neck.

"Your own sister." Nelda's voice was low.

"What?" Tilicea stuttered.

"You would kill your own sister for some trivial ideology."

"If it's so trivial why have you brought us to this?"

The Empress' face changed, her cheeks becoming pale and her eyes watery. She looked up at the prophetess.

"I've always admired you, Tili," she croaked.

"Stop, Nelda." Tilicea eyes widened. "Stop."

"I've always wished we could get along."

For a moment Tilicea's blade on the Empress faltered. Before she could regain its position, Nelda flipped her over onto her back, and the prophetess smacked her head on the ground. The Empress now straddled her, her own blade at Tilicea's throat. Her eyes were wide, but not like Tilicea's had been. They widened with her smile.

"You're still the same, Tili," Nelda said. "Just as foolish as you always were."

Just then an arrow struck the High Empress' back. She gazed at her sister, smile slacking, then lost her balance and tumbled over. No one moved, not even the army men who had pledged to fight alongside her. A pool of blood formed on the ground. Tilicea searched for the assassin.

Joachim's fingers still stung with the release of the arrow.

CHAPTER TWENTY-NINE

A CONTRACT SIGNED IN BLOOD

The atmosphere around Ithra's Keep had changed. Once the Empress was dead, the remaining soldiers of the High Council's army fled north. General Ares sent a small army to follow them but not to strike them down. Rather, he wanted to make sure they didn't disturb any common folk on their way to Minerva's Pass.

The remaining soldiers hailed Joachim as a hero. Not only had he saved Tilicea, he also killed Empress Nelda, the woman who led the oppression of the people and committed monstrous acts.

After a short celebration, the Keep cleaned up. Under the guidance of General Ares, all bodies, rebel and High Council army man alike, were to be buried at a site just west of the Keep on the Southern Plains: the newly-named Joachim's Hill. Soldiers put out the remaining fires with the hydration runestones, and plans to rebuild the damaged portions Ithra's Keep commenced.

Tilicea brought them back up to her chamber on the fourth floor. She had sent for the transportation runestone again, and an aide waited for them as they entered. The aide handed it to her.

Joachim and Baruch could finally return home.

"What will become of Zalm now that the Empress is gone?" Baruch asked.

"The fight will continue," Tilicea sighed. "Even though Nelda isn't able to lead the High Council, it will not cease to exist. Unfortunately, there is still a battle to be fought against those who worked alongside her and fed her power."

A feeling of defeat grew inside him. Joachim didn't realize how hard it would be for Tilicea and her people to be free. It seemed to him they had won the fight, only to discover there was much more to do.

"Don't worry, dear Joachim." She put a hand on his. "A major battle has been won. We are much closer to gaining the freedom we deserve. The south is free."

She held the runestone out in front of her. On the smooth face of stone, Joachim saw three parallel lines.

"Do you have everything?" Tilicea asked.

"Yes," he said. "I have the eye, the egg, and the half quart of blood in my rucksack."

She took a piece of parchment from her pocket. "I have written down the prophecy for you to take with you in case Zupay wants to know what ingredients we have gathered."

Joachim put it in his pocket.

"Excellent," she said. "Let's join hands."

They did as she said, the runestone carefully held in the grasp of both her and Joachim's hand. Baruch held a lantern in the hand that joined him with Tilicea.

"Are you ready?"

They nodded, and she closed her eyes. A bright light grew in the room, soon consuming the stone of the walls. A familiar breeze pulled at Joachim's cloak. The air became cool and bright. Just as the light became blinding, it faded away.

They were in a cave lit only with Baruch's lantern. A wall of stone with two painted handprints stood before them.

"This is where I leave you."

He turned to her. Tilicea had tears in her eyes. She hugged them both, and for the first time, Joachim approached her as a friend. He held her tight against him, and when she pulled away, he too felt tears on his face.

"Thank you," he said, "for everything. If it weren't for you, I doubt we would have made it through Zalm alive, let alone able to gather the ingredients we needed."

"You're very welcome," she said.

She lingered and smiled. She then closed her eyes.

"Remember, my friends," she said. "Sometimes freedom is not won without perseverance and sacrifice."

With that, a white light grew in the cave. As whispers echoed down the passages, the light expanded before fading away altogether. When Joachim could see again, Tilicea had disappeared.

Baruch placed his hands on the prints on the wall. The cave shook like it did when they had first entered Zalm, but Joachim wasn't anxious about it this time. It was like seeing an old friend, visiting a long forgotten place that once held such wonder. The wall in front of them glowed momentarily and then became transparent. It felt like home.

They walked through the barrier to the other side. Back on Earth the air smelled different. He took a deep breath. Though he knew their journey hadn't ended, the air cleansed him. Each inhale brought him closer to his village, closer to Darcie.

After a small meal of their remaining bread and meats, they walked, guided only by the firelight. It had taken them only twenty minutes to travel from the transparent wall to the mouth of the cave when they first came to Zalm nine days ago, but it seemed to Joachim that they walked for much longer this time. Each thought that passed through his mind was of his wife.

Finally there was light in the distance. It was faint at the start, but as they moved closer they knew the exit was near. Baruch extinguished the wick of his lantern. But there was something else there—someone, a figure standing in the morning's light.

"Welcome home, Mr. Joachim and Baruch."

The voice made his heart race and his face warm. Zupay leaned against the stone of the cave. He smiled. Joachim eyed Baruch. The man looked uneasy. He must not have expected to see the demon leader so soon. They hadn't spoken of a plan to ensure the village's safety. If anything went wrong, Zupay was in complete control.

"I assume you have brought me the ingredients," he said, "or else you would not have returned. And you are a day early, at that. I'd like to see them now."

He held a hand out. Baruch turned to Joachim and nodded. He took the rucksack from his shoulders and emptied the three objects on the ground. Before Zupay stood the eye of the Druid, the gold glowing in the light. Next, there was the harpy's egg, looking so discolored that Joachim was sure it was long dead. Lastly, the thick blood of the Undine sat in its glass container.

Joachim took the parchment from his pocket.

"*In order to achieve immortality, one must obtain the window to the Great Druid's soul, half a quart of blood from the enchanting water nymph, and the Harpy's child still unborn,*" he recited. "It's signed by Tilicea Shorciman, the Black Oracle herself."

Zupay snatched the parchment. He read the words aloud again, and a smile graced his lips. It was a wide smile, a sick smile—the smile of a man who had surely gone mad, or was on his way there. Zupay called forth three demons that hid in the trees of the jungle behind him. They took the ingredients and scurried away.

"I'd like to thank you, gentleman," the demon said. "But unfortunately your efforts have been in vain."

Joachim's heart dropped. What did that mean? Why were they in vain? Had Darcie already died in captivity while he and Baruch gallivanted around Zalm?

"What are you talking about?" Baruch barked.

"Our creatures invaded your village two days ago," Zupay said. "The contract has been broken."

"How?" they both cried.

"It seems while you were gone, a band of your people staged attacks on my colony," Zupay said. "They tried to unsuccessfully poison my people, and when they failed, they escaped captivity twice. During their second attempt, they contaminated my water supply."

Joachim's eyes widened, and Baruch's mouth dropped.

"As you can attest, that was not part of the contract," Zupay said. "As such, the contract is invalid. Your entire village has been under occupation and is at the will of my power."

"You can't do that!" Joachim yelled.

"Joachim is right," Baruch protested. "We gathered the Black Oracle and the ingredients for your potion. You can't hurt anyone!"

"But Baruch," the creature started, "you didn't mention in the contract that you would organize an uprising in your absence."

The two of them were silent. They didn't know how to reason with the demon leader, and frankly, Joachim feared they couldn't. Though they hadn't organized the attacks, they had taken place all the same and left them without any further options.

The contract was indeed invalid. All the color had drained from Baruch's face.

"Come and retrieve Mr. Baruch and Mr. Joachim, please," Zupay called out. "They too will face death for breach of a contract signed in blood."

At his word, demons appeared from the trees. They came into the cave and grabbed their limbs. Joachim resisted and was successful in throwing a few of them off, but they gained control and dragged him into the jungle.

Baruch didn't struggle at all, but unlike their transport to Guluki the expression on his face was not so smug.

"What do we do now?"

Tabitha sat on a rock, her head in her hands. Trent repeated the question, but she waved him off. She hadn't imagined this could happen. Well, she knew it could, but she had hoped. But then again, hope was proving to be a disastrous instrument.

What was their plan? Trent was insistent. She had no plan.

"We can't go back to the village," Trent said. "And it's a good thing we didn't wait at the caves for Rae. It sounded like Zupay has just come from there, and I thought I could hear Joachim's voice."

His eyes were serious. She wished he would stop talking so she could think. She needed him to stop talking.

"They've been captured," he said. "What do we do now?"

"Will you shut up?" Tabitha hissed.

They had been on their way to the caves when they heard something in the distance. Before they knew it, creatures moved right for them. They waited in the trees, silent and invisible, terrified they might be caught anyway. As they were deciding what to do, Tabitha and Trent heard the creatures return, and from the sounds, they had taken human hostages.

Zupay and his demons had made it to the cave before them. They'd taken the ingredients and captured Joachim and Baruch.

"There's nothing we can do," Trent said lowly.

"Yes, there is," she retorted. "We two remain free and so does Rae. We can find a way to free the village and kill the creatures. If Rae was successful then there's no way to repopulate the colony for at least a short while. We can get them while they're weak. We have to kill them all now."

"And how do you propose we do that?" Trent asked. "With some sticks and leaves and some invisibility ointment?"

"We have to go back to the village."

"Are you out of your mind?"

"No." Tabitha glared at him. "You said it correctly, Trent. We can't do anything useful with sticks and leaves. However, we have the invisibility ointment. We can use it to sneak back into the village, gather supplies, and create a new plan."

Trent cursed and kicked up pebbles on the ground. She had

never seen him so angry, but she didn't blame him. It seemed the closer they got to defeating the creatures, the farther they got from that exact goal. She, too, wanted to throw a tantrum and kick things, but that wouldn't help.

"Are you done?" she asked.

He rolled his eyes.

"Now, I can continue alone, and you can go turn yourself in," Tabitha said. "But know that won't solve anything. The creatures will still prevail. They will continue to occupy the village and probably kill us all."

He huffed.

"Or you can quit acting like a child and help me."

"What about Rae?" Trent asked.

"He's probably in transit between the colony and the caves," she said. "He'll arrive and wait for us there. But we can't stay. We'll go back to the village, and once we've retrieved the supplies and information we need, we'll return and meet him. By then we should have a better idea of what to do."

She sounded more confident than she really was. Her years as a village elder allowed her to do so, but it was still a lie. All had gone wrong. Everything they tried. It was foolish now to believe they would still succeed, but what other choice did she have? They would be lucky to have time to do all the things Tabitha planned.

"Fine." Trent's voice was calmer. "We'll apply some more ointment and go to the village, but if you think you'll be able to talk to either Joachim or Baruch, you better reassess your plan. We'll be lucky if they haven't killed them yet."

Rae watched in the trees as the creatures took Baruch and Mr. Joachim away. He had waited for nearly an hour, and the sun began to rise, but Trent and Tabitha never came. Zupay and his demons did instead.

Where could Tabitha and Trent be? Why weren't they waiting at the cave? Did they perhaps know Zupay would come and decide to go somewhere else until he was gone?

Rae came out from the trees once They left. He was no longer invisible. In fact, he had run out of the ointment altogether and discarded the jar on his flight from Zupay's colony. From the conversation he just heard, he was happy to know the hemlock worked this time. He didn't like the way Zupay spoke though.

If he didn't act fast, the village would certainly pay again for his actions.

He emerged into the clearing in front of the cave. He examined the ground, but only footprints from Zupay and his demons crowded the dirt. Inside the cave he could see footprints from Baruch and Joachim. He looked around again, eyeing the trees carefully. There was no sign of Tabitha or Trent anywhere.

Maybe they hadn't reached the cave yet and were still coming to them. Whatever the reason, Rae sat down on a rock and took some dried meat from his rucksack. He decided he couldn't go back to the village now. He should wait.

He rubbed his eyes. The plan was ruined. It was all over now. The demise of his village was imminent, and his own survival was questionable. Joachim and Baruch would die too. Though he tried to keep his mind clear of those thoughts, he couldn't stop them from coming.

Ultimately, he was responsible for the breaching of the contract signed in blood. They would all die.

It was his fault.

CHAPTER THIRTY

THE VISION

The High Council has fled Minerva's Pass," General Ares said. "Our troops will be communicating with our spies in the north to see how Zostrava has reacted. I don't want to become overconfident, but I believe our battle has been successful. Without Nelda, a thorough plan and a vision for a repressed Zalm are fragmented."

Tilicea could see his face had brightened since the battle and that his gaze no longer looked heavy and far away. She examined the faces of the other army men in her office. They, too, wore expressions of relief. These were new faces, she thought. The new faces of Zalm.

"Excellent," she said. "Then let us continue with the effort to rebuild Ithra's Keep and send word to citizens in the south. Let them know the Empress is dead and freedom is within grasp. Once we receive word from the north, we can appropriately take action."

The men nodded and a few even applauded her. They hugged her and clapped her on the back. Soon, they all had left her chamber except for General Ares. He embraced her again and kissed her. Letting her go, a smile stretched across his cheeks.

Though she smiled back at him, she hardly felt happy. It was one thing that so many had died in the battle, but her sister had also. Through the many years of estrangement, she never stopped wishing things could be different between them, that they could be true, loving sisters. But none of that mattered now. The right path was rarely easy, and she could tell this would haunt her as the hardest thing she had ever done.

"We did it," he said.

She snorted. "It isn't over."

"This is the beginning of the end, my love," he said. "The rest of our lives wait for us, and we can live without violence and without the High Council."

"Such optimism, General Ares," she teased.

She went to her desk. From the top drawer she took her pipe and a small pouch. She took dark green herb, one she knew General Ares had seen before, and placed it in the pipe.

"Can I trust you to record for me?" she asked.

"Of course," he said. "What is it you seek to know?"

"Anything the gods are willing to say. I wish to know what they plan for Zalm now."

The general sat on the edge of her bed and watched. Tilicea took a corked bottle from her pocket and smeared cream on her arms and legs. She then took a match, struck it against the wood of the table, and lit the herb inside her pipe. The smell was bitter and spicy, and as it came closer to her nose, it burned. But she inhaled.

With each pull of smoke, she grew paler and paler and sunk deeper and deeper into the armchair. Finally, she let the pipe drop from her fingers onto the floor. General Ares watched her as she swayed back and forth, her head finally resting on her shoulder.

The noises started to grow. Though the Keep resonated with many noises, these were different—whispering. As they reached a crescendo, light started to glow.

The room became unbearably bright. General Ares closed his eyes, but the magnificent light penetrated even that. And then came the heat. He sweated underneath his clothing. At last the light faded.

Tilicea's head hung forward, her eyes narrow and her skin glowing.

With a loud gasp, Tilicea fell to the floor. Her hands rolled into her chest, and she closed her eyes tight. General Ares flinched to go to her, but he knew better than to interfere with the will of the gods. Tilicea had warned him against it many times before.

As he watched her, she muttered. The words were inaudible, but they became louder and louder. They grew to a normal talking level, words he didn't understand but ones he had heard from Tilicea's earlier trances—guttural, throaty, rapid.

Just then, she began to scream. In all the trances he had watched, he had never seen her do that. It made his heart race. The sound was piercing and seemed to be layered with the voices of many others. She writhed on the floor, her limbs curled tight into her body and tears squeezing from her eyes. It took all the general's will not to go to her aid.

Her eyes tore open. The glow drained from her face.

Tilicea stood. She looked around the room with wide eyes. She saw General Ares, seeming not to recognize him. She stared at him for a long moment.

"What did you see?" he asked.

"We must assemble an army and head north." Her voice was shaky. "Bring me all the transportation runestones you can find."

"Is it the High Council?" he insisted. "What did the gods show you?"

She sat down in her chair. Her eyes were somewhere distant and didn't focus on anything. Tilicea shook as if a cold breeze swept around the room, but the world outside grew hotter with the afternoon sun. The prophetess tried to slow her breathing.

"It wasn't the High Council. I was not shown anything from the gods regarding our trials."

"What then?"

She cleared her throat and wiped her eyes. They finally met his.

"It was about Baruch and Joachim," she said. "Something has happened in the other world. The contract has been broken, and Zupay will show no mercy.

"He will kill them all."

CHAPTER THIRTY-ONE

RED ON THE OCEAN WAVES

The creatures hauled Joachim past the library and down the path to the rest of the village. Through the blood blurring his vision, he could see that much of the library and Baruch's workshop was destroyed. Burnt shards of building and mangled bodies lay on the ground of the clearing. Zupay's creatures had taken over the village and claimed it as their own—their territory marked with blood.

As they came to the center of the village, Joachim saw not only insurmountable destruction but a presence so immense it made his chest hurt. There were many more creatures than he had ever seen before, even in their own colony in the jungle. He couldn't see any villagers. He feared they were all already dead.

Zupay brought them to a spot near the fire pit and said something to his creatures. With a call, They sprang around the village, pulling open the doors to dwellings and dragging scared villagers outside.

In the crowd, Joachim saw familiar faces, ones he had grown up with. Each one was covered in dirt or blood, and their eyes bore a fear so real it rendered them colorless—almost lifeless. As the last few stumbled out in front of him, he noticed some of the villagers were missing. He didn't see Trent or Rae or Ophelia, or the older

248

woman who lived up the path, Tabitha. They must have been the villagers the demon had spoken of who broke the contract. Where were they now?

The last people to come out of the dwellings made his stomach drop.

His mother called his name as she saw him. Darcie bounded toward him. Immediately a creature pulled at her arm and held her back. Though Joachim struggled to get to her, more creatures did the same to him. Tears ran down her face, and she spoke to him, but he couldn't hear her words over the creatures.

"Enough!" Zupay's voice rang loud. "Turn and face me."

Baruch turned willingly, but Joachim did not. He kept his eyes on Darcie, hers on his. He saw she clutched her stomach, nursing the small hump of a child.

The creatures pushed him, but he was unwilling to move.

"Take them to the ground."

They pulled him down onto his stomach. The sand stung his face. Claws dug into his back. He cursed aloud, but Baruch beside him was still silent. He could hear Darcie's cries. The demon leader held a long knife in his hand.

"They will be the first," he said. "They will be a reminder to all in this village to heed my leadership or face the wrath of my power."

The words rang in his ears, but it was as if Joachim didn't hear them. He focused only on the Darcie's weeping. He tried to look up to see her, but every time he moved, a creature pushed him into the sand. He could only lift his head enough as to see the satisfaction plastered onto Zupay's face.

"Do you have anything to say, gentleman?" The demon beckoned.

Joachim looked at the old man.

"So, this is it, Baruch?"

"Not now, Joachim."

"Then when?" He could feel heat tearing through his chest. "He's going to kill us!"

"We have failed. There is no hope for us here."

Joachim's anger for the man was almost as intense as his hate for the monster that brought his village to ruin. He could tell Baruch knew he implored him, but the man didn't look back. Perhaps Baruch had given into their fate after all.

"Are we done?" Zupay asked.

He held his breath, feeling the fire of anger come over him. The fire of the hunter.

"I'm not!" Joachim yelled.

He pushed upward. The creatures on his back fell off him, and Joachim launched himself to his feet. Shrieks filled the air. Before he could turn around, they were on top of him again. He pushed the first two and sent them rolling through the dirt, but his strength soon ran short. He was overwhelmed. The creatures dragged him down again.

They pinned him on his back.

"Just like your father."

Joachim saw Zupay's smirking face in front of him.

"The man never knew when to give up," he said. "He never knew when enough was enough. He never knew when he had lost."

"Good!" Joachim spat. "Because I have not lost. Even if you kill me, my voice will live on. These villagers will never let you control them and treat them like your food supply."

"Oh, but they are, Mr. Joachim." The creature played with the blade on his fingertips. "And if they think they can be as insolent as you have been, my creatures and I will have no problem killing them off. I will see that we get them—every last one."

Zupay held the knife above Joachim's face. He etched the blade along his cheeks and then grazed it over his throat. The demon's eyes were wide, and his creatures laughed maniacally. Darcie called out from the crowd, her screams barely audible over them.

"And to prove it," the demon leader said. "I'll start with you."

He pressed the blade to Joachim's throat, the pressure building. He closed his eyes. Though he tried to silence his mind, he couldn't help but acknowledge the fleeting thoughts. He thought of his father and of Ben, the two men he could only hope to join in death. He thought of Darcie. He thought of the child who would grow up without him.

Another to grow up without a father.

He could feel the knife moving on the flesh of his throat. He thought to scream, but no sound left his lips. He heard the screams of the villagers. Darcie's rang the loudest in his ears, his arms clawing toward her as the jungle faded away.

The sky beyond the palm trees now shone so bright.

Father.

ﾁ ﾆ ﾌ ﾞ ﾖ ﾟ ﾟ ﾟ ﾟ ﾞ

Something burst through the trees—figures emerging from the path. The man leading the commotion struck down two demons with arrows, and the men that followed killed the others who attacked them. Zupay looked at them, his eyes wide. Darcie could just see the man's face through the blur of her tears.

Rae led an army into the village.

The boy set an arrow to his bow and pointed it at the demon leader. As he released it, it sliced through the air and whistled as it passed by. The creature cried out, and the village fell quiet. Pale green blood seeped from a wound in Zupay's stomach.

"Your wrath in this world has ended, Zupay."

A woman emerged from the ranks of men and stood beside Rae. She had dark hair flowing down her cloak, and she held a bow in her hand. She glared at him.

"I am the Black Oracle," she bellowed. "I have come to rid this world of the demon leader. I have come to rid this world of you, Zupay."

He began to laugh. "You're a fool. Without me, there will be no one to keep my colony from feeding."

The creature stumbled back, holding the arrow lodged in his stomach.

"I'm sure we can handle them." Tilicea readied a second arrow and pointed it at him.

Zupay called out just as Tilicea planted it in his head. The creature stumbled forward and then fell on his side, green blood seeping from the wound and blanketing the dirt. Everything remained still. Darcie wished the creatures would flee, that Zupay's death was enough for the villagers to win. But she knew better.

With a screech, the creatures began to move. They intended to kill.

She needed to get to Joachim. If he wasn't already dead.

$$\text{ク と ブ ‹ ⟨ ⟨ ⟨ ⟨ ⟨}$$

The screech burned Trent's ears, and he saw the creatures mobilize. He struck one down as it lurched toward him. Though Rae had brought the help of the Zalmish rebels, the number of creatures never seemed to diminish. Trent swatted at them. He tried to look through the chaos and find Joachim's body. Before Rae and the Oracle came, Zupay's blade was right at his throat. The chaos kept Trent from seeing the final moments.

But now Zupay was dead, and he feared Joachim was too.

He saw Darcie move toward the fire pit and toward Baruch. The old man was kneeling down where Joachim lay.

Trent hoped he hadn't lost another friend. Not like Ben—not yet.

The battle moved to the bottom end of the village and toward the beach. He didn't have time to wonder or mourn. He had to fight.

Sand layered the ground underneath his feet, and he could hear the sound of the ocean behind him. He killed another creature, and its blood splattered into his eye. As he wiped it away, another jumped onto him and knocked him over. He managed to keep its teeth from finding the flesh of his neck. Before he could push it off, he heard a whimper, and more creature blood fell onto his chest.

Someone pulled him to his feet.

He blinked, not recognizing who helped him up or who had killed the creature attacking him. He expected to see Tabitha or another villager, but a familiar boy smiled at him. He looked much older than Trent remembered, and he had seen him not long ago. He looked like a hunter.

"Rae, you're here," Trent said. "How did you get that army?"

"I was waiting for you and Tabitha at the caves and watched the creatures take Joachim away before I could reach him. While I tried to think of what to do, Tilicea and her people came through the cave and told me they were here to help our village."

"Well, it's almost over, my friend," Trent said. "Zupay's dead."

"What about Mr. Joachim?" Rae asked. Trent felt a knot in his throat. "I saw Zupay with the knife."

"I don't know," he admitted. "But there's still a chance he's alive."

Trent dragged him out of the battle and into the jungle. The sounds of fighting meshed with the roaring of the ocean. In the trees though, there was no one.

"What are we doing here?" Rae asked.

"We need to find a way to end this battle quickly," Trent said. "I won't stand the killing of our villagers at the hands of these monsters anymore."

"So, what do we do?"

"I have a plan."

Rae followed Trent through the jungle. They zigzagged around tree trunks and leapt over rocks, heading back toward the center of the village. Once they reached the area, they slowed and listened. The battle was on the beach.

"There's Tabitha," Trent said.

Rae followed his pointing finger. He saw a figure moving through the trees.

"Did you get them?" Trent asked.

"Yes," Tabitha said, her naked body covered in war paint. Rae had to admit she looked a little frightening—and a little ridiculous.

"Tilicea gave me whichever ones she had."

"Well, all we need is three," Trent said. "General Ares said he'd take care of the rest."

Tabitha opened a pouch and held out three tiny stones. On the face of each stone, Rae saw a glowing red dot.

"What are they?" he asked.

"They're runestones," Tabitha said. "In Zalm, they are used to conjure up magic."

"Magic?" Rae almost laughed.

"Yes," Tabitha said. "Watch."

She held the stone so the red dot faced away from her and into a clearing in the trees. With a twitch of her wrist, the entire jungle filled with a light and a roar. Rae shielded his face, but when he realized the other two didn't do the same, he moved down his hand. From the stone, Rae saw fire.

"Where did you get these?" Rae asked.

"General Ares," Tabitha said. "I had worked with him some time before, back when I entered Zalm and obtained the invisibility ointment. He and the Black Oracle have a plan."

"We're going to burn them all?"

"The creatures can't swim," Trent said.

Rae knew that. He remembered the time after his mother spoiled their plan, and a creature pursued him in the jungle. It fell into a river and drowned.

"So?" Rae asked.

"We'll use the fire to drive them into the ocean," Tabitha said. "If we execute this properly, they'll all drown."

Rae's eyes widened. "What if they come toward us?"

"Then they'll burn," Trent said.

"It's understood then," Tabitha said. "We don't have any more time."

Tabitha took Rae's hand and ran down the path that led to the beach. Though it was the probably the best they could think of in such a short time, Rae wondered if it would work. How could three fire runestones drown an entire demon army? Even still, how could they be sure not to burn their own allies?

They reached the beach, and he knew they had no time to re-evaluate. Tabitha gave Trent and him each a runestone. Rae gripped the stone tight in his hand.

"Are you ready?" Tabitha asked them.

They nodded.

"On my word."

He looked out at the battle. It was hard to tell the difference between creature and human. Much of it was a blur, and weapons flew through the air. Rae calmed himself. He hoped no humans would perish because of another one of their questionable plans. He prayed no more villagers would die for him.

He prayed for Mr. Joachim.

Trent called out to the beach. Rae thought this was the call to use his runestone, but Tabitha held his hand back. The battlefield cleared of villagers and armoured rebels. They ran into the jungle. The creatures, too confused at the retreat, remained on the beach.

"Now."

All around them erupted fire. Rae soon realized it was not from their three runestones alone. There were more following the plan. He saw that the rebels from Zalm had runestones, too, and walked onto the beach from the trees.

"Onward!" Tabitha bellowed. "To the water."

Flames soared through the air as they reached the licks of ocean waves. Though the creatures tried to brave the fire, They found only death.

Soon They splashed like the jumping fish at dusk. Their screeches echoed through the jungle, but the runestones remained a constant assault. The splashing stopped and dead creatures floated face down on the rolls of the sea. After a time, only fire pouring from the runestones remained in front of the army of villagers and Zalmish rebels.

It glowed red on the ocean waves.

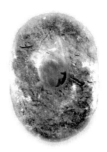

CHAPTER THIRTY-TWO

A NEW ERA

Tilicea and her army left soon after the creatures had drowned in the ocean. They helped clean up the village, tackling the bigger structural issues and helping to bury bodies of villagers and rebels at a special spot in the jungle behind Baruch's new workshop. As they came to the corpses of the creatures that perished on the ocean waves, they noticed the bodies were gone, carried away by the tide. Tilicea and her people then said their final goodbyes and promised to visit. They went back through the caves that would take them to Zalm.

The ingredients to the immortality potion had to go too. They had to be destroyed. Tilicea insisted that it was the will of the gods, that immortality would do ill in the wrong hands. Even in the right ones, it would cause pain to those who outlived their families and friends.

But Joachim didn't need immortality. He had escaped Zupay with little more than bruises and cuts. In fact, he'd been more injured on hunts.

The following night, he and Baruch disposed of the ingredients to Zupay's potion in the fire pit. They smashed the harpy's egg with a hammer and burned the solidified contents inside, scattering the ashes into the ocean. They shattered the vial of Undine blood along the logs of the fire, the liquid hissing in the flames like the familiar song of the water nymph. As for the Great Druid's eye, they buried it with the other casualties from the battle.

They kept Tilicea's prophecy though. It was a reminder: a reminder of the battles they fought, a reminder of the fight for freedom in both Zalm and in New Earth. They kept it as a reminder that they had a friend just on the other side of the caves.

And then it happened. One afternoon, Darcie went on a walk with Alena. She felt something strange in her. It started as an odd twitch of a muscle, but soon became widespread through her stomach. For the first time since her kidnapping, she seemed to remember the gift bestowed on her, a gift that warranted meaning in her and Joachim's life.

Darcie felt the first movements of that new life in her womb.

Six months had passed since then. Darcie had awoken one night and gone into labour. The next morning she gave birth to a beautiful, healthy girl. They named her Tilicea, in honor of the woman who fought for freedom not only in her homeland but also in the village of her friends.

But during all that time, the village had run out of meat. They prepared a hunt, one that would be devoid of the fear of Zupay and his demons. The need to hunt brought an odd feeling to Joachim. It made him feel young again, ready for the relish of intrigue and adventure. But he wasn't going on that adventure, not this time. He'd stay with his daughter.

Instead, a new hunter readied himself.

"Where is he?" Joachim asked.

"I don't know," Trent replied, "but we can wait. Tell him I'll meet him by the workshop with the other hunters."

Rae had been missing all morning, and now that the time drew close to their departure, the hunters began to worry. Would he decide not to go with them? Would he stay in the safety of the village out of fear for the jungle?

"I'll go look for him," Joachim said. "Someone ought to have seen him."

Joachim crossed the clearing of Baruch's library. They had repaired much of the damage to the building, but many of the books inside had not survived the destruction. Baruch had taken on the task of writing down much of his knowledge to pass on to future villagers. He also wrote a few new books, ones describing the new creatures and plants that existed in the jungle after the Great Death. One even detailed their great journey into Zalm.

Joachim passed the path leading to Tabitha's cabin and continued down to the center of the village. The old recluse had retreated to her loner lifestyle, but she never failed to chat with passing villagers who found themselves curious about her. She even opted to eat with the village a few nights of the week, contributing foul smelling teas she prepared herself.

Joachim found Alena salting and drying meats with a few younger girls near the fire pit.

"Have they left yet?" she asked.

"Not yet," Joachim said. "They're waiting on Rae."

"Where is he?"

"I don't know," Joachim said. "I haven't seen him around the village all morning."

She smiled. "I know where he is."

Alena wiped bits of dried meat from her palms.

"Follow me," she said.

$$\text{⅄ ⅃ Ӿ ⅎ Ɛ ⅁ Ƈ ⅋ Ƌ ⅍}$$

Though baby Tilicea now lay in a crib of bamboo and grass pillows, Darcie's back still ached. She looked down at her daughter. At long last she was quiet. Even though Darcie had a moment to sit and relax, she didn't. She watched the little girl in her peaceful slumber and thanked the gods she was healthy.

"May I enter?"

Darcie turned to the voice. She thought it would be Joachim, but he'd just come to watch her feed and was seeing Rae off to his first hunt. From the open window, she saw Baruch stood on the porch. She smiled and nodded. He came into her home and stayed at a length. His eyes looked puffy and his face long.

"Is everything all right?"

"No," he croaked.

Her eyes widened, and her chest ached. Not again.

"What happened? Is everyone okay?"

"Yes," he said. "Everyone is fine. I just came to tell you something, something that I should have told you long ago. I do not wish to distress you by telling you this, but I know that I cannot ignore it any longer. You deserve to know the truth."

She looked at the man. He seemed on the brink of tears, and she could see that each word pained him. Though her chest panged in discomfort at what he said, she went to him and touched his arm.

"No, Darcie," he said. "You don't understand—"

"I do, Baruch," she said. "I know what you're going to say."

"You... what?"

"I know what happened to them," Darcie said. "My people and my old village. I know what Zupay made you do, and I know how my family ended up here."

"How did you find out?" Baruch asked. "Did another elder tell you?"

"No," she said. "I found it in a journal in your workshop. I snuck in one afternoon while you were on a hunt to get the key to the library."

Baruch looked at her then gazed at the floor, shaking his head. She could see his shoulders shuddering in sobs. She lifted his face to hers.

"It's okay," she said. "What happened wasn't your fault."

"Yes, yes it was. There were other options. We should have thought of a plan. We could have banded together and killed the creatures many years ago. All of this could have been avoided."

The words brought tears to her eyes. She also wished things could have been different. But they weren't. Her parents were gone. Her people were gone. But so, too, was the horror Baruch fought against. No one else would have to experience it again.

"But you didn't," Darcie said. "And it's over now. The creatures are dead and so is Zupay. He can't control us or force us to live in fear anymore. We've won. And we made it this far because of your leadership—because of you."

"I'm… I'm sorry," Baruch said.

Darcie hugged him.

"I forgive you," she said. "You only ever did what you had to for this village. Sometimes those choices were hard, but know I don't blame you. No one does."

She released him and noticed he smiled. He wiped the tears from his eyes.

"Thank you."

In the crib behind them, the child cooed. Darcie and Baruch moved to her. As Baruch gazed down, his face brightened, and he smiled much bigger than he had a moment ago. Darcie smiled too.

"She looks so much like you," Baruch said. "So much like the both of you."

"Really?" Darcie asked. "I think she looks a lot like Alena."

"No, I don't see it. Look. She's got Joachim's eyes and his scowl."

Darcie laughed and sighed. "Yeah, that much is true. I just hope she won't inherit his cynicism."

The man lowered his hand into the crib, patting young Tilicea's head. The baby grabbed hold of his finger.

"Do you want to know the best part of it all?" Darcie asked.

"What?"

"Tilicea and generations of children from now on will never have to live the horrors we faced," Darcie said. "Zupay is gone."

ﾗ ⅃ ﾌ ⅄ ⏃ ⅂ ⏃ ᛐ ⅄

Rae gazed out at the ocean, sitting on the Black Rocks his father had shown him all those years ago. The swelling waters blanketed his face in salty mist and his feet in coolness. He had a rucksack slung over his shoulders filled with enough supplies to last him three weeks.

His parents would be proud of his first real hunt, even if they weren't there to see him off to it.

After the Zalmish rebels left, Rae assisted Alena in the reconstruction of the village. During that time he was able to deal with all he had neglected during the nine days of torment. He accepted his parents' death, something that bubbled up to the surface every now and then. He accepted his own failures, too, and tried not to blame himself for their consequences, for the death of the villagers he might have caused. He vowed to live the rest of his life in their honor.

The threat of the creatures was gone, and he accepted he could live a new life in the village.

A new era.

He had found himself another family. He wanted to raise Joachim and Darcie's daughter like a sister, passing down stories and skills Ben had taught him. He pledged to become a more integral part of village life. He wanted to hunt. He wanted to build a boat to sail up the coast. He wanted to explore the lands they called home.

Another rush of sea blast tickled his face, and he heard voices. He turned. Joachim and Alena crossed the rocks. Clearly she had not taught him how to traverse them smoothly.

"The hunt is leaving soon," Alena said. "Will you be going?"

"Yes," Rae said. "I just wanted to be alone for a bit. I wanted to say goodbye."

"Goodbye?" Joachim asked. "You'll be returning, I presume."

"I hope so."

"Good," Joachim said. "Because little Tilicea will be missing her older brother."

Rae stood up and hugged the man. His hug felt nothing like his father's, and Rae felt guilty for thinking it might. It was a different kind of warmth, one from a friend, one of reassurance. Perhaps he could get used to it.

They walked back along the rocks toward the village. Rae took one last look at the ocean. He wanted to savor the view and remember it until the moment when he would return. He just needed to cherish it for a little longer so he could draw on its memory when the hunt seemed too much, when the jungle was too much.

"Wait," Rae said.

They turned around and faced him. What Rae saw at sea made his chest fill with a rushing feeling and his head buzz. He couldn't believe it. He rubbed his eyes and looked out again. He was sure he saw something.

"What is it?" Alena asked.

He could do nothing but point.

The two followed his finger and looked out across the ocean. They, too, didn't believe their eyes, perhaps too tainted by all the years of uncertainty. But as Joachim and Alena stood and stared, smiles came to their lips.

Gliding along the line where sky and ocean touched, they saw a group of black smudges. They didn't dive under the sea like whales did—they moved across the water, heading left. The stories Rae's father had told him so long ago were true all along. Rae was stupid for doubting him. Even his mother was right too. He wished there was a way he could let her know.

Boats on the horizon.

ACKNOWLEDGEMENTS

Firstly, I'd like to thank my parents. Raising an angsty dreamer can't have always been easy, but I am grateful for all your support and for the ice cream (it really does make everything better). I'd like to thank my brother. I know you still plan on taking over my old bedroom, but know that the bed is staying and I have dibs on the desk. Thank you also to the rest of my crazy, big family. You all know how to have a good time. Keep it that way.

Secondly, I'd like to thank everyone involved in creating *The Black Oracle*. I may have written it, but I would not have been able to do it without your help. So, thank you Sarah and Matt for being my beta readers and for telling me exactly what needed to change. Thank you to Megan, Priya, Charla, Rachel, and Christopher for still wanting to hang out with me even when I was being a grumpy writer. Thank you to everyone at Curiosity Quills Press: Lisa, Eugene, Andrew, Nikki, Clare, Mollie, and Alexandria. Without all of you, this wouldn't have been possible. And a special thank you to Katie for everything you've done for me.

Lastly, I'd like to thank Phil. Thank you for believing in me. Thank you for putting up with me. Thank you for being amazing and for helping me believe that one day, I can be.

ABOUT THE AUTHOR

Michael Cristiano is a Canadian writer. His relentless obsession with fiction began long before he could even spell the words 'relentless obsession'. He spent most of his childhood getting lost in fantastical masterpieces, learning foreign languages, and attempting to be published by the age of thirteen. Though he's off by a few years, The Black Oracle is his debut novel.

Website: www.michaelcristiano.net
Facebook: www.facebook.com/MichaelCristianoOfficial
Twitter: www.twitter.com/mcristianowrite

THANK YOU FOR READING

Please visit http://curiosityquills.com/reader-survey
to share your reading experience with the author of
this book!

The Actuator: Fractured Earth, by Aiden James & James Wymore

On a secret military base tucked in a remote desert mountain, a dangerous machine lies hidden from the American public. Known as "The Actuator", this machine is capable of transforming entire communities into alternate realities.

Meanwhile, an unknown saboteur dismantles the dampeners. The affect is catastrophic. The entire world is plunged into chaos, and familiar landscapes become a deadly patchwork of genre horrors. It's up to Red McLaren and his band to set things right again. They must survive their journey through the various realms that separate them from the Actuator, where ever-present orcs, aliens, pirates, and vampires seek to destroy them.

Valcoria: Children of the Chrystal Star, by Jason King

History repeats itself like a song. The verses may vary, but the melody is always the same. The eastern empire of Aukasia has a new leader, a man who means to bring war to all the land. Yet, even in all his bloody ambition, he does not realize that he is but the puppet of a greater evil. Only the Kalyra—The Children of the Crystal Star—can stand against what's coming. Only they can protect the world of Valcoria from the mad hatred of the fallen god, Aedar. A new verse of the song has begun. The last verse.

CPSIA information can be obtained at www.ICGtesting.com
Printed in the USA
LVOW11s0555190515

438951LV00005B/193/P